ARMY OF THREE

Maxwell J. Hammond

First paperback edition October 2025

Cover art by Ashley Hammond

Book formatting and design by Opeyemi Ikuborije

Edited by Melissa Prideaux

ISBN 979-8-218-85815-5 (paperback)
ISBN 979-8-218-85816-2 (eBook)

www.maxwelljhammond.com

CONTENTS

Maxwell J. Hammond is a science-fiction writer and music enthusiast with an engineering background.

Born in Sacramento, California, by age 10, his journey took him to the beautiful forest suburb, Beaverton, Oregon.

When he was younger, he wrote music to express himself.

In his late 20s, he ended up in Modesto, California, where he met the love of his life and started a family.

CHAPTER 1

The Fassbinder Family

Have you ever met your wit's end? Been devastated by the pain of grief, rendering your conscience lost? As I sit on my pedestal of guilt between a rock and a hard place, I debate the hardest decision of many lives. The world is an utterly dark place, barren of hope, but there is still a glimpse of potential in its lasting endurance. This place where we are now. I can see a beautiful world before us. A child-like first perspective of this reckoned reality. Subjective innocence. Surrounded by the bane of my accomplishments, my life haunts me.

As the rain falls, hitting my forehead, it trickles down my mind. Passing my tears, it continues downwards as my thoughts transcend. What is justice but an immunity to understanding? Circumstances are not neatly defined as one or the other. Black or white. We live in a contentious world of gray. We live in a nation where our wants compete with the value of our needs. Only those who have experienced true loss understand what they need. No ecstasy in excess is true. Life is about finding your balance. Where discontentment thrives, bad things will follow.

August 15th, 1997. The eighteen-year-old boy prepared himself in his room for the big night. He strapped a bulletproof vest over his all-black outfit. His weapon, a metal sparring staff that could split into two. The night was young.

"Axel! Your brother is waiting for you in the garage," his father yelled up the stairs.

"I'll be down in a moment," he responded.

Axel was a tall young man, standing around six foot three. His medium-length hair was a dirty blond shade. His eyes a deep brown with a hint of green caressing the outer rim of his irises. He sat down on his bed facing the analog clock on the wall in his room. Reflecting on his life and how it had led up to this moment. His eyes gazed into the clock. Time slowed down. Each tick of the hand flooded his mind with anticipation. His memory drew those words his father used to tell him in his adolescence: "You can either be a good man or a great man, but in life, oftentimes, they are very different things."

Those words resonated through his mind. Each tick of the clock's hand took him a year further into his past.

He remembered when he was eleven years old. Before he had discovered his ability. He was practicing with his older brother, Karl. Karl was born with his power, as was his grandfather before him. Karl was gifted, his surreal attributes making him hardly considered mortal. On this particular day, fate was in the air. The brothers were attempting to jump across a long gap between two buildings downtown. The gap must have been at least ten feet long, and the buildings over three stories high. Karl made the jump with ease. When Axel headed for the gap, his momentum failed him, and he completely missed his landing. He hit the side of a fire escape, breaking his leg, then tumbled down onto a dumpster, shattering his ribs. His limp body slid down the side onto the ground as his brother hurried to his aid. Karl rushed him to the hospital. By the time the brothers arrived, all of Axel's injuries were miraculously healed.

The young man shook his head, trying to clear his mind. This was the moment he had been training for. The clock's hands passed their vertical peak. He finished getting ready, then hurried downstairs and out the door. He headed to the garage. As he took his first step through the garage door, Karl greeted him. Karl stood at a broad six foot five. A couple inches taller than his younger brother. Wide shouldered with a very fit build. Dressed in a leather jacket and blue jeans.

"'Bout time. You ready, brother?" Karl asked him.

"I've never been more ready in my entire life," he answered.

Karl smirked. He reached into his jacket pocket and pulled out some black leather fabric. After he handed it to Axel, he explained, "It's a mask. It won't shroud you from people we know, but it's just enough to deter camera footage from identifying us."

Axel nodded in understanding. The two then loaded everything they needed for the big night into their dad's car, a 1975 cherry red Pontiac GTO in mint condition.

"So much for low profile," Axel remarked as they got into the car.

The two embarked on their mission, driving through the starry night. Down a single lane highway out in the boons.

"How about some tunes to get us in the mood?" Karl proposed.

He turned the radio onto the local rock station. "TNT" by ACDC came on the station. The radio always knew how to set the mood, Axel thought.

They drove for nearly an hour until they reached the city, driving through a tunnel in the dark. As they exited the other side, the city lights lit up the sky. The brothers were dazzled by the city ambience. Living out in the country, they didn't often experience the sky in this manner.

Karl looked for an exit that would lead to a seemingly low-income neighborhood. Inherently, struggling people tended to commit more crimes. He took them into an old beat-up area by the railroad track and found an alleyway to park in. Once he'd pulled the Pontiac over, he put the shifter into park and flipped the ignition into accessory mode.

"Now what?" Axel asked, curious how their plan was going to play out.

Karl turned on his police radio. "We wait."

Their task was clear, their motive pure. They had the upper hand in pursuing crime compared to their opponents. No one would see them coming. The lurking wretched filth of the slum would have scattered like roaches in direct light if a blare of a siren went off.

The two waited silently, listening to a few routine transmissions communicated over dispatch.

Finally, they got something. "Shots fired on Prescott Avenue. Assailant is wearing a gray hoodie, heading southbound," a woman's voice stated.

Karl started the car and peeled out, heading in that direction. He floored the gas pedal to the ground, speeding up to sixty miles per hour in a forty-five zone.

"I remember Prescott is this direction, but I don't know which way from us he's gonna be." Karl creased his brow in frustration.

"Just turn left and let's hope he was further south," Axel suggested.

They approached Prescott, and Karl slammed on the breaks, skidding the car into a drift around the corner.

"That's him!" Axel spotted him off to the right.

The man in the hoodie jumped a fence and ran through a back alley. Karl slammed on the brakes.

"I'm gonna look for him on foot. You follow me in the car," Karl said.

Axel nodded. "Okay, go, go!"

Karl jumped over the fence after the guy with the hoodie and began sprinting down the road, going thirty miles per hour. Axel sped off in the Pontiac, heading around the block to try and corner him.

Karl caught up to the hooded man. The man jumped another fence into someone's backyard. Karl grabbed the fence and ripped it out of the ground, breaking the metal links from the post. He hurled the heavy, fifteen-foot-wide fence behind him.

"H-h-how the hell did you do that?" the criminal stuttered.

Karl took a step toward him with no response. The man in the hoodie pulled a small Glock out of his sweater pocket, pointing it at Karl. "Stay back or I'll shoot you."

Karl did nothing. Just stood there.

Meanwhile, Axel had exited the car that was parked on the other side of the house they were behind. He snuck around to the side gate and discreetly approached the hooded man.

"GET OUT OF MY WAY!" the hooded man shouted at Karl just as Axel jumped over the fence behind the assailant and swung his metal staff into the criminal's head, knocking him to the ground, unconscious.

He bent down and worked quickly, slapping some police-grade cuffs on him.

Three police cars came swarming in, looking puzzled as they stepped out of their vehicles. The criminal was lying on the ground, seemingly unconscious, his hands cuffed. No one else in sight. The brothers had fled.

"Did you see that? Damn, man, that was exhilarating!" Axel said enthusiastically as they headed home in the Pontiac.

"You did good, Axel. You did real good. That's what I call teamwork right there. Grandpa would have been proud of this moment," Karl told his brother.

They drove back to the old country town they lived in, arriving at their home right at dawn. The Pontiac pulled into the long gravel driveway. They parked in front of an old, country-style, two-story hand-crafted log cabin. Before it stood a stained maple deck attached to four hardwood posts supporting the balcony above. On the porch, their father, Peter, and Axel's best friend, Russ, waited for the brothers' arrival.

Peter bore a great resemblance to Karl. With dark hair and blue eyes, he was wearing his usual heavy vest with a ball cap on. Axel spotted Russ first before he even stepped out of the car. He stood out with his distinctive red locks of hair and the flannel shirt he always wore.

"How did it go?" Peter Fassbinder asked his sons.

"We successfully took down an armed suspect without anyone getting hurt. The Police have him now," Karl explained.

"Wow that's awesome, guys," he responded.

"That's so cool, man," Russ interjected. He walked over and gave Axel a fist pump. "So, you guys are gonna let me join on the next trip, right?"

Karl and Axel looked at each other with concerned expressions. "Um…" Axel started to reply.

Russ interrupted, "Kidding, of course."

They laughed and headed inside for breakfast. The brothers and their dad sat down at a large wooden dining table in the center of the room. Russ walked over to the kitchen counter to plate everyone up.

"Mr. Fassbinder, where are the napkins?"

"At this point you know my kitchen better than I do, Russ. Where did you put them last?" he asked playfully.

The brothers giggled a little and shook their heads.

"Right, on it." Russ figured it out.

"Your grandfather would have been very proud of you boys," Peter told them.

Russ walked over and placed everyone's plates in front of them.

"But Mom wouldn't be?" Axel asked his father, frowning, his tone serious.

Russ paused, setting a plate in front of Axel, looking at Peter, who then looked at Karl.

After a moment of silence, Peter answered, "Axel, your mother…" He paused, holding back his conviction. "No, she wouldn't have been. But that's why… She wanted you boys to have a normal life. We always disagreed on what would happen when you boys came of age."

Axel stared at his father with a blank look. He looked down at his plate, then stood up, pushed his chair in and walked up to his room without a word. Peter looked down, swallowed by grief. A moment later, he followed Axel up the stairs to his room.

He knocked twice on the door; with no response, he opened it. Axel was sitting on his bed with his head in his hands. Peter walked over and sat down next to him.

"Your mother would be proud of whatever man you decide to be. I just wanted to be transparent with you. She asked me to promise her that I would never let you boys become like your grandfather. She respected him. That wasn't at all the problem. That just isn't the kind of life any mother would wish for her children. I saw things differently.

"You know, when I found out about my father's abilities, I was five years old. He was working on his car and knocked the jack stand out. The car fell on him. I witnessed it all. He pushed the car up with hardly any struggle and moved it to the side away from him. When he realized I'd seen him, he told me about his power. He felt like it was necessary because he needed to make sure I knew that I wasn't invincible like him.

When he told me I was just an ordinary boy, I was crushed. Then he explained that my son would be like him. I began focusing my whole life on raising this perfect man. Now I'm blessed with two. As selfish as it seems, I wanted to live my dream through Karl. And now you as well. This world needs heroes, and I believe our family was bred for that task."

Axel lifted his head up and put his hands on his lap. He turned toward his father, met his gaze, and asked, "Is it true that we're the first generation of Fassbinders to have more than one child?"

"Who told you that?" his father asked, looking concerned.

"Karl. When we were kids. He said that every generation in our family only had one son until me. Was I a mistake? Was I meant to be a Fassbinder?"

Peter stood up and moved in front of Axel. He kneeled on one knee and lifted his son's chin up with his two fingers.

"My son, you are a gift to us all. Of course you were meant to be a Fassbinder. No other family could bear a child with as great a talent as you."

Axel smiled. "Thanks, Dad."

When Axel lay down to sleep, no dreams visited his rest that day. He got up around three in the afternoon, a few hours after lying down. He used his landline phone to call Russ's house and told him to meet at the river, their usual hangout.

Axel walked down the trail behind their house, which led to a circle of trees. In the center there was a big boulder to sit on. Russ was sitting on it, waiting for him.

"What's up, man? Is everything alright?" his red-headed friend greeted him. "You seemed pretty upset earlier. I've been worried."

"Yeah, I just needed some time to collect myself. I waited so long for that night to come, when it did it almost felt like... I don't know. Different."

"Well, you spent the last seven years focused on one thing. I can imagine you'd have mixed emotions about it. If it makes you feel any better, I could only dream of doing something like that."

Axel walked over to one of the large tree trunks and put his hand on it, leaning his head down toward the ground.

"I do feel like this is what I'm meant to be doing. I made my father proud, my grandfather, and Karl. Part of me just wonders what my mom would say if she was here. You know I've always felt somewhat responsible for her death. If she didn't have me, she would still be here today."

"Hey, man, you can't think like that. She knew the risk months ahead of time. She would have made the same decision to choose you over her again and again," Russ comforted his friend.

"I guess deep down I just wonder if my dad or Karl ever blame me. If they really love me like I think they do or if it's only a façade."

Russ walked over to Axel and put his hand on his shoulder. "Honestly, man, coming from a broken family myself, I have never seen so much love between a father and two brothers before. You are blessed, remember that."

"Thanks, Russ."

"Now let's hit up the river, it's like ninety degrees out here."

The following weekend the brothers went out again. They began making a habit of heading down to the city every Friday and Saturday night. As time passed, the brothers earned somewhat of a reputation with the locals.

A couple of months had passed since the night with the hooded man, and they were sitting down for breakfast when their father said, "I heard about you boys from someone in the shop this morning. Some old timer was in getting a quote for some maple countertops and asked me if I had heard about this superhero phenomenon down in the Bay Area. I told him I had not. He said that people were calling you boys, the 'Army of Two.' Two masked men fighting off armed criminals. That was a proud moment. I thought you boys ought to know."

Axel and Karl looked at each other with big grins.

"Well, it looks like we have a name," Karl remarked.

"I like that. Well, there's no going back now," Axel added.

February 11th, 1998. On a stormy night, nearing three in the morning, the brothers heard a call for a fire in a fourplex building. Multiple gunshots reported. The brothers drove the Pontiac to the destination. When they arrived, they saw the building was engulfed in flames.

"Oh man, that's not good," Axel commented.

They got out of the car and jogged over to the building entrance. Karl opened the door as a powerful gust of smoke pushed them back.

"Is anyone in there?" he yelled into the building.

The brothers waited for a moment with no response. They looked at each other, and Axel nodded. A moment later, they entered the building, the smoke pouring out profusely.

Axel looked down the hallway to see two dead bodies on the ground, both armed. He ran up to one and checked their pulse. He looked at his brother and shook his head, confirming a negative reading. He evaluated the corpses, noting that both of their guns were melted at the tip of the barrels. His gaze rose upwards, and he peered into the remains of the hallway. In the darkness, he tried to focus his vision. The flickers of the flames distorted his view. He saw a figure at the end of the hall. Just a silhouette. He blinked a few times, trying to make out what he thought he saw. Two red eyes bore into him from the dark humanoid.

"Hello?" Axel addressed the figure.

With no response, the two brothers waited for a few seconds.

Suddenly, a hooded figure came running out at them, holding a little girl in their arms.

"Get out, quick!" a woman's voice yelled at them.

The hooded woman ran straight between the two and out the door behind them. The brothers looked to see the house's structure was compromised. They ran out of the building with haste.

"What happened here? Are there any more people in the building?" Karl confronted the woman.

The woman wore a cloak draped around her, and a hood covering her head. She set the little girl down.

"What's your name?" she asked the girl.

"Abigail," the poor girl answered softly.

"Were your parents in there, Abigail?"

She shook her head no.

"Abby!" a woman yelled from across the street.

A middle-aged blonde woman jumped out of her car, leaving the door open, and hurried over, picking the girl up and hugging her.

"Thank you. Thank you... My daughter is okay," the woman said gratefully. "I had to run to the corner store and figured she was safer at the apartment."

"Maybe take her with you next time," the shrouded, heroic young woman told the mother.

The brothers felt out of place, witnessing this scene. Karl looked at Axel awkwardly. Usually, they were the ones who got the thanks.

Sirens blared around the corner. The Army of Two and the hooded woman all looked down the road to see a fire truck and two police cars on their way.

"That's our cue," Karl commented.

The three heroes fled a block down and crossed the street. They headed down a small alley between brick buildings.

"Who are you?" Karl asked the mysterious woman.

She looked to be about five foot six. Under the black cloak she wore a black leather, skintight outfit. She lifted the hood from her head to reveal gorgeous, piercing blue eyes and pitch-black hair.

"I could ask you the same question." She paused for a moment, studying the two. "Wait a second. I'll be damned. You're them, aren't you? You're the infamous Army of Two."

"I guess we have earned a bit of a reputation," Karl answered, borderline flustered.

"I thought you would be older," she scoffed.

"You need to have a little youth in you to do what we do," Axel interjected.

"So, what happened in there? What did you find? And are you going to tell us who you are now?" Karl asked.

She sighed, hesitating. "As far as I could tell, the perpetrators had some business that had gone wrong with one of the tenants of the building. I was in the area and heard gunshots. So naturally, I intervened. My name is Azrael, if you must know. And your names are?"

"I'm Karl, this is my younger brother, Axel. You just happened to be in the area and decided to intervene? Why do I get the feeling an average young woman wouldn't go running toward the sound of gunshots in a building on fire."

"Fine. I knew about the gunshots ahead of time. For the last couple of years, I've been fighting crime around the county. I'm just a little better at keeping a low profile than you two. So, you probably haven't heard of me. I also don't have a catchy name like you guys. I think the only thing I've heard a witness call me was 'the witch'."

The brothers looked at each other with puzzled expressions. "The witch? Why? And how exactly does a one-hundred-and-ten-pound woman fight off armed criminals?" Karl was determined to get answers.

She looked down the alleyway in both directions to make sure they were alone. She then whispered an elusive sentence in what seemed to be ancient Latin. Her eyes began to change color, turning a crimson blood red. As she held out her hand in front of her, out of nowhere, fire began to materialize. It then expanded, getting bigger, forming a six-inch diameter ball of flame that hovered above her hand.

"My powers are hardly limited. I can move things without touching them, heat objects, cool objects, and bend elements such as fire."

The Army of Two's eyes lit up, astonished by what they had seen. Karl wondered if she was the reason the building had caught fire.

"How did you obtain these abilities? What happened to you?" Axel asked.

"You know, honestly, it's kind of personal. We did just meet. Do you guys wanna grab a drink and we can get to know each other a little better?"

"A drink? Are you even old enough to drink?" Karl asked.

"I'm twenty-two, but I went to bars before I was of age, so that doesn't matter much."

"Well, Axel's only nineteen and hasn't had anything alcoholic before, so that's probably not the ideal place for us."

"I can speak for myself, Karl. I think if I'm old enough to risk my life fighting dangerous men armed with weapons as lethal as assault rifles, then I'm old enough to have a drink," Axel said brusquely.

Azrael grinned in an almost sinister manner. "I like that. I think that's pretty reasonable, right, Karl?"

Karl exhaled slowly. "Alright, well if you know somewhere that won't ID him, I guess a few drinks won't hurt."

"Are you guys on foot or…?"

"Our car is parked a few blocks down. Maybe we should go the long way around in case any of the emergency responders are still there."

They all agreed. The three of them made their way to the Pontiac. When they got to the car, Axel opened the door for Azrael and put the front seat down. She climbed in and sat in the back. The Army of Two got in, and they headed off. They drove about five miles into the industrial district of the city until they arrived at a small dive bar with parking out back.

Karl pulled up and parked the car. "Looks like a dump," he commented.

"Well, it's the only place that won't identify us as our alternate versions or ask for identification cards, so you gotta enjoy it," she explained.

They continued into the bar. Azrael walked in first, followed by Karl, then Axel. The bar was narrow with a couple of dart boards on one wall to the left. A juke box and some tables to the right. In front of them was the bar with only five seats. One old man sat there with a Budweiser in his hand. The Army of Two and Azrael all sat in a row next to him. The bartender walked over.

"We'll have three hefeweizens, please." Azrael slapped a twenty on the bar.

The man nodded and got their drinks.

"So, you come here often?" Karl asked her.

"You know you ask a lot of questions. I come here almost every morning after a long night of fighting crime. It's the only bar in town that doesn't ask questions and doesn't close for the state's mandated four-hour alcohol prohibition."

"Right... Well, that's reassuring. And I'm sorry if it seems like I ask a lot of questions. I guess we just don't meet many people and well... you're the first person we have heard of outside of our family that has any type of superpower or whatever it is that you possess."

"Outside of your family, huh? So, all of you are superhuman?"

Axel chimed in, "Not all of us. Only a select few. You may have heard of one, though. The Patriot? That was our grandfather."

Azrael's eyes widened in disbelief. "Your grandfather was the first real-life superhero? Wow, that's awesome. What ever happened to him?"

The brothers looked at each other with dismay.

"We're not so sure, to be honest," Karl explained. "He went missing when our father was pretty young. Long before either of us were born."

"Well, I'm sorry to hear that."

They were interrupted by the bartender setting their drinks on the bar in front of them. "Thanks, Mitch, we'll need another in about five," Azrael told him as she took a big drink from her ale, then let out a satisfied sigh.

She looked at the brothers, then at their drinks, as if to say, *Drink up!*

Karl took a sip off his and turned toward Axel. Axel hesitated slowly, lifting the glass to his lips. He tilted it and took a small taste. "A little bitter."

"You'll get used to it."

"I know we just met, but I honestly need to know. How did you create that fire back there?" Karl pressed.

"I don't know if this is the best place to talk about certain things," Axel commented, gesturing his head toward the old man sitting next to them.

"Don't worry about Bill, he's an old Vietnam vet. He has no clue what's going on around him," she reassured them. "Hey, Bill, who's running for office next year?"

The old man turned in their direction, a crazed look in his eye. "That goddamn, bloodthirsty Nixon will win every time," he yelled violently and followed with a chug on his bottled beer.

"See, you don't have to worry about Bill. He's here 24/7. I'm pretty sure he sleeps out back too. How I got my abilities is a little disturbing. I'll tell you, but it's pretty heavy, and I don't want you to think differently of me. I'm actually starting to like you guys, which is unheard of for me. I'll tell you if you promise I won't scare you off.

"I promise," Axel said.

"Karl?" she asked.

"Yes. I promise."

"Well, it started with the most tragic moment of my life. When I was thirteen years old, my parents were brutally murdered in our own home." She paused, looking at the wall. She took a big drink of her beer. "Another round, Mitch."

Turning back toward them, she continued. "I remember that night vividly. I relive that moment almost every single day. It was a couple of minutes past midnight. There was an intruder in my room. His intent was never fully determined. He broke through the door, and I screamed. My Dad came running up the stairs. When he got to my room, the intruder shot him dead on the spot. My mother, after hearing the gunshots, grabbed our family rifle to help. When she entered the room, the gunman shot her twice before she had a chance to lift her weapon. Debatably the most haunting part of it all was after he killed my parents. I'll never forget how he looked at me and said, 'You are your own worst enemy.' He then turned the gun on himself and pulled the trigger. Blood everywhere."

She stopped because she started trembling. Her hand was shaking.

Karl put his hand on her shoulder. "You're okay. I… I don't know what to say."

Axel, with tears in his eyes, commented, "That's horrible. I can't believe you had to go through that. Especially at such a young age."

"Yeah, it's unbelievable. Some men are made of pure evil. The worst part is probably that we're pretty sure he didn't know any of us. It was some random catastrophe. Something else disturbing about it was that the police were never able to identify the murderer. Something wrong with his fingerprints and DNA.

"Anyways, I wasn't just telling you about this for your sympathy. The reason why is because of what came after. After the loss of my parents at such a young age, I didn't deal with it well. All the emotions from the grief. Living with a foster parent that didn't understand me. It was terrible. I couldn't go on like that. How could someone move forward after experiencing such chaos, so much pain. I began spending a lot of time at the public library. Researching into some dark subjects. I found some books that I shouldn't have. I started studying witchcraft."

The bartender interrupted her with the next round of ales. The brothers just sat there, completely invested in her story.

She continued, "I discovered a spell that supposedly would summon a demon that could grant you a wish in return for a great price. I took the book into the woods and chanted the spell. *Blood costs blood* was its name. When I completed the ritual, the demon appeared. It was far more frightening than I could ever imagine. However, I wasn't scared for a moment. It asked me what I wanted. I told it that I wanted it to bring back my parents. It could not complete this wish. So, I asked it if it could grant me the power to overcome any man, so that I could avenge my parents. The demon told me it could grant this wish at a great cost: When I died, my soul would never rest but would go to hell for eternity. I made my blood pact with the demon, and instantly it granted me powers beyond imagination."

She finished her story, and both the brothers just sat there, leaning toward her, speechless.

Finally, Karl said, "I don't even know what to say… I've always thought of demons as more of a spiritual or metaphorical subject. To think of someone interacting with one, let alone making a deal with one, is just inconceivable." His tone was condescending.

"I understand about making rash decisions. I mean, you did what you felt you had to. I'm sorry that you were led to take those kinds of measures," Axel said.

"Yeah… no going back now. Now you guys know my big dark secret. Basically, everything there is you need to know about me, to be honest."

The brothers both grabbed their ales and drained them.

"I think we'd better get going. It's almost seven. Do you have a phone we can reach you on?" Karl asked.

"Yeah, of course. I have my own apartment and have a landline there." She pulled a pen and paper out of her pocket. "Never know when you need to write something down. Especially doing what we do." She wrote down her number and slid it across the bar to them. "Hope to hear from you guys. It was nice meeting you and getting to know each other a little."

Axel looked at Karl with a sorrowful face, then said, "It was a pleasure meeting you, Azrael. You'll definitely hear from us soon."

Karl left the bar and walked out to the Pontiac. Axel followed. They headed home. On the drive there was an awkward silence. For thirty minutes, neither brother made a peep.

Finally, Axel said, "So… I'm guessing we aren't going to see her again?"

"She seems nice, but aren't you a little skeptical too? I mean, at least she was honest, but that is a lot to take in," Karl replied.

"It is, but we all have our own demons. Hers are just more real than ours. I really liked her. Shouldn't we at least give it a shot?"

Karl didn't respond. He just focused on the road. After a few minutes, he turned the stereo up.

Axel started getting angry. He turned the music off. "Aren't we supposed to help people? Maybe it's not just protecting them from physical danger. I feel like she needs us. And honestly, maybe we need her. Maybe I need her."

"Those are very strong words to say about someone you just met," Karl lectured. He paused for a moment or two. "Alright, Axel. We'll give her a chance. Tomorrow night, you give her a call, and we'll see how it goes. It's gonna take me some time to warm up, though."

The younger brother nodded. The brothers got home and rested, and that night they gave her a call and arranged to meet down in the city near where they had met. Parked in an abandoned parking lot they waited for her. The brothers were both watching off to the left where they assumed she would be coming from. Suddenly, a hooded figure knocked on the passenger window by Axel, startling them.

"Give me all your money!" a woman's voice demanded.

Azrael laughed and pulled her hood off, revealing her face to them. Axel joined in the laughter, then noticed Karl's stern expression and instantly matched his.

"That's not funny," Karl remarked.

"You should really try to enjoy the little things," she told Karl.

The brothers got out of the car and walked over. They stood in a circle with Azrael.

"So, what's the plan?" Axel asked his new colleague.

"Well, I have a personal preference to pursue crime on foot. I actually have a portable two-way radio that I managed to figure out how to get the police radio channel on. I say we head into the city and keep the radio on till we get something."

The two nodded. The three heroes embarked on their first night together. Shortly after walking around in the abandoned old industrial district, they heard a transmission just for them. "Armed Robbery on Barnes Road. There are four armed suspects."

"Four of them? You guys each get one, and I'll take two. Sounds perfect. Barnes Road is only about a mile from here," Azrael told them and started running in that direction.

The brothers looked at each other curiously, then followed.

"Hurry!" she yelled.

They ran around a few quick corners and arrived in front of a big building with beige pillars near the door. The glass door was shattered.

Azrael slowed down to a walk and pulled her cassette player out of her pocket. She put in her favorite album by The Romantics. "What I like about you" played on her headphones. She walked through the building entrance, followed closely by the brothers. Inside the broken glass doors, the bank opened into a twenty-foot wide by thirty-foot-long open room. One robber was off to the left behind the register. Two were toward the right looking through the cabinets on the wall. The fourth robber was nowhere to be seen. All of them wielded AK-47s. They all stopped in their tracks simultaneously when they saw a beautiful, hooded woman with headphones walk into the bank so casually.

She looked at them without a speck of fear in her eyes. Her voice muttered a spell in Latin. All three of their guns began heating up. They heated up to the point where they couldn't hold onto them, and they threw them on the ground in front of them. Axel stepped in the door behind her. He split his staff into two metal batons. He smirked and looked at Azrael.

The three robbers ran toward them. A man to the right came in with a right hook toward Axel. Axel dodged it and hit his chest with his right baton then turned against his initial swing with a second blow from his left baton to the back of his attacker's head. The next robber ran up behind Axel and scooped their arms under his in an attempt to put him in a hold. Azrael clenched her fist and sent it into the side of his head, knocking him back. Axel turned around and did a one-hundred-and-eighty-degree spin, hitting the robber on the forehead, splitting it with the back of his left baton.

The third man charged them just as Karl dashed behind him and grabbed him by the back of his neck. He threw him five feet into the concrete wall, where the impact shattered multiple bones. The fourth robber entered the room, coming from the vault with a bag of cash in each hand. He looked at his three accomplices scattered across the room, then his gaze fell on the three heroes. He dropped the bags and tried to flee the scene. Karl swiftly ripped a metal file cabinet off the wall and hurled it at him. It smashed into him, knocking him to the ground and leaving him incapacitated.

"That was a little too easy," Axel commented.

"Short and sweet as I like to say," Azrael replied.

"Maybe we'll make a good team after all," Karl said, his tone apologetic.

He was reinspired. After the first night with Azrael, the brothers went home and told their father about her. He was very pleased to hear they had expanded the team.

Army of Two wasn't a suitable name anymore, now that they had a new member. The three vigilantes built up traction and became known across the country as the infamous Army of Three.

A few months after meeting Azrael and continuing to grow as a unit, Axel asked her a question that had been on his mind since they had first met. Karl was off on his own solo mission. Sitting on a roof top, watching the city lights, Axel turned toward Azrael. "Do you think... Maybe this morning you might want to get together for breakfast or something?"

"Are you asking me out?" she asked him in disbelief, but she was smiling.

"I mean, maybe. I don't know. Should I be?"

She chuckled. Grabbing her pen and paper, she wrote down her address. "Pick me up at eight."

At 7:15 that morning. Axel drove to her apartment complex downtown. He parked and waited, looking in the review mirror, trying to fix one of the locks of his bang. When he saw her approaching the car, he was awestruck. She looked beautiful. Her hair was curled with a bow. She wore a deep blue skirt with a matching blouse. He felt underdressed. She opened the passenger door of the Pontiac and sat down.

"You look..." He paused for a moment, flustered, trying to come up with the right words to say.

"Beautiful, I hope?" she finished his sentence uncertainly.

"Yes, sorry, I've never seen you in this light before."

She blushed and looked out the window.

Axel started the car and exited the apartment complex. They made their way to a diner in the old town.

Over breakfast, they chatted about their nights performing acts that some might call vigilantism. Axel felt that their connection seemed stronger than before. Something special and real was growing between them.

After that morning, Axel and Azrael continued having their casual dates from time to time. Another month passed, and he invited her to his special spot in the woods where he went to get away from the world. He drove up onto a small gravel road near his family's house and parked behind by the forest. It was approaching dusk. As the sun hit civil twilight, it shone across the looming lake. The trees glowed with a special tint. He opened his door and stepped out, walking around to open the door for Azrael.

"Close your eyes," he told her.

She covered her eyes with one hand and held his hand with the other. He led her down the trail to his favorite spot. The middle of a circle of trees. They were very tall old redwoods. In the center of the trees was the rare-looking boulder.

"Do you trust me?" he asked her.

"Is this like a trust fall or—?"

They snickered.

"No, but do you trust me?"

"Yes, of course."

Axel pulled down her hand from her face. With his other hand he stroked her hair behind her ear. He leaned in and kissed her gently on the lips. She kissed him back. He pulled away from her. She opened her eyes and tried looking into his.

"You had to bring me all the way out here for that? We should have come here sooner."

Axel smiled and looked away. "I just wanted to make it special. This is my sanctuary. I've been coming here since I was a little kid."

She looked around, astonished by her surroundings. "It's gorgeous. These trees must be hundreds of years old. Maybe thousands."

"They were here long before we were and will be here long after. I…" He paused for a moment not sure if he wanted to continue his sentence. "This was my first. You were my first."

"First what?" She pondered for a moment. "That was your first kiss?"

He nodded awkwardly. "Well, here is your second."

She put her hands around his head and planted one on him. They spent the next few hours together just sitting on the boulder. She leaned into him, and he held her tight with his arm around her shoulder.

At one point he stood up and walked over to the tree in front of them. Pulling out his Leatherman, he started etching into the bark.

"What are you doing, honey?"

Axel finished his project without responding. He took a step back to show her. A heart, carved in the tree with their names in it. "So we never forget."

She smiled. This was that pivotal moment in his life where suddenly everything made sense. He knew what his life was meant for. It had a deeper meaning than just trying to help others.

Azrael and Axel fell in love. The following year included some proud milestones. They both got jobs and decided to move in together. Axel began working as a carpenter at a cabinet shop. Azrael became a bank teller at the most prestigious bank in town. The new couple found a one-bedroom house in a pleasant, friendly neighborhood and had to have it. Life had never been happier. Axel felt like he was living a dream.

They made an effort to make sure that their romance did not affect their night job with Karl. In the last year of fighting crime for county and state police, the three of them had reduced major crimes by over ninety percent. The heroes had been working on a mission to shut down a drug smuggling operation that had been ongoing for quite some time. A few weeks prior, they had finally found the source and put an end to it once and for all.

The federal government began losing millions in the worldwide drug trade. So Big Brother, the dirty hand behind the government, tasked the deadliest department of mercenaries known to man to eliminate the three heroes.

June 27th, 1999. Three black SUVs arrived in front of the one-bedroom house that the new couple called home. It was around three o'clock on a Sunday afternoon. Axel had taken his new green Honda Civic to the corner market to get some eggs for their late breakfast. Twelve men exited the three vehicles, armed to the teeth. Two snuck around back, a few, set up base around the perimeter. One of them placed C-4 on the front and back doors of the house. Azrael was lying on the love seat in the center of the living room, watching her favorite sit-com, *Friends*. Nodding in and out of sleep, wearing her favorite matching pink pajamas, she rested, waiting for her significant other's return.

Right as Azrael was on the verge of sleep, the mercenaries burst through three windows whilst detonating an explosion of C-4 at the doors. They breached the house in all directions. She immediately awoke, stood up, and began to murmur a spell. All the mercenaries' weapons began heating up. Before she finished her sentence, a fifty-caliber bullet pierced through her neck from the window behind her. It burst through her neck and out the other side, preventing her speech. Sniper at six o'clock. As she was riddled with bullets from all angles, she dropped to the ground, drawing her last breath before hitting the floor.

Moments later, Axel pulled up in front of the house in his green Honda. He had a dark feeling like death was breathing down his neck. He immediately noticed the three SUVs. He then looked at the devasted opening of their home. His heart sank. He approached the house with a steady jog. He couldn't fathom something terrible could have happened. *She must be okay*, he thought to himself. He walked in the doorway, his eyes dashing around the room. They locked onto the most horrific sight anyone could lay eyes on. Azrael's body in the middle of the room.

The intruders opened fire on him. He took bullet after bullet, step after step, as he moved toward her body—her disturbing corpse. The one good thing to ever have happened to him was lying dead before his eyes. Her beautiful face was so pale and blank. If only he had gotten home sooner. He dropped to his knees and held her head in his lap in tears. The mercenaries slowly devastated his body with automatic weaponry. Every bullet was rejected instantly from his body, healing the wound. But he was ready to go. His life had been with her, but from that moment on, it no longer would be. He was ready to join her in death.

A few weeks ago, he had bought her an engagement ring that he had been saving for, with plans to propose the following Friday. In the woods, under the starlight where they would go to get away from the stresses of the world. Right by the tree where they had their first kiss. The feeling of holding the cold, absent skin of the one you love in your hands is something you never forget. He kissed her cheek while he held her body. Stroking her hair behind her ear one final time, he whispered to her, "I will see you again, my love."

Tragedy spawns many things in a person and changes who you are. As he was torn apart by bullets, one of the mercenaries approached him from behind, wielding a machete to attempt to decapitate him, hoping that would prevent his healing ability.

"Do it," Axel muttered to the man. The mercenary raised his arm for the kill. Just a moment before Axel was gone forever, the wall exploded behind them, and the roof collapsed onto everyone in the room.

As the dust, rubble, and smoke cleared, standing there was Karl Fassbinder. During the raid, Karl had been tipped off that there was a price on their heads and had headed for Axel and Azrael's place with great haste.

One of the attackers started to get up and lifted his gun toward Karl. Karl swiftly picked up a giant chunk of concrete and hurled it at the gunman, smashing him completely, killing him on impact. Karl ran over to where his brother had been and dug through the rubble until he found the crumpled-up dangling parts of a body barely held together. Karl tossed Axel over his shoulder. He paused when he saw Azrael did not make it. He knelt and closed her eyes as he grieved for a moment before he jumped up and ran out front, carrying his brother. He loaded Axel in the passenger side of the Pontiac and hopped in the driver's seat, heading for their family's house in the countryside.

CHAPTER 2

Hunting or Hunted

Everyone who has lost someone has that one image that repeats itself. That specific moment that flashes through your mind every time you remember them. It could be your biggest regret or your greatest experience. Out in the country, under the moonlit sky, Axel sat on the roof of his childhood home, looking down at the gravel driveway. Reflecting through the tears pooled in his eyes was a vision of Azrael stepping out of the Pontiac. His memory of their first kiss drew a smile on his face. He clenched his fists and stood up. He had to go on, he thought. He climbed through the window within the flared gable dormer into his room and walked downstairs. He went for the front door as discreetly as possible to avoid an awkward conversation with his dad. As he reached for the door he was interrupted by his father's words.

"Leaving already? Another trip with your brother?"

Axel paused with dread. He slowly reached for the handle.

"Can I at least ask when you'll be back?"

"Next week."

Peter turned the light on in the kitchen. "Russ called again today. I had to start deleting his messages on the answering machine. There have been too many. He's worried about you. We all are."

Axel's hand trembled. "I'll be fine," he responded as he opened the door and slammed it shut behind him.

July 15th, 2000. Axel and Karl had sworn they would get their revenge, and they had gotten it. Fifteen higher-up government executive assassinations completed, three left to go. This included everyone responsible for or involved in Azrael's murder. Next on the list, Tyler Murtagh. He oversaw the departure of the mercenaries, knew their intent, and did nothing to prevent it. His family was on vacation, and he was home alone for the evening.

On a humid summer night just after ten o'clock, the Army of Two arrived in their dad's old muscle car. Pulling into the driveway, Axel turned to Karl and made a smart-ass remark about the place and overpaid government employees.

Karl wore dark blue jeans with a black hoodie under a leather jacket. Axel was also dressed in jeans and a hoodie with a black collared military jacket. Before exiting the vehicle, they put on black bandanas covering the lower halves of their faces. They finished their shroud by covering the rest with their hoods, then headed inside, ready for the kill.

Approaching the door, Axel tossed a hand grenade at the entrance. It blew a hole near the handle as the door fell back into the house. The noise startled Mr. Murtagh, leading him to rush downstairs to see what caused it. When he saw a tall man, his face concealed by a hood and mask, carrying an automatic handgun, step through his shattered front door, he froze on the stairs, eyes wide with terror.

The vengeful brother lifted his weapon. He fired a horizontal line across his prey's legs, cutting them in half with the stream of bullets. Mr. Murtagh fell down the rest of the stairs, screaming in pain. His legs dangled, barely attached to his waist. He dragged himself to Axel's feet in tears, begging for his life. With no remorse, Axel finished him off—one bullet to the heart, another to the head. The brothers then poured gas all over the house and set up some explosives by the body. They fled the scene, peeling out and lighting a trail of gas.

Behind them, the whole house exploded, leaving a mushroom-shaped cloud of smoke. The Two returned to their headquarters where all the information pertaining to those responsible for the death of Azrael was held.

The ADA, aka the Anarchists of Democratic Associations, was another form of government that answered only to justice not to Big

Brother. An independent intelligence agency with the people being their primary concern. Some knew of them as Anonymous. They had sought out the brothers shortly after the tragedy and made a deal with them. They would give them all of the names of everyone responsible and in return the brothers would owe them an equal number of kills. For every revenge mission Axel and Karl achieved, they received a task to carry out for the ADA.

The brothers drove downtown and parked on the side between two buildings. They got out and walked around the corner to a big building with large glass windows for walls. An agent greeted them at the door.

"Good morning, Miles," Karl said to the doorman.

"It's a pleasure to see you Agent Gold." He paused and looked at the younger brother. "And of course, Agent Silver. How is this magnificent day treating the both of you?"

"Not as good as it's treating you evidently," Axel remarked sarcastically.

"Very well then, Mr. Black is awaiting you in his quarters." The agent opened the door for them and gestured inside with his head.

The brothers entered the building. Inside was a large open room with two staircases wrapping around the walls to the left and right. Directly in front of them was a long hallway that led to the elevator. They continued down the hall and up the elevator to the third floor. When they arrived at Mr. Black's office, he was standing by his desk waiting for them. He was around Axel's height. Maybe six foot three. His skin pale, with dark hair, cut short and very well kept. He wore a fully tailored suit, like most of the agents.

"Good work on your last mission, agents. You are truly making a difference. Ridding the world of all this corruption. As agreed, the agency will decide your next task."

He walked over to the Two and handed them a manila envelope full of documents. "Here are your next two targets. Chris Evenson is next on the list. He is rarely isolated or alone. This weekend he is on a hunting trip upcountry by his lonesome. This would be an opportune moment for your business. This meeting is adjourned."

The brothers nodded, then headed off to their next destination. They drove for a few hours upcountry and found a small motel to set up home base. After checking in, they headed to their room. Axel immediately dug into his bag and pulled out a bottle. A fifth of Pendleton Whisky. Before the loss of Azrael, he could barely finish a beer on his own. Ever since then, he could hardly go without a drink. Drinking almost every moment of every day. He took a few heavy swigs of his bottle. Holding it tight.

"Careful with that stuff," Karl said.

"I'll be fine. I don't need to be careful with this one. It's not like if I miss a shot, I might ruin a family. It's just animals out here."

"You…" Karl wanted so badly to tell his lost brother how he really felt. He worried about him daily. He held back. "You're right."

They prepared their weapons and gear for the hunt.

"Won't be needing any silencers on this one," Axel joked.

Karl just nodded with a half-hearted smile, struggling internally. "Give me a swig of that," he said after deciding he needed something to take the edge off as well.

He took a few drinks from Axel's bottle of liquor. The brothers then left the hotel, ready for the kill. They entered the woods near the cabin Chris Evenson was supposedly staying in. Axel had a particular distaste for the woods. So many memories of them brought him to misery.

They quietly walked in between rows of trees, each standing around five feet apart from one another.

"It's peaceful out here in the boons," the older brother commented.

"Something like that. I find it kind of hard to find peace in anything nowadays. I was thinking it's kind of ironic that we're hunting someone that is himself hunting something."

"Not sure if ironic is the best way to put it, but yeah, you could say that."

"You must be pretty happy that you got the title Agent Gold," Axel commented, a jealous edge to his tone.

Karl instantly stopped in his tracks and turned toward him with fury in his eyes. "Just to be clear, I'm not happy about any of this. In fact, in this range of excellence I would rather be considered bronze."

"That's catchy. Maybe if you ever have a solo act that will be your new name. Karl Bronze, the Army of One."

Karl gave him the least amused look he was capable of.

They were interrupted by an unknown voice in the distance. "Howdy."

"Damn it, I hate when they talk," Axel commented.

"What are y'all doing out here?" Chris asked the brothers. "I could've accidentally gotcha." Suddenly, he stopped in his tracks. "Careful. Don't make a move."

The Two turned around to see what he was looking at. About ten feet behind them was a full-grown mountain lion with its cubs.

Axel sighed. "I'm not doing this today." He turned toward Chris and pulled out his revolver, aiming at Chris's head.

"Wait!" Karl yelled as Axel fired a bullet.

The mountain lion became enraged and charged the brothers. Karl pushed Axel out of the way, and he tumbled to the ground. Karl was then tackled by the great feline. He fell on his back, holding the lion's paws back from his face. The beast's strength was so great even Karl struggled to control its flailing claws. He wrestled with it for a moment, then managed to get out from underneath the creature, throwing the beast a few feet away. It turned back and charged as Karl rolled to his side and onto his feet.

The lion then leapt toward him; he sent his fist into the side of its head. The beast stumbled around, disoriented. Karl ran over to a hollowed-out tree stump lying on the forest floor near him. He lifted it in front of him and split it vertically in two. He walked over to the mountain lion, which was still stumbling around. With much remorse, he stabbed the sharp half-log through its back, pinning it to the ground. The beast exhaled one last time. Its cubs ran away, frightened.

"What the hell is wrong with you?" Karl demanded aggressively.

"I'm sorry. We had to kill him. I figured the longer we waited, the harder it would be."

"You're probably right. In the future, just communicate, please."

The two left the woods and went back to the motel. They packed up in a hurry and headed to their next mission. First, they took the cherry red Pontiac back to their shop where they stored all their extra artillery. Every time Karl looked at the Pontiac, the cherry gloss looked a tad more blood red. His mental wellbeing was becoming compromised. The brothers collected what they needed for the mission and headed east on a road trip across state lines.

Zachary Morris was their next head for the slaughter. This job was a little more complicated than the last. He was at work, in a government building surrounded by businesses. They parked out back in the alleyway. Karl tossed Axel up to the fire escape, and he let the ladder down. The two climbed the fire escape up to the third story. Karl picked the lock and the moment he pulled the door open, he received an extremely high-voltage shock. A crackling explosion knocked him back off the fire escape, and he fell multiple stories to the ground. Axel stepped back near the railing, avoiding the shock.

It's a trap, Axel realized, raising his sidearm in front of him and entering the building. When he stepped in, he saw the building was clear, absolutely no one in sight. But then he received a few sporadic gunshots to the chest. His body quickly rejected the bullets and healed the wounds. He shot at a desk and a pillar—the only objects he could see that someone might be hiding behind. Another round of bullets streamed across his chest. *Where is he?* Axel thought. He unloaded his clip, firing it from side to side in front of him. Just before the clip was empty, he got a hit.

A bullet stopped midair, floating above the ground, surrounded by red fluid. The fluid started from the front and came toward the back of the bullet, dripping down a faint outline of a cylindrical shape tapering downward in size. *Perhaps a man's leg?* Axel thought. He reached for his second clip on his belt. The second he looked down to grab it, he felt his chest being repeatedly stabbed by an unseen source. He swung in front of him and connected with something, hopefully a head. In response, the younger brother received multiple strong blows to his head. These were no mortal man's punches. He hadn't felt this level of pain since he used to spar with Karl.

Axel felt an arm wrap around his forehead from behind. He felt his throat being slit all the way open. Deep. Cutting straight to the bone. He felt the blade on his spine, scraping back and forth. Right before his spine gave way, Karl leapt over the ledge behind them.

Noting the blurry movements of the stealth figure, Karl grabbed its chest from behind and reached around to seize the invisible arm holding the knife. Now that the figure was closer, he realized the active camouflage didn't work as well, and he could see the shape of a man's body. He grabbed the figure by its left shoulder and spun, throwing it as hard as he could into the neighboring building. All he could see was blood splattering the wall where it must have impacted. Then a moment later, he heard a thud as the figure must have hit the ground.

By the time Karl helped his brother to his feet, Axel's throat wound was sealed shut. The two hurried down the ladders, then jumped down from the bottom story to the ground ten feet below. When they got to the circle of blood, Karl kicked where he thought the body had landed, failing to make contact with it. He looked around the area and then at Axel and nodded his head to the right toward their escape. The two fled to the car and peeled out in a hurry to get off the radar.

"We need to find somewhere low key," Karl told his brother. "I don't know what that was, but what I do know is that was a setup, and we are more than likely being tracked. We need to find the smallest, low-profile town we can and lie low for a couple days."

"You think the agency was in on it? They should have been the only ones to know," Axel said, wondering if they had been betrayed.

"I don't think so, but there is no way to know for sure. We will wait it out and find a safe way to contact Mr. Black when the time is right."

They drove further east along the highway till they found a small town they had never heard of. Charlston city, population twenty-five hundred.

"Perfect." Karl took the exit.

They pulled up to an old beat-up gas station neighboring a small shopping center. "I'm gonna go in and pay. You should find us something to eat."

"I'll see what they've got," Axel responded and walked over to the shopping center. It was small, with four stores attached in a square shape. The lost brother wandered down the sidewalk until he found a burger joint. As he stood in the long line waiting to order some food, a weird shiver passed over his body. He turned around and looked down the sidewalk, where he saw a woman walking away from him with long black hair. She seemed oddly familiar. Axel just stared curiously. The woman stopped in front of the salon next door. She turned to her left, revealing the side of her face. A face Axel could never forget. Azrael?

Axel pursued her immediately, power-walking in that direction before speeding up into a jog. He ran up to the door and opened it. When he looked inside the nail salon, the familiar woman was nowhere to be seen. He walked up to the lady at the counter. "Did you see a young woman with long black hair come in here?"

"That's not very specific. When?" the lady asked.

"Just now. She just walked through the doors."

"I haven't had any customers for at least thirty minutes," she told Axel in confusion.

Axel left the salon and stepped out of the parking lot, looking around him. She was nowhere to be seen. It couldn't have been her… He headed back to the car where Karl was impatiently waiting.

"Where's the food?" Karl asked, disappointed.

"I… it was too long to wait."

"Whatever. I guess jerky will have to suffice. We should go."

They drove for five minutes to find a bed and breakfast. "Maurine's Inn. Sounds promising," Karl commented sarcastically as they pulled up and parked.

Once inside their room, Karl locked the door and closed the curtain. "I'm getting really tired of these motels. I can't wait to have somewhere I can call home again."

Karl waited for a moment and after Axel didn't respond, he said, "You alright?"

Axel just stared at the wall. His face blank. After a minute, he spoke. "I swear I saw Azrael today at the shopping center."

"Axel... you gotta…"

"It wasn't just a memory this time. I really saw her. It was real."

Karl became angry. "Look, we just got ambushed by something or someone that was invisible, man! Are you not the least bit concerned about that? Like that maybe they might come back. How much did you have to drink before you thought you saw her?"

"I was sober. I haven't had any since this morning."

"Don't tell me that. You're never sober anymore. I've seen you when you think I'm not looking. Gulping down your goddamn airplane bottles of whisky."

Axel stood up and grabbed the keys. He stormed out the door.

"Where are you going?" Karl called after him.

"To stock up. I need a drink," Axel told him as he got in the car. Karl went back into the motel room, shaking his head.

"Goddamn it!" he yelled and smashed the bedside table to bits.

Axel drove the Pontiac back to the little strip mall where he had seen a liquor store. He went in and grabbed a few bottles of Pendleton. While he was at the checkout, he asked the clerk, "Have you noticed anything strange around here? I swore I saw someone I know, but I'm sure that it couldn't be her, and I'm trying to figure out if I'm losing my mind."

The clerk was a young man around Axel's age wearing a large black shirt and a ball cap. His face turned serious, and he gave his coworker a concerned look. The coworker, an older man in a polo, matched his expression.

"This town is known for strange happenings. It's best not to get involved," the older man answered in his stead.

"Let's say I do want to get involved. What happened here?" Axel asked.

The man in the ball cap shook his head. "We all see things from time to time. As long as you ignore them, you'll be fine."

Axel smacked his hand on the counter with a hundred-dollar bill and aggressively asked the man. "What happened here?"

"They say quite some time ago there was a secret government operation. As the story goes, some form of classified division of the government was testing some experimental technology here in town. Supposedly, they opened a gateway to hell. That gateway was never closed… So, they say. With everything I've seen in my ten years living here, I'd say they're right."

Without hesitating, Axel asked him, "Where can I find this gateway?"

The man wrote down the directions on a piece of paper and handed it to Axel. He bought his liquor and got in the car. After pulling around behind the building, he opened a bottle and took a few drinks. How could he go on? What was the point of it? Growing up homeschooled, he hadn't experienced his fair share of human interaction. No girlfriends, only a couple of friends in general. Although his family was close-knit, they were few in number and couldn't give him what he needed in the next phase of his life. When he met Azrael, their connection felt divine. A match made by the heavens. He knew where his destiny lay. But fate had played a trick on him yet again.

He drove to the location the clerk had directed him to, a very old cemetery with a large Victorian-era building in the center. The building dated back at least a couple hundred years. *This must be it*, he thought.

After parking the car, he walked over to the entrance. He lit up a Lucky Strike cigarette he had been saving for an occasion. He felt a drop of rain fall upon his cheek. He looked up to see the clear sky above him. The wind began picking up out of nowhere. The rain fell, drenching his smoke. A short wooden fence surrounded the graveyard. He put his hand on the gate to open it. Just a moment before he stepped on the holy ground, he was startled by an unknown man's voice.

"Sad sight, isn't it?"

Axel paused and looked to his side to see an old man who seemed to be the groundskeeper, holding a rake in his hands.

"Seems lonely. No flowers. Not a single visitor. All of these lost loved ones left forgotten."

Axel turned toward the man, and in a distraught manner, he replied, "No loved one is ever truly lost or forgotten."

"Maybe they should be. Sometimes in life things happen that are out of our control. Death is only natural. To deny death is to deny life itself. No man is exempt from death, judgment, or fate."

Axel responded, "Love has no bounds, no limits, and it cannot be undone. I will do what I must."

He proceeded to push the gate open, and after one step into the graveyard, thunder roared. Looking over his shoulder, he saw the man had mysteriously disappeared.

CHAPTER 3

The Gateway

The path to the building must have only been fifty feet from the entrance, but for every step he took, it seemed he was a step further away. The sky began getting darker at an uncomfortable pace. Thunder roared as lightning flashed without a single cloud in sight. After walking for some time, he arrived at the door. He went for the handle, but it was locked. He knocked twice and attempted to look through a mail slot in the door. The inside of the building seemed like a completely normal house at first glance. He knocked again three times and then heard loud footsteps that sounded like someone big was walking down the stairs, approaching the door with haste. The footsteps stopped at the door, and a moment later, the door swung open.

He drew his weapon with his right hand. A sawed-off double-barrel Winchester that he rarely used. In his left hand, he held a cheap pocket LED flashlight. He walked through the door holding his gun in front of him. Once he was fully inside the house, the door slammed shut behind him. He was unfazed by the supernatural anomalies, knowing exactly why he was there.

He continued into the house down a long hallway with a red rug. He shone his light down the rug all the way to a small door that appeared to lead to a basement or closet. As he approached the door slowly, he noticed a single picture on the wall to his left and focused his light on it. He approached it, trying to make out what the picture was of. When he got close enough, he realized it was a picture of him and Azrael with two children. Heaven couldn't bless him with such a sight. The image began to change. It turned then, into a picture of his family, his mother included. He watched as his mother began to fade out of the picture. Soon after his father faded away, then his brother. Leaving only himself in the portrait. He noticed his face began to change. His smile turned to a grin. His cheeks turned pale, his eyes black. The face became so foul and frightful he knocked the picture to the ground, breaking the frame as it landed face down.

He knelt gently and lifted the side to flip it back over. At the same time, he heard three knocks from behind him. He turned around to see the door at the end of the hallway was no longer there. He turned back in front of him to find the portrait and rug were both gone. He stumbled back to the entrance, confused. On his way, he noticed the rug again, now leading up the stairs. He followed the red rug upstairs with his gun out, now beginning to question the situation he had found himself in.

At the top of the stairs, he entered a room with a high ceiling. At the end of the room, three doors stood evenly spaced apart. He heard a sharp, high-pitched piercing tone that formed a scratchy, painful voice.

"Beyond you lie three judgments. Humanity needs correction. God gave man life, and in return, man gave God only death and destruction. Behind the first door, God bestows grace upon humanity, granting everlasting happiness. Behind the second, He will grant grace only to the just and good-hearted. Behind the third door, justice will have its course. Every man, woman and child who has sinned will rest in their divergence, and the fate of humanity will be accomplished."

Axel hesitated for just a moment. He stepped toward the third door. Then quickly he walked through the second. He suddenly realized he had just walked in through the front door. *Impossible*, he thought. Immediately he noticed the red rug was back in its original location. His light followed it down the hallway to the door that was now back in its original place. He ran at the door with a steady jog, ripped it open and stood in awe at the sight of a plain wall.

He screamed and yelled, "Damn you! I demand an entry to hell. Where is the gatekeeper? I have the price to pay." In a moment of silence his flashlight flickered and died. As the last bit of light seeping into the house faded away, the floors creaked, the house's tears. In the peak of darkness, he heard an old, deep, powerful voice reply, "The gatekeeper greeted you when you first arrived at the gate. You are already here."

On a bright summer's day in the spring of 1985 two young boys headed down to the river on a calm Saturday. Running through a path in the forest on their way to the swimming hole, they skipped in excitement. The younger boy, who had messy, dirty blond hair, wore a jean vest with the sleeves cut off. In front of him was his older brother who had deep brown hair. He was wearing a baggy old army shirt from his grandfather.

"How much you wanna bet I'll beat you to the ledge?" the blond boy told his brother.

"I'll bet dad's BB gun," the older child responded.

They both ran up to a cliff leading down to the swimming hole. As they approached the ledge, they sped up and dived off. Twenty feet down into the water, the younger brother landed in the center in the deepest point. His brother was not so fortunate. He had jumped too far with too much power. He missed the deep spot and smashed his head directly into a rock. When the younger brother surfaced, he saw what had happened.

"Karl!" he screamed violently. He swam over as fast as his arms would pull him.

Karl didn't have a scratch on him. "I'm okay, Axel."

Axel stood up, now in the shallow part of the river. He stared at his brother like he had never seen him before. "I saw you hit the rock... How are you alive?"

Karl looked at the ledge they had jumped from, trying to think of a lie to cover up the truth behind why he was okay.

Karl suddenly awoke from his nap. He went to the motel lobby and grabbed some coffee. He sat in his room enjoying his cup of coffee while awaiting his brother's return. After a couple of hours had passed since Axel left for the store, Karl became worried. He gathered all of their belongings and checked out of the motel. After checking out, he walked a few blocks down the road till he found an old beat-up car, seemingly abandoned. He broke the window, unlocked the door, and hotwired the car. He peeled out as discreetly as possible.

He drove to the liquor store. When he arrived, he looked around the parking lot; the Pontiac was nowhere to be seen. He continued inside and asked the clerk if he had seen his brother. "He would have bought a few bottles of whisky. A tall, young blond man." He described him to the clerk with the ball cap.

"Well, he was here… He had a lot of questions about the town. He needed answers as to why he was seeing someone that couldn't have been here."

"And what did you tell him?"

The clerk's face fell. "Umm, I told him what I'll tell you. It's best not to get involved in the strange happenings in town."

Karl reached over the counter and grabbed him by his shirt. "What else did you tell him?" he demanded angrily.

This was enough for the clerk to tell him and give him the directions to the gateway. Karl left the store, walking out in the parking lot toward the stolen car. As he passed a large Suburban that he had parked behind, he noticed two police cars parked on each side of the car.

"Damn, that was fast," he muttered to himself. He continued walking, trying to play off any connection with the vehicle.

One of the police cars turned his lights on and pulled out, driving up next to Karl. He stopped walking. The officer that pulled him over hopped out of the car. The other officer did the same and made his way over to the Fassbinder brother.

"Where you headed?" the first officer asked.

Karl looked at the officer's shoulder and saw his sergeant patch. "I'm looking for my brother, Sergeant. He was supposed to pick me up here hours ago and never showed. I just decided to start walking and hoped he would find me along the way."

"It sure looked like you were about to get into that car back there," the sergeant replied. "Is that your car?"

"No, no, I definitely was not."

The sergeant questioned him further. "Where does your brother live? Does he live with you?"

Karl was far from home and had no legitimate reason for being in town. He started to realize there would only be one way out of this. "We're from out of state but I must be on my way. As I said before, my brother is missing, and I'm worried about him. Thank you for your service."

He turned around and walked in the opposite direction of the officers.

"Stop right there!" the sergeant demanded as Karl heard the click of his gun being readied.

He stopped immediately.

"We're going to need you to come with us."

Karl turned around, facing his potential foes. "My name is Karl Fassbinder. If you don't know who I am, you don't want to. Please let me leave in peace and all of us will get home to our families safe," he warned them.

With his gun drawn, pointed at Karl, the sergeant declared, "Put your hands on your head and get on your knees or we'll shoot."

Karl gradually lifted his hands above his head. He then placed them on his head and knelt. The sergeant walked around behind him, grabbing one hand, putting it behind his back and cuffing it. Advancing to the other hand with haste.

"Stand up," he demanded.

Karl rose to his feet. Checking his peripherals, he noticed both officers' guns were holstered. Karl ripped apart his handcuffs, devastating them. They shattered so fast, metal shards sprayed like dust in the air. He pivoted a full one-eighty at an impossible speed. He threw one blow into the sergeant's chest, which sent him flying five feet into the air and slamming into an SUV. He then pivoted his left foot back, turning ninety degrees and leaning forward. Bending his knees, planting his feet, he launched himself forward.

The other officer reached for his sidearm. Karl dashed ten feet forward in a split second, ripping the gun out of the officer's hand.

Crumpling it up with just his left hand, Karl grabbed the center of the officer's uniform with his right hand, lifting him a few feet off the ground.

"You should have listened to me."

He threw the officer a few feet back. Just enough to knock the wind out of him. The sergeant, however, Karl may have hit a little too hard. He walked over to examine him. His body all slashed up, with fragments of steel and fiberglass from the SUV embedded in him. Karl checked his pulse and got a positive reading. Thank God. The sergeant would recover in time, but his wounds were severe.

"What have I done?" Karl muttered with great remorse.

He got into the original stolen car and drove off to find his brother. When he arrived at the destination, he saw the Pontiac. Yet Axel was nowhere in sight. Karl stepped out, inspecting the graveyard. He couldn't see anywhere Axel could have gone. No fences or buildings.

He heard a man's voice from somewhere off to the left. "You won't find what you're looking for," the mysterious man stated.

Karl turned around to see an old man wearing worn grey coveralls over a collared white shirt, with a fedora hat upon his head.

"Please, sir, have you seen my brother?" he asked. "Our family has been through a lot. We don't have much left but each other. Do you know where he is?"

"It's not where he is but who he is that should be your concern. Sometimes things happen that change people forever. He will return, but he will never be the same."

Karl was then startled by an unbearably loud, deep noise. It sounded almost like an aircraft carrier horn. He turned to see what was causing it. He looked upon a darkening sky, though only the sky above the graveyard had blackened. He saw a red crackling light in the center of the cemetery that looked like red lightning. Beginning and ending nowhere, jolting up and down. The lightning then moved back and forth horizontally. The noise continued to get louder as the red light expanded its perimeter. Bouncing around in a circle now. He noticed a minute space in between the red mysterious lightning and could see a dark red building through the gap. The gap was getting bigger. The light became brighter and brighter until he couldn't even handle looking in that direction. He looked away, protecting his eyes.

The noise came to an abrupt stop as the light disappeared. He smelled something so rancid he almost puked. The worst smell he had ever experienced. He turned back to see a fence standing before him. Decorated in skulls. Dripping with flesh and blood. At the top of the fence was some writing in an ancient language he did not recognize. Maybe Latin. He regretfully opened the gate, stepped through, and gazed upon a giant building with skeletons for walls. A bone door was actively bleeding, as if it were still alive.

He approached the building and opened the door. Once he opened the door and stepped into the house, he heard cracking noises. He looked up to see the whole house was collapsing on top of him. As it fell apart, parts of the structure hit the ground and deteriorated on impact. The dust cleared, and Karl stood in his place, his arms raised above him, shielding his head. He lowered his arms to see his brother before him. He was on his knees and naked. Axel's back was covered in long bleeding gashes that appeared to have been caused by years of torture. Why hadn't they healed? Axel slowly rose to his feet and turned toward his brother. Karl's face turned to a partial smile. He was just happy to see him alive at this point.

"Axel! What happened to you? What have you done?" Karl demanded.

Axel looked up with a blank, emotionless face. His eyes locked with Karl's, showing no expression. As if he had never met him before. He walked to Karl, then right past him toward the gate. Karl just stood in place, shocked. Trying to figure out what had happened and why his brother did not recognize him.

Axel exited the gate and headed out into the road. He turned to see two police cars coming in his direction. They stopped alongside him. They must have received a call about the building collapsing.

"Sir, are you okay?" the first officer asked him as he got out of his squad car and walked over to him.

After no response, the officer put his hand on Axel's shoulder, worried about him. His hand started aging at a visible rate. Maybe thirty years a second. He tried to pull his hand back, but it was stuck. His hand disintegrated into nothingness, leaving a nub at the end of his arm.

Axel turned around and grabbed the officer's throat, quickly snapping his neck, then tossing him to the side. The other police officer called in for backup and drew his firearm. He opened fire on Axel. Axel walked toward the officer at a steady pace. Unfazed by every bullet he took. The officer finished his clip, watching as all of his bullets retracted from Axel's body. Instead of reloading, he decided to run in the opposite direction.

Axel lifted his hand in front of him in the direction of the officer and turned it slightly sideways. The officer's legs both broke all the way through the side in the same direction and angle of Axel's hand movement.

The officer crawled away and screamed, pleading. "Let me go, please, I have a family."

Axel grinned in a very sinister tone and raised his hand again. Out of nowhere, he was tackled to the ground. Karl, in one fluid motion, lifted him up and chucked him through the police car, and he burst out the other side. He rolled ten to twenty feet on the ground.

Karl tossed the officer his sidearm. "Try to hide," he briefly directed him.

Karl looked back at where Axel had landed to see he had vanished. Karl ran to the Pontiac and headed back into town. Where the hell had he gone?

CHAPTER 4

When Hell First Arrived

A couple of hours before sunset, Karl headed back west out of Charlston toward the city. He arrived shortly after sundown. When he got to town, he went straight to a neighborhood market to use the payphone. He parked and walked to the door. He noticed two people standing outside arguing on their cell phones. He went in and grabbed a few snacks and a coffee.

"Slow day?" he asked the cashier.

The young woman ringing up his items responded, "Not exactly. Apparently all the credit and debit systems are down. Everybody is getting mad at me, but from what I've heard, it's everywhere in town."

"That can't be good. How could that be?" he asked her.

"Beats me. Is this everything?"

"Yeah…" Karl went outside and put a few quarters in the payphone. He dialed the number he had memorized for the direct line to Mr. Black. The number dialed. It went directly to a busy tone. He hung the phone up and right as he did, it rang back. He answered.

The head of the agency spoke. "We need to meet. Immediately," he told Karl.

"Wait, how did you know—" Karl responded, but was interrupted.

"Meet on the top of the parking garage at the intersection of J and tenth street. We'll expect you in exactly thirty minutes."

The call cut off. Karl set the phone down, wrinkling his brow.

Back in his car, he drove to the meetup location. He gripped the wheel firmly as he thought about the last words he had said to Axel. *What end have I driven him to? He needed guidance, and I sent him away.*

On top of a five-story parking garage he found two black Cadillac Escalades parked with a car space in between them. He parked between the SUVs and got out of his car. He walked around back to find two agents dressed in their typical all black suits. Agent Black stepped out of the back left door of one of the SUVs.

"So, in four hours your brother managed to shut down the nationwide trade system. He wiped every bit of information at every bank clean. The whole nation is in chaos. Riots, protests, all hell has broken loose," Mr. Black explained.

Karl looked over the barrier and down at the street. He was in disbelief.

"It isn't him. He found a gateway to another dimension, and I fear that what came back was not my brother at all."

"You're telling me that one of the most dangerous men in the world is now being controlled by a being from another dimension? You know what you need to do." Mr. Black handed Karl a piece of paper with directions on it. "This is where all the hackings originated from. We're not sure he's still there, but it's a start."

Karl looked at the paper, then back at Mr. Black's face. He stepped closer to him. Uncomfortably close, face to face. "You want me to kill him? There must be another way."

"You saw what he did to those police officers. There is no other way."

"He's my brother. You find someone else to do it if it must be done."

"There is no other that can complete this task. You know this. If you look deep within yourself, you'll understand. Think of all the death that would be on your hands if he is left to do his bidding."

Karl closed his eyes and meditated for a moment. He opened them and grabbed the paper. then nodded at his superior and continued off to complete this dreadful task. Axel was in Los Angeles. The reason for this was unknown, but it appeared his intent was to create chaos, so somewhere within that population would be an ideal start.

The older Fassbinder brother had a seven-hour drive ahead of him. He stopped at a gas station, filled up his tank, and was on his way. Headed south on the interstate he drove as fast as he could. Around eighty miles per hour. Throughout the drive he had difficulties focusing on the road and his mission. A plethora of memories and scenarios bled from his mind. He fought his distractions as hard as he could. His eyes became heavy and fell shut for just a moment.

"Check," the young blond boy declared as he moved his bishop into his brother's king's line of sight. His brother smiled and then moved his knight, blocking the attack.

"Nice try," the older brother responded.

"Who's winning?" their father asked while sitting on the couch behind them in the living room. "It's a pretty close one."

The blond boy told his dad, but then continued, "I might actually get him this time."

The brown-haired brother moved his queen. He took his opponent's rook, cornering the king. "That would be checkmate."

"No! Aw, man, I was so close." The three laughed together. "You're next, Dad."

"Oh man, sounds like my time as reigning champion is almost over," their dad playfully responded. He walked into the kitchen to grab a soda.

"I feel like you're the queen, Karl."

Karl looked at his brother, upset. "What's that supposed to mean?"

"It's like each piece has their own superpower, but the queen has all of them."

Karl smiled. "I guess I'll take that as a compliment.

His younger brother looked down with a sad face. "I wish I was special like you."

"Hey, it's okay, Axel. You are special. We are in this together. We're going down to the city tomorrow with Mr. Price, remember? I'll make you a deal. If you promise not to be sad, you can practice jumping buildings with me when we're there."

Axel's face turned from a frown to a smile. "Deal."

A loud horn blared at Karl. He opened his eyes to see he was veering into the other lane. He quickly corrected himself. When he reached the city limits of LA he noticed the difference right away. No open businesses. Mayhem everywhere. The roads were closed off because of the riots. He parked and continued on foot into the city. The streets were in ruin. Parked cars were burning, as were some of the shops. The whole metropolis had become a war zone.

He approached the credit agency's building far into the city. The place where Axel had supposedly hacked the online trade. He walked to the door to see it was destroyed. Shattered glass coated the ground beneath him. He stepped through the opening, continuing into the building, where he observed the aftermath of the havoc that must have taken place. It was no surprise that the building was abandoned. However, he expected there to be possible corpses. If his new foe had been there before him, he expected some evidence. Yet there was not even a single body in sight.

He walked down the hall to the elevator. As he reached for the button, he was interrupted by the ding of the elevator arriving. The doors opened, revealing it was empty. He entered the elevator and looked for the number pad. When he gazed upon it, the numbers became transparent and began to change, before stopping and forming numbers once again. He saw there were thirteen floors, and between twelve and thirteen there was a button for twenty-three. He pressed the enigmatic button and ascended to the unknown.

The light flickered all the way to the mysterious floor. When the door opened, the floor he arrived at was pitch black. The elevator light turned out. He walked forward into the unseen. A voice questioned him, "Why are you so willing to save a man who has always resented you? Who has always envied your might, and who now dives greedily into the depths of the unknown in search of undoing justice?"

"He's my brother, and family means everything in this world," Karl answered.

"*Is* he your brother? What is truth but reassurance to our nobility. Blinded by your love for your brother you leave your fate unmet," the voice lectured.

"Who are you to question my fate?"

Suddenly a pale face became visible directly in front of Karl, only a foot away. It screamed, "I am the question of fate!"

Karl fell backwards startled by the supernatural event. The lights turned on, revealing Axel, sitting in a chair across the room maybe twenty feet away, facing the opposite direction.

"Brother, you must be in there somewhere. You need to find a way back," he pleaded.

Receiving no response, he approached Axel. When he got closer, he could see Axel was different. He stepped in front of him as his brother looked up. His face was as old as time. His skin, the palest of whites. His eyes, black crevices leading deep inward. Axel grinned frightfully as he stood up and picked up Karl, hurling him into the wall fifteen feet away.

A different, powerful voice spoke from Axel's mouth, "I am humanity."

Karl fell to the ground and looked up to see Axel was gone. He was then picked up from behind and thrown into the center of the room. Karl stood up from his blow, sensing another attack from behind. He leaned his left shoulder down, catching a fist, and threw Axel to the ground in front of him. A desk was lifted up in the distance by an unseen force and thrown into Karl, knocking him down, away from Axel. Darkness engulfed the room, rendering Karl blind again.

"You're far too late to prevent his destiny. If you defeat me now, it will only postpone the inevitable," the voice in Axel declared.

"I create my own destiny," Karl replied.

He closed his eyes and held his breath, triggering his other senses. After ten seconds he could hear his own heartbeat. He moved his hand behind his back and grabbed hold of his pistol. He canceled out all the other noises, including his heartbeat. He focused all his senses on the noise surrounding him. Then he heard it. The heartbeat next to him.

In one fluid motion he spun at his target, unsheathing his pistol in that direction. He fired one single shot. Silence. A moment later, a thud.

The lights turned on as he looked down at Axel's body in front of him. A giant hole in the middle of his forehead where the bullet was lodged. He dropped to his knees and took out his Leatherman. Using the plyers, he shoved them into Axel's head, retrieving the bullet from his brain. Karl held his brother's hand. He sat there and prayed for some time.

After ten minutes had passed, he had almost given up. A tear streamed down his cheek, dropping to the ground. Just as he felt it, he felt his brother grasping his hand.

Karl looked toward Axel. His eyes opened. All he could say to his brother was, "What have I done?"

September 13th, 2000. Some weeks after the incident in the City of Angels, the Fassbinder brothers had been keeping a low profile. It was time to get back to business. They only had two kills left for the ADA. After everything that had happened, the agency deemed Axel a threat to humanity, and for good reason. They did not want him to live freely. However, Karl had insisted that they would finish their contract, and his brother would never be deemed a threat to humanity ever again. The agency was wary of this agreement. But Karl had already proven his ability to subdue Axel if needed. They believed in Karl's determination and had no intention of burning bridges with such a valuable asset as him.

The two were at a motel planning their strategy. This mission was trickier than most. Three armed guards and potential innocent civilians involved. Mark Caine was their target. He was one of the executives that had made the decision to bring back the drug trade. This man was debatably the most responsible for Azrael's murder.

"We need to be on our A-game for this, Axel. No civilian casualties. There has been far too much blood on our hands already," Karl told his brother.

Axel sat at the end of his bed, looking at his hands with disgust. "I honestly don't know if I can even kill again, man. After everything I've done. All the death that I've caused because of her… Maybe I wasn't myself. Yet, I put myself in the situation that caused all of this. The last fifteen months I've been trying to make things right for her. But now that I look back at it, she would never have wanted any of this. If she were here today, she wouldn't be able to bear the sight of me. What have I become?" Axel's eyes flooded with sorrow.

Karl walked over and sat next to him, placing his hand on his shoulder. "You did what you thought was right. All we can do now is quit while we're ahead. The fact that you want to stop now… I mean it's better late than never. Honestly, I've been done for a while now. Since our first few kills. I just wanted to support you out of respect for Azrael. Grandpa fought crime for years and only took two lives. Both times were only to save another's. We have strayed so far from what we were meant to be. I don't even know what side we're on anymore. The Fassbinder family creed is to liberate the oppressed. We have only created more oppressed."

"So, what are we going to do about the mission?" Axel asked.

"Well, we can't just call it off. We owe them too much. We'll bring Mr. Caine to the agency and let Mr. Black fulfill his judgment himself. It's about time for him to do his own dirty work."

Karl stood up and reached his hand down to Axel. His lost brother was finally found. He smiled and grabbed his hand, then stood up. Axel wrapped his arms around his brother and held him tight. Karl held him back.

They headed back to their hometown where their base was located. When they got there, they packed up all their weapons from the shop and prepared to embark on this final task.

On the way to the city, they passed over an old wooden bridge. Karl pulled the car over and parked. He collected all their guns and artillery and put them in a duffel bag. The two walked out to the side of a cliff.

"To a new beginning," Karl stated as he threw the bag off the cliff.

The Army of Two headed back to their car and drove to their final destination. They pulled up outside a government building in the middle of downtown. They found street parking right outside. Karl turned to his brother and as he pursed his lips to speak, he was interrupted. A loud smash with an impact to his head. The Pontiac had been T-boned by a large truck that was going fifty miles per hour. Karl, being the driver, was on the side that got hit. While disoriented he sluggishly lifted his head up and looked through the truck windshield. An Uzi popped up and began raining fire on them. He stood up, breaking the roof, bending it in the direction of the incoming fire. Then, he continued to bend it in half to prevent the bullets from piercing all the way through. He ripped Axel's seatbelt off and helped him out of the car on the other side. As Axel's only power was defensive, and they had just thrown away all their weapons, Karl needed to get him out of the fight.

The brothers crawled behind the car that was parked in front of them and sat with their backs against it. The driver of the truck got out and walked toward them with an Uzi in each hand, rapidly firing at the two. Karl ripped the passenger door off the car they were hiding behind and threw it like a Frisbee at the gun slinger. As it hit the attacker, the door hardly lost its momentum. It picked them up and carried them five feet into the truck they'd come out of.

Karl heard a strange noise that sounded like a big machine powering up. He turned to see a giant man standing ten feet behind them holding a large cannon-like rocket weapon. The barrel of the cannon glowed with an unbearably bright blue light. The cannon fired a beam of blue energy directly into Karl, sending him through the line of parked cars. He traveled at least fifty feet in a straight line, bursting through vehicle after vehicle then smashing into a steel post connected to a bus stop.

Axel zig-zagged toward the man wielding the cannon. When he got close to him, he realized the man's size. He must have been at least seven feet. Maybe three hundred and fifty pounds with a muscular build. Axel quickly grabbed the gun. He swung it in a semi-circle counterclockwise, against the turn of his opponent's trigger arm. The gunman grunted in pain, letting go of his gun. He then punched Axel's face twice in quick succession. Following the attack, he picked him up by his shirt with one arm and smashed him into the car next to them.

Karl, already recovering from the massive damage, stood up and looked down at his shirt to see a large hole burned through. Some of his flesh was lightly scorched. He felt the burn immensely. Pain—this sensation was unfamiliar to him. This burn was like nothing he had ever felt. This weapon was not from this time, he determined.

Karl sprinted toward his brother, moving at least forty miles per hour. He traveled the seventy feet in a matter of seconds. He tackled the giant man jumping toward him with his hands first. He knocked the man on his back, swinging his own legs over using the momentum from his tackle to land. His feet planted as he used his upper body to finish the throw, hurling the giant twenty feet through the air. His opponent's body hit the pavement and rolled another ten feet. Karl turned toward Axel to see the original gunman advancing on him. He could now see that it was a woman. She spun her foot in a circular motion, kicking Axel in the side of his head. She pulled a knife out, pressing it to his throat. Axel grabbed her arm, holding her back. Karl being only ten feet away, planted his feet. He leaned forward, bent his knees, harnessing his energy and focus. He then released himself, jumping the whole ten feet instantly.

Karl threw one punch to the woman's head, immediately disorienting her. He then threw her on her back a few feet away.

"We need to get out of here," Karl warned his brother.

He walked to the nearest car, broke the window and hotwired it in a few moments. Axel joined him as they drove off with great haste.

The giant man walked up to the woman who was now getting up herself.

"What the hell was that?" he asked his partner. "He didn't say anything about a superhuman bodyguard."

"It doesn't matter what he is," she replied. "We have a mission. The fate of our world is in our hands. If we can't overpower him, we will outthink him. How do you kill a bulletproof man?"

The giant's face became briefly confused, then very concerned as he replied, "Time... if we do this we'll be stuck here forever."

"Whatever means necessary? The benefit outweighs the cost, Maverick," she told her partner.

"Us being the cost… Alright, Tara, I'm with you. Show them why we call you Terror Smith," Maverick replied.

They got into the truck they arrived in and followed the two to the destination they had been instructed to go to if Axel fled. Speeding up to seventy miles per hour in a forty zone, they caught up to the Fassbinders within minutes. Terror Smith was driving the truck and rammed it directly into the rear of the little sedan the two had escaped in. Karl lost control of the car and crashed it into a covered bus stop on the side of the road. The assassins got out of the car and strode over to the wreck.

Maverick took out a rectangular advanced-looking piece of technology. He turned the screen on and selected 'one hundred positive' as the amount. He set the device on the ground in front of him and took a few steps back. The two hitmen both stood about five feet behind the device. They raised their automatic weapons at the car and rained havoc upon it. Karl opened his door and ran toward them. He stepped on the device and instantly, it generated a ten-by-ten room around him. It then opened into another dimension, sending Karl through a wormhole into the future.

CHAPTER 5

To Bridge the Gap of Time

November 11th, 1925. A new age was among the land of the free. The invention of automobiles and the defeat of the soviets in World War One dominated the newspapers. Leonard Fassbinder had been with his wife Lucille for over a decade. They prayed often for her ability to carry a child to be restored. They were on the cusp of forty and knew that their time for this opportunity was limited. As for the history of the family, every generation was only capable of conceiving one child. In every other generation among them, the child would be gifted with certain abnormal traits. Some might call them abilities rather than abnormalities. These select members of the family inherited superhuman qualities—surreal abilities such as superhuman strength, being able to lift ten times the amount the strongest men on Earth could lift. Very enhanced speed and endurance in athletics. As well as being intensively invulnerable—they had skin like leather.

Taking this into consideration, Leo knew he must continue his line. He was born of the mortal existence. He knew that his son, one day, would inherit these god-like traits. Considering the importance of this family, it was imperative that he have a child. The middle-aged couple was then blessed when they found out that Lucille was indeed pregnant. Nine months later, their son Donathin was born. He was one of the members blessed with that extra something.

Don grew up on a ranch with his parents near a small town in the western United States. He tossed bales of hay from age five. He would eventually carry the cows around for exercise. In high school, Don wanted so badly to play football with his friends, but his father, Leo, regretfully forbade it. He was afraid that Don might hurt one of the other teenagers. Don struggled to have a normal childhood, unable to express himself in certain ways, including physical activities that normal kids around him participated in.

On December 7th, 1941, the Fassbinder family had known about the war going on across the Atlantic. This was the day the war came to their homeland. When Don found out about the attack on Pearl Harbor, he was furious. He felt like this was something he was meant to intervene in.

April 11th, 1944, a few years after the U.S. joined the war, Don turned eighteen. On his birthday, he headed down to the local military office and enlisted without his parents knowing. He went home that day to find his father waiting for him on the steps of his childhood home. It was a particularly windy day, the sun fading in and out of the sky. Leo stood above six feet with his black hair streaked with gray. He wore an old flannel shirt with blue jeans and dusty cowboy boots.

"You feel better now?" Leo asked his son.

Don looked around to confirm he was talking to him.

"What do you mean?" he asked his father.

"Do you feel accomplished or important? You're my son, you didn't think I would know where you went off to this morning?"

"Umm, I was just…"

Leo interrupted him, "I went to great lengths to have you deferred as a farm hand. Then you turn around and enlist anyway. Son, I know some of your friends were called off to the war. I know you feel like this may be your calling. This isn't your fight. Maybe you weren't meant to be called in the draft."

"It's everyone's fight, Father. If helping make the world a better place isn't my calling, then what could it be? Who are we if we don't stand up when someone bigger is pushing us around?"

Leo smiled and walked over to his son. He brushed the back of his fingers down his cheek. "My boy… You will be a better man than I ever was. I never told you this, but I served in the First World War. I was in the Battle of Cantigny."

Don's eyes lit up. "What? Why didn't you tell me?"

"After what I saw in the war, I didn't want you to experience what I did. I was no hero. There was no valor, only bloodshed. If you see battle, son, you will never be the same again. Know this before you step on that boat. I will always love you no matter what you decide."

Don did not take his father's lecture lightly. However, he knew exactly what he had to do. A month later he received his call to arms in the mail. The United States Army recruited him, unaware of the quality of service he may later provide. In boot camp, Don deliberately suppressed his abilities to avoid drawing attention to himself. His family had managed to keep their abilities a secret from the public thus far. He had no intention of changing this. After three months of boot camp he had made a couple friends who were to be by his side in his platoon. Carlos Lopez, a young Hispanic man from down south. Jackson Henderson, who was from New Jersey and their platoon leader. An older sergeant named Nick. Nick had enlisted after his older three brothers had fought and died in the war.

The four newly found friends were sent off to Britain to set up camp before their big battle. Upon arrival, they helped erect tents. That night they all shared a tent and popped a bottle of Glen Levit scotch. Carlos handed cigars to the other three and then lit his own.

"Always wanted to go to France. Just thought it would have been under different circumstances," Jack told the crew.

"I don't know if Nazi-occupied France counts," Carlos disputed the sentiment.

"Drink up, boys. This could be the last drink for any one of us," Nick stated pessimistically.

"Don't be so sure. The whole world is coming together for this strike. They're extremely outmanned," Don commented.

Carlos chimed in, "Don't listen to the sergeant, he's just a bitter old man.

"The shores of Normandy have never been defended by such a legion. Let's just hope God is on our side," Nick responded.

The group passed around the bottle until it was finished. Don stepped outside the tent and looked up at the deep blue sky.

"It seems so quiet and peaceful," Nick said, pulling back the tent entrance and stepping out with Don.

"So why are you here? Your paperwork said you were deferred but then voluntarily enlisted anyway? You gotta have something you're running away from to be dumb enough to join this war."

"I live in a small town near the West Coast. Half of the men in town were sent off and never returned. I guess I feel as if it's my responsibility to contribute my life on my family's behalf."

"That's very noble of you. You'll definitely make some of the other guys feel better. A lot of these guys feel like prisoners. It's hard going into battle alongside men that don't want to be there. I'll look to you to keep the others together when the bullets fly."

Don nodded to his superior. "Why do they call you 'old man'? How old are you?"

Nick laughed and shook his head. "I just turned thirty. In military years, that's old. Most of these guys don't make it past twenty-five."

"Wow, okay, well at least we have you with us."

"I wish it were that simple. Get some sleep. We leave in four hours," he told Don.

Don lay down, uneasily rolling back and forth, unable to rest properly. It was time. June 6th, 1944. Don and his military platoon loaded up in the square-shaped landing craft. They departed their base, on the way to the beach of Normandy. Commencing Operation Neptune. The roar of the ocean crashed over the boats. The platoon was drenched in seawater.

"Try to keep your weapons as dry as you can!" the sergeant yelled.

They approached the beach. Once they were close enough to see the beach, they realized what this was. A slaughter. Don looked off the boat to explosions across the shoreline. The noises of gunshots rang in his ears. His platoon was getting closer to the shore.

"Were getting off here," Nick declared, letting down the boat's ramp. "We'll have to swim the rest of the way!"

The sergeant led the platoon into the water. Being too deep to stand, they all fought the sea's current while holding their guns above their heads. Flashes went off in all directions. When they got to the shore, the platoon split into three squads heading in different directions. The four companions and the rest of their squad kept right. They hid behind a barrier by the waterline.

"Lopez! You handle the guard tower to the left. Henderson, you cover him. Fassbinder, you're with me. The rest of you, just try not to get shot." The troops all nodded simultaneously. The sergeant stood, and as he did, a bullet went straight through his helmet, splattering blood onto Don's face. Don crawled up next to him and rolled his body over to see the remains of his face.

"Fassbinder, get down!" Carlos yelled at him.

A line of bullets from a turret sprayed across them. A few hit Don and deflected off his body. He looked to see Carlos, Jack, and three other soldiers were all hit. The remainder of the squad fled to the water in fear. Jack crawled over to him. Carlos was gone. Don ran up to Jack and grabbed his chest, pulling him behind some sandbags standing only a few feet off the ground. Jack's legs were cut through.

"Get out of here, Don."

Don stood up, angered. The gunman on the turret rained fire onto him. Don's body was immune to this weapon. He ran through the sand up to the wall and leapt at it. He smashed an arm into the wall, digging it a foot deep. He climbed up the twenty-foot-tall wall while being fired upon. Multiple allied soldiers stopped, awestruck. Don climbed the wall to the top and hopped over the side. Three Nazi soldiers were manning turrets and paused, confused, when they saw him. *Impossible*, they thought.

Don charged at them. He punched through the first soldier's head, exploding it on impact. He turned around and grabbed another, throwing him off the wall down to the beach. The soldier on the turret turned it toward Don. The Great Fassbinder dashed at him, and in one fluid motion, he picked the Nazi up and split his body in half. Don grabbed the turret and ripped it out of its post. He dropped down and opened the gate for his men. He headed into enemy territory, firing the turret into enemy soldiers. Walking down a dirt road surrounded by bomb shelters, he destroyed his foes by the masses.

A tank turned into his line of sight further down into the base. Don threw the turret down and sprinted toward the tank. He got close and jumped up on top of it. He then ripped open the hatch and dropped his grenade into the piloting compartment. His efforts led to the allying army breaching the shore. The battle was won solely because of this.

Later, when Don returned home, he would receive a Medal of Honor for his efforts. He would bring with him the scars of war. Internal scars, not those of the flesh. After witnessing the chaos that came with firearms firsthand, he developed a distaste for them.

March 13th, 1945. Don finally arrived in his home country after being gone for six months. The house was different. A bed had been moved into the living room, and he walked into a doctor by his father's side.

"Don!" Lucille, his mother, yelled as she ran up and gave him a hug. "We tried writing to you. I wasn't sure if you were going to be back in time."

"In time for what?" he asked his mother.

He grabbed his father's hand. "Father, you look ill. How long was I gone?"

"My heart condition finally caught up with me. I read in the paper that you were quite a hero. I was wrong. You know your destiny better than I ever have. I'm proud of you."

Don spent the next few months by his father's side until he passed away at sixty-eight years of age.

He used his inheritance money from his father and invested it in starting a carpentry business. A couple of years later, Don met his future wife, Carrie, at a rodeo near his hometown. Carrie's maiden name was Mccoy. She came from a very wealthy family and was a highly desirable woman in town. Some might call her a trophy wife. Don won her over with his wit, handyman skills, and his ability to make her laugh. Women were also very fond of military men back in that day.

Don and Carrie conceived a child shortly after marriage, when Don was only twenty-two. He was named Peter.

When Peter was five years old, his father received a letter from the Army. Carrie, her hair in blonde pigtails, wearing her favorite black dress, walked out to the street to check the mail on an ordinary Friday morning. She was disappointed when she saw what was there. She went back inside to find her husband and son sorting through their classic baseball card collection.

"Don… You got something important in the mail," she told him regretfully with her southern accent. She had moved from down south a couple of years before meeting him. Her family was practically royalty where she was from. He set down the cards he held and hurried over. He kissed her cheek and asked, "What is it, honey?"

When she handed him the piece of mail he saw the stamp on the front. His face sank. The letter was from the Army, addressing Don as the hero he was. It asked more of him. He immediately slapped on his jean jacket and got in his old yellow Plymouth. He drove to the military base nearby.

When he arrived, he arranged a meeting with the superior officer who had sent the mail.

"Mr. Fassbinder, it is my pleasure to meet you. You did our nation a great deed that day, nine years back. We need to ask one more request of you."

"I was relieved to find out that because of my combat medals I didn't have to complete my four years of service. I have a family now and want no part in anything you could have to offer."

The officer seemed disappointed. "Well, it isn't what you think. We aren't asking you to join infantry or to be any part of any war. We are creating a new elite team for special forces. I have a crew of the highest expertise soldiers in any division."

"So, like the Army Rangers?" "

Similar to that, but more covert."

"I will talk to the missus and see what I can do."

Later that day, Don had a fight with Carrie about whether or not he should join this new military division. He decided to train this new special force that was called the Green Berets. For the following three years he trained the elite division of the Army. During this time, he grew apart from Peter and Carrie, only coming home every couple of months. While training this task force he came up with a motto that he would later bring home with him. *Liberate the Oppressed.* This phrase gave a new meaning to the Green Berets and the Fassbinder family.

In the summer of 1955, Don went back home to his family. He caught up on business at the shop and focused on raising his boy again.

A couple of years passed with everything going well. His and Carrie's relationship was back on track and blooming once again. As for Carrie and Peter, this was the ideal scenario for them. Yet Don still felt like he was missing something. Even after playing such a significant role in the greatest battle of his time and training a force to be reckoned with. He knew his life had some other deeper meaning to it.

On a calm Sunday around nine in the morning, Don and his family were watching the local news on their new television. A story aired about a bank robbery that ended in a shootout with police, resulting in multiple civilian casualties. One of the victims who had been shot dead was a local that happened to be a regular at his wood shop. This particular event bothered Don greatly. He thought maybe if he was there, things could have ended differently.

After a couple of months of feeling heavy-hearted about the tragedy and reflecting on how he was underutilizing his gifts, he finally decided what his life was meant for. He became the first real-life superhero and went by the title The Patriot. The name was a shout out to himself and his father for serving their country.

The evening that he decided to act, he told Carrie about his plans. A mask covered his face. He wore a red-and-blue striped jumpsuit with an American flag for a cape. Don tried to explain himself to his wife. She walked into the kitchen where he was waiting for her. When she looked at him, she did a double take.

"Are you kidding me? You look ridiculous! What is wrong with you? Why can't you just stay please. Are we not enough for you? You've already done so much for this country and even the whole world!"

"I'm not like you, Carrie. The blood that runs through my veins is not of human mortality."

"I know, Don… I've always known. I'm not worried about you getting hurt. I just need you. Pete needs you. I get it there is evil out there that is left unchecked. The world needs someone like you… but not you. Please."

Don gave her a look that said, *I'm sorry.*

He left just past eleven at night.

October 5th, 1957. Don Fassbinder aka The Patriot began his new crime-fighting career. For six months he drove to the city in high hopes of making a difference. Over time, his wife's resentment grew. She eventually had enough. Don refused to give up the burden that came with his new title. So Carrie left Don. After a long night out, he came home at about 3:30 in the morning. She was gone. No note, no phone call. Just a ten-year-old boy with a heart shattered to pieces.

Peter sat on the couch in the parlor, staring at a family portrait.

"Pete?" his father addressed him.

"She left dad… She left for good."

"I know, son. This isn't going to be easy to take in but… I need you to go and stay with the Price family for a bit. I think it's the best place for you until I figure some stuff out."

Peter stood up with tear-filled eyes and walked up to his father. He pushed him aggressively. "You're going to leave me to!"

"No, son. It's in your best interest. They will take care of you, I promise."

The Price family legally adopted Peter. Losing his family hurt Don deeply, but at no point did he regret his decision. He then moved to the Bay Area and began making a real difference. He left the title to his house and ownership of the shop with Mr. Price so that one day, when Peter came of age, he would have something his father had left for him.

The Patriot became a big deal. First, he was known across the city. Then the county, then the state. Soon enough his name was well known across the nation. He had previously thought his disguise was clever. Until one day, the U.S. government made contact. They knew who he was.

In the fall of 1965, he was recruited for a top-secret mission. Somewhere in the Nevada desert a covert military operation took place. Dwight Heisenberg had been working with experimental technology for the better half of his life. After two failed attempts in the last five years, he finally believed he had solved the equation to travel through time. They were focused on creating an entrance, but what he needed to figure out was actually the exit. The other side of the wormhole. A gateway needs an entrance and an exit to function.

Dwight's multidimensional theory stated that there were at least nine or ten other dimensions. He believed they could be manipulated—to enter the dimension in one time and come back from the dimension in another. What he had been missing before was not the how but the when. In his previous attempts Dwight aimed for smaller gaps to increase his odds. However, after further studies, he decided to try something new.

Dwight's lead physicist and molecular engineer, Nelson Hunter, had perfected the device multiple times. Every time the machine was used, the electrons and serum combined to create antimatter. This destroyed the machine every time it failed to bridge the gap. Due to this, Hunter had to reconstruct the machine perfecting its flaws three times.

In a government lab a hundred feet beneath the surface, they prepared to power up the machine. Their target, the year 2035. Dwight stood behind a glass wall, staring at the machine. This time, he was sure. They had tripled their energy output to ensure the dimensional breach. Something was going to happen regardless of what. Don Fassbinder was the most resilient man alive and the perfect specimen to endure this unknown, alternate dimension. Don blindly volunteered, unaware of what he had signed up for. The Air Force had told him he would be saving the world.

The elevator arrived at the subterranean facility. The doors opened. Don stood in his casual civilian garments. Wearing a plain black T-shirt and blue jeans. Around his neck was a chain necklace bearing two rings, each engraved with a name—Carrie and Peter. He towered over the two soldiers that stood by him on each side. He had inherited his father's height. He stood around six foot and four inches. His hair was black and messy. His eyes had a sharp blue sting to them.

The facility was divided into two different rooms. The elevator opened into a small ten-by-ten-foot chamber. On the opposite side was a glass wall with another door. Behind this wall was a larger forty-foot-long and ten-foot-wide room, where the machine was assembled.

Dwight looked at the two soldiers standing beside The Patriot and nodded. One of the men gave Don a pill that would temporarily give him amnesia. He took the pill and advanced through the other door toward the machine. The machine was about six feet in all directions. A glowing sphere of energy spun in the center, while two bearing-like pieces of metal rotated around it.

Dwight looked at Hunter and nodded once again, indicating it was time. Nelson Hunter began powering the machine up. The power went out as a loud noise came from a rift materializing from within the machine. Red lightning shot out of the machine in all directions. Multiple soldiers and scientists were hit and dissolved into dust.

Dwight yelled, "Shut it down! Shut it down!"

He quickly realized that Hunter was among the deceased. He ran toward the machine as a second wave obliterated everyone except for Don. He stood there in a mental trance from the drugs he had been given. Alone with the machine. In his blurry mental state, he noticed his surroundings starting to age rapidly. He fell to the ground unconscious.

CHAPTER 6

2100

The room was small and uncomfortable. As Karl traveled through time, the box emitted sporadic lines of red and blue electricity. He felt his stomach knot and his insides project out of him. He threw up so intensely, blood and bile spewed everywhere. The most unimaginable pain coursed through his entire body, and he felt as if he was dying over and over again. Suddenly, the pain ended abruptly as the box stopped electrifying. He heard mechanical noises from above. He looked up to see the box opening and the sides folding down. The roof turned into the walls as the walls turned into the floor. Before he knew it, he was only standing on a rectangular device.

It was surprisingly dark out, considering how bright it was in the afternoon when he had left. He examined his surroundings to find he was in a barren wasteland, inhabited by nothing but desert and ash. The air was thick with smoke, ash and the remnants of great fires. This made it nearly impossible to see further than maybe twenty feet away.

He picked up the device that had taken him to this hellish place and began to fiddle with the mechanism. The rectangular device had a slot where it seemed like the screen belonged. However, the screen was dead and unresponsive. He couldn't find any way to get it to respond. After realizing he might be trapped here, he began to ponder what had happened to Axel, and where the hell he had been sent. *Water,* he thought to himself.

In emergency situations, people often die from dehydration before anything else. He grabbed the device, beginning his journey into the abyss. Everywhere he passed there was a rancid smell. Like the stench of a thousand rotting corpses. After walking in one direction for a few hours he noticed that he sank deeper into the ash or sand he was walking on. This made it much more difficult to walk. Every step took a lot longer. He noticed the temperature was far colder than it should have been. Maybe thirty-five degrees. He felt waves of heat across his face, brushing with gusts of ash. He could hardly see anything, only maybe a couple of feet in front of him now that the hour was late. He came across the first sign of anything other than desert when he saw concrete structures in the ground. *These must have been basements to houses once upon a time*, he thought to himself.

Unexpectedly he heard a throat clearing noise from somewhere in the distance.

"Hello? Is somebody out there? I'm a peaceful man. I don't know where I am or what's going on."

He waited five seconds without a response and asked again. "Is someone there? Please, I'm far from home. I need direction."

"You bring no peace," said a raspy old man's voice in the distance. Karl saw two red slits looking like the eyes of a serpent appear in the pitch black just ten feet in front of him.

"What are you...?" Karl asked the being fearfully.

The eyes approached him, and when they passed out of the smoke, he could see they belonged to the disturbing, animate corpse of a teenage girl. He heard a growling noise. Suddenly a hand grabbed his shoulder from behind. He turned, pushing something back in the darkness and started running as fast as he could. He ran harder and faster than he had ever run before. At first his pace wasn't very quick because of the deep, heavy sand weighing down his strides, but he powered through it. He ran so fast that he rose above the sand, no longer dipping each foot down into it. All of his weight was being lifted, with his momentum preventing him from falling into the ground. He must have been traveling over one hundred miles per hour. Which was over double the fastest he had ever run up to now. He covered ten to fifteen feet between each stride.

As he lifted his foot while running, it caught on something. Perhaps a rock. It sent him tumbling through the wasteland moving over one hundred miles per hour. His body flew through the air, dangling and hitting impact after impact. Until eventually he crashed into a giant boulder, bashing his head against it and falling unconscious.

When he awoke, he had a blanket laid over him. A canteen of water was by his side. With no hesitation, he began chugging the water, not caring where it came from.

"I'm surprised you survived the night. One lucky son of a bitch."

Karl looked up to see who had spoken. He was surprised to see a ten-foot-tall robotic humanoid with a giant turret for a hand standing before him. In the center of the machine, he noticed a glass visor, and behind it he could see a man's face. Karl lifted the canteen and splashed his face to try and clean off some of the debris.

"What the hell, man? It took me weeks to fill that. Do you know how hard it is to get purified water nowadays?"

"Are you human?" Karl asked the machine.

"I could ask you the same question. Seeing as how the boulder I found you near had a giant head-sized hole with blood all around it. Yet, you seem to be completely fine."

"I've just had a lot of concussions in my time, and you could say I'm a little hardheaded."

"Well, seeing as how you're the first seemingly normal person I've seen in maybe a year, I'd like a little more detailed explanation than that," the robotic man said as he raised his weapon in Karl's direction.

Karl put his hands up. "It would help me explain if you could first tell me where I am."

"You're in the United States of America. Or what's left of it," the man replied.

Karl paused for a moment, deep in thought. They didn't send him in a portal through space but through time.

"What year is it?" Karl asked.

"Well, that has no straightforward answer. What was left of organized civilization was calling the new era—A.E. That's 'After Earth'. The last living civilization lives on the moon, and based on information they gathered, the apocalypse occurred around 2035 A.D. This is the year 65 A.E. Which would translate to about 2100 A.D."

"One hundred years?" Karl cried out to fate, falling on his hands in agony.

"I'm guessing you're not from anywhere near this time. Based on the extreme reaction," the robotic man commented.

"I was with my brother. We were ambushed by mercenaries from the future. Well, I'm assuming that's where they were from. They sent me here."

"Damn. That really blows. Well, the first rule to survival is to never be in the open at night. It's a miracle you're alive. My name is Sergeant James Tyson. Me and my combat squad were sent down in search of civilization or renewable resource sustainability left after all the bombs destroyed everything. We were delayed. We had no idea what we were in for. We landed at night. Within minutes of landing, half of us were down. Almost all the other half followed not long after. The only reason I survived was because I was the only cybernetic in my squad. So, the Mecha-Unit protected me.

"It was devastating watching all my brothers in arms die so horrifically. That was about two years ago, and I've only met one other human that wasn't one of those things since."

"You've been alone for two years in this shit hole?" Karl said. "My problems don't seem so bad all of a sudden."

They both chuckled.

"Is there anywhere to get something to eat and maybe catch a buzz?" he asked James.

James smiled as he answered, "Follow me."

Karl followed the friendly mechanical giant to where he resided. After walking for half an hour or so, the new companions arrived at a long yellow pole standing alone in the flat desert ruins.

"We made it," James stated cheerfully.

Karl stopped walking, puzzled, thinking James must have lost his mind. James walked up to the pole and lifted it up, revealing a hatch or door of some sort attached to the end. His Mecha-Unit then opened. In the chest area, the metal separated just before the arms and legs, revealing James's real body, showing his extreme atrophy. He must have been fifty pounds underweight. His skin looked like it had never seen sunlight. The palest of whites. At his wrists and ankles, he unplugged electrical cords that were connecting his body to the Mecha-Unit. He lifted his leg to step down from the mech. He stumbled and fell when climbing up and out of it. Karl caught him and helped him to his feet.

They both climbed down a ladder into a three-foot diameter hole. After a few steps down, they found themselves in a small room that James said used to be a bomb shelter. The room was not tall enough for either to stand up straight. Nor long enough to lie down flat.

Hunched over, James inched his way to one corner. "Let me see what I got in the kitchen."

He dug through some boxes and pulled a small can out. He handed Karl a can of pork and beans and a bottle of Crown Royal Black whisky.

"No flatware," he told Karl with a fat grin on his face.

Karl ripped open the can with his bare hands and aggressively poured the beans and meat into his mouth. After finishing the can he took a big swig of whisky.

"So… I need to go back in time one hundred years somehow," he told James.

James laughed for a moment, then replied, "That's no easy task. If it is possible. However, you seem like there's something special about you, and I could definitely use a companion in this hell of a world…" He paused for a moment in thought, then continued. "I think we could make an arrangement of sorts. I need help with my mission. I was sent down here to find a place called the Temple of the Past. When I did, I realized I was strongly outmanned. If you help me get to the temple alive, I'll find you your time machine."

"You got a deal." Karl shook hands with James.

"In a few hours it will be dusk again," James said. "So, we'll have to stay the night here. It's a little cozy."

The two of them passed the bottle of whisky back and forth until they both fell asleep, half sitting, half lying down. At sunrise, they awoke and packed all the provisions they would need to bring for the long journey. James boiled some water on a camping stove. After brewing some old coffee, he poured it into the two cans they had used the night before. He handed Karl his coffee. Karl looked at it, disgusted, with a facial expression that said, *Really?*

"I rinsed it out," James told him with a sinister smile.

Karl took a drink and spat out an old bean.

James pulled out a map that he had drawn. "Alright. So, the temple is about fifty miles from our current position. There are two paths that we may take. Neither are ideal, but it would take us far too long to walk all the way around. We need to minimize the number of nights, otherwise we probably won't even make it to the temple."

Karl looked at the map, confused, trying to decipher the drawings.

"I'm not much of an artist. I get it," James said.

"No, it looks fine. I'm just trying to make out what I'm looking at."

James pointed out where they were at and where they were going. "When I made the journey before, I had to take the higher road. I call these the sinking hills. They're old skyscrapers that are now covered with sand and ash. You just need to watch your step, otherwise you may sink down a hundred feet or so." He reached under some clutter and pulled out an old, dull machete. "Here. Something to defend yourself with."

After they finished their coffee and discussed the route, they departed through the wasteland toward their destination. James used his location indicator device built into his Mecha-Unit to direct them. Fifty miles to go to the destination. According to their route, they would have to stay the night somewhere on the way.

They traveled for hours and hours through the desert of ash. No structures in sight, everything barren. The sky was a constant grayish orange shade. The sun remained hidden behind the smoke. The wind started picking up as they headed up in elevation when they reached the Sinking Hills.

"Watch your step," James warned Karl. The hills appeared to just be sand and ash. Their path was made of thin metallic plates laid on the ground before them.

"What are these plates we're following?" Karl asked, raising his voice.

The wind blew harder and harder. "Solar panels! They were used in the past to conduct electricity using the sun! You'll only find them on the top of buildings. Pretty cool stuff, actually."

"Never heard of such a thing," Karl responded as he almost lost his footing, quickly correcting himself. About thirty minutes later, he stumbled again and noticed a few wide oval holes in the ground. He peeked over them and looked down at deep bottomless crevices.

Becoming anxious about the silence and their dangerous route, to distract himself, he asked, "So, how old are you, James?"

"Take a guess."

"I don't know… mid-fifties?" Karl said, trying to gracefully shave off a few years.

"Damn. That's harsh. Didn't know I looked that bad. I was thirty-four when I landed about two years ago."

"Oh… I didn't mean anything by it."

"Don't worry about it. I know I look like shit. I was just messin' with ya. It's a combination of the smoky air, the malnutrition, and other factors. Being a cybernetic, I'm not supposed to exceed a certain number of hours in the Mecha-Unit. It kind of drains the life out of you. But given my circumstances, I spend more time in it now than out of it."

He then lost his train of thought and stopped in his tracks. He turned to the side, then looked behind them and back in front. He seemed very confused.

"Is everything alright?" Karl asked him.

"Umm, well the path changed. I'm not sure. It's been maybe eighteen months since I was here." Karl scratched his head, trying to keep it together.

"It looks like it keeps going," Karl suggested.

"Looks can be deceiving."

Karl walked past him in the direction they were heading. Instantly, the ground he stepped on fell out from underneath him. James swung his left arm and caught Karl right before he fell into the darkness. James pulled him up and helped him to his side.

"Thanks, that was close. So, what do we do now?" Karl asked him.

"We don't have enough sunlight to risk anything. We'll have to take the lower path. Unfortunately."

They made their way back down the hills. Moving as fast as they could, now running out of time before dark. James moved as quickly as he could in his Mecha-Unit. They headed down into a valley of sand. Karl noticed hundreds of little holes, maybe a foot wide, across the ground. Some were bigger, up to two or three feet in diameter.

"I didn't take this way because of the worms," James said. "I'm not sure what they are or where they came from. Honestly, I don't know if they'll even mess with us. Let's just try to hurry across."

They walked carefully but hastily across the sand. The ground was hard and packed down, unlike everywhere else Karl had been in this landscape. The valley was only about a mile long. When they approached the final stretch, James stopped Karl with his robotic hand on his chest. Karl gazed upon a three-foot-wide, dark brown scaly worm-like creature partially buried in the sand before them. Only its belly was visible. They gradually made their way around the creature, and it disappeared under the sand.

"That can't be good," James whispered.

A moment later, the slimy belly then revealed itself again in front of them. It was almost as if it knew their route and was blocking them.

"Get ready to run," James told his companion.

He lifted his turret at the belly. *Boom!* The belly exploded, splashing nasty slimy parts of the worm-like monster onto Karl. Instantly, they felt the ground shake. They ran the last twenty feet out of the valley and right as they stepped off the packed sand, they saw hundreds of the creatures swarming the body.

"I'm gonna add a worm pit to my map when we get back."

They both laughed awkwardly.

With only maybe an hour left until sundown, they came across a cave that had some human-like clothing articles near the entrance. Maybe there was a safe place to stay the night within, Karl thought.

"Don't remember this being here," James commented, looking puzzled.

"Should we scope it out?" Karl suggested.

"We don't have much of a choice. We're running out of sunlight."

They walked up to the cave entrance that was large, round, and open.

"Smells like death," Karl remarked.

"Everything smells like death now."

Inside the cave there was a narrow corridor.

"Well, I vote you go first, considering my weapon is a busted machete and your arm is a giant turret," Karl said.

James laughed and replied, "If you insist."

He proceeded to enter the cave. Karl followed. James's Mecha-Unit had two small lights on each side of the visor, as well as a bigger light under his turret arm. They walked through the tight corridor that opened into a room.

In the corner, James spotted a sleeping bag, shone his light on it, and asked quickly, "Anyone in here? Are there any of the living here?"

Karl, without a moment's hesitation, threw his machete at the sleeping bag that appeared to have some form of body in it. It stabbed through the center all the way to the ground. James turned his suit steadily a whole ninety degrees to make eye contact with Karl.

"Never too careful," Karl reassured him.

James smiled and replied, "Truer words have never been spoken."

Karl approached the sleeping bag and went for the zipper, slowly crouching.

"I don't think you need to... they're not going anywhere," James explained, respecting the corpse.

Karl looked at James, then back at the corpse. He kicked the body fairly hard and waited for a response. "Good enough for me," Karl commented.

They readied themselves to continue down the next corridor of the cave. James looked at the tunnel before them and realized his Mecha-Unit wouldn't fit any further.

"You explore on foot, and I'll keep watch by the door," he suggested to Karl.

He opened the hatch on his suit to hand Karl a flashlight. "It's the only one I got besides the mech's lights, so don't lose it."

"Of course. There's nowhere I want to be without light."

Karl continued down the tight corridor further into the cave. He walked for quite some time without finding any more rooms. His path became narrower and narrower, turning into a tunnel leading almost directly downwards. The ground crumbled beneath his feet, sweeping them from underneath him. He lost his balance and fell on his back, skidding down the tunnel, which veered steeply downwards. He plunged twenty feet into a pit.

The ground beneath him didn't feel solid. Quickly, he stood up and shone his light where he had landed, revealing horrific corpses by the dozens. He moved his light all around the room to see it was full of bodies on bodies, and then shone it in the hole he had come through. He climbed through the corpses, centering himself under the hole. Leaping up fifteen feet, he planted his arms against the walls on either side of him. Digging his hands into the rock, he climbed back up.

When he'd made his way back to the first room of the cave, James asked, "How did it go?"

"We need to go. We should find somewhere else."

"Dusk is upon us. There's no going anywhere, the creatures of the night with be lurking soon," James said sorrowfully.

"There were a bunch of bodies in a giant tunnel leading into the earth..." Karl said. "Did you bring any of that whisky?"

"Just my flask full, but it will get us through the night," James replied, handing Karl a flask out of his Mecha-Unit.

Karl took a drink, then his expression turned serious. "So, what is this task that you need me for?"

"The reason why I was sent to find the Temple of the Past was because of certain items that lie in the temple. Supposedly, after all the bombs went off, there was a group of survivors who departed on missions to gather great mementos to remind mankind of history. They also gathered useful objects such as engineering blueprints and scientific documents. The most important of all these items were the seeds. They have seeds to recreate the trees, fruit and all the beautiful life that was taken from us. Andromeda has plenty of green but not enough. With the ratio of people to plants, our renewable oxygen won't last much longer. I need to find the temple and save Andromeda, but it is no easy task."

"So this Andromeda, it's your home?" Karl asked.

James nodded. "It is mankind's home. It's all that's left. A city-province on the moon, protected by a wall of glass. A stone burgh garnished with plants and trees. I can still smell the sweet roses in the windowsill, hear the brook flow through town as the children harmonize with laughter, feel the cold foam from a freshly brewed ale from the space tavern."

Karl chuckled lightly. "Sounds like my kind of home. So, how do we get to this temple?"

"The temple lies in the center of a giant maze. I didn't even make it to the maze. Outside of the entrance to the maze there is a beast so great and terrible no mortal man would dare face it. This is where you come in. I need to know what you're made of. I need to know if you're confident in completing this task."

"Whatever cost to get me back to my time. You can do that right? Get me back to my time?" Karl asked.

"The original blueprints and schematics to the first and only ever invented time machine are also in the temple. If we prevail, we will both get what we need," James assured him.

"That's reassuring. 'If' we prevail. Well, I'll sleep to that sentiment," Karl commented sarcastically.

"One last thing, how is your mech powered?"

"Solar. Everything was becoming solar back before the nukes fired. The light powers me, you could say."

Karl smiled and nodded as he lay down. Although they were both tired, they did not sleep until morning.

CHAPTER 7

The Temple of the Past

A couple of hours after falling asleep, Karl awoke abruptly to some fumbling noises. He panicked and scrambled for his flashlight. He turned it on and shone it around the cave, then pointed it at the corpse in the sleeping bag and saw that it was moving. The corpse was now animate and aggressively trying to get out of the sleeping bag. *The machete must be pinning it to the ground*, he thought.

"Get up! Get up quick!" he yelled at James.

James woke up immediately. His face was blank and dazed from his dream state. He stared at Karl for just a moment, confused, then started to acknowledge the situation. "What happened?"

"We got a hell of a situation," Karl replied.

James sluggishly rose to his feet and climbed into his Mecha-Unit. He raised his blaster arm at the corpse. *Boom.* He fired a round into the creature's chest, exploding the body and decorating the walls with it. They paused for a moment in silence, then heard a noise in the distance. It was very faint. Almost like a crumbling sound. Then some kind of pounding noise. As the pounding got closer, it sounded more like footsteps. The steps moved quickly, multiplying and hastening.

The two companions looked at one another simultaneously.

"Run," Karl said.

They headed for the exit of the cave. Right before they made it out, James was tackled by vicious demonic living corpses. They piled onto him, all slashing and biting at his mech. Karl, who was in front of James, turned around and grabbed his arm. He swung the mech one hundred and eighty degrees and launched James ten feet onto his back outside the cave. Karl turned to the wall of the cave and sent his fist into it. The impact crushed the rocks supporting the entrance. As one of the creatures ran on all fours at Karl, it got close enough to leap for its strike. But before it could, the mound of rocks above the cave came crashing down on the monstrosities.

Karl ran over to James and helped him to his feet.

"Where have you been all my life? Thank you," James said appreciatively.

It was pitch black outside. Not even a hint of moonlight. They heard some rustling around in the rocks. Both turned toward the destroyed entrance of the cave. Karl shone his flashlight at it. Suddenly, a hand burst through the rocks. A second immediately followed. Karl and James started running toward their destination. Out in the open in the dead of night, they heard screeching noises all around them.

"Four thousand meters till our destination and a couple of hours left till sunlight. I don't know what to do." James was panicking.

"Just keep running! We'll figure something out," Karl assured him.

James's Mecha-Unit only gave off enough light to see maybe a seven-foot perimeter around them. The fastest James's mech could move was maybe five miles per hour. This gave them at least thirty minutes until they would arrive at the maze.

Out of the darkness, three humanoid creatures came scampering toward them on all fours. All of them had the same glowing red serpent eyes. One of the monsters approached Karl from behind. As it leapt to attack, he turned toward it. In midair, his palm grabbed its face, and he crushed its head in his hand. He threw the creature's body off to the side. He looked to see James was struggling to swing at two creatures attacking him. James seized one and threw it onto its back, following up with a blow from his weapon, ending it. Karl grabbed the third creature from behind and with one hand to its head and one to its shoulders, he quickly beheaded his foe.

Another dozen of the monstrosities appeared, surrounding them. They all stood up on their two feet simultaneously. Another dozen appeared behind them. Before Karl and James knew it, they were surrounded by maybe a hundred of these foul beings. Seeing mostly just eyes all around them, they felt doomed.

"Aim for the chests," Karl recommended.

"Damn it. I only have one shot left," James replied.

It would appear they were damned. No escape, only fight. The creatures all began walking forward slowly toward them. Karl bent his knees and leaned forward, placing one foot slightly in front of the other. He focused his strength into his legs. He positioned his shoulders for perfect aerodynamics, then launched himself ten feet ahead into the wall of monsters. He pummeled them with both of his fists before bursting through, ripping their chests in two. He swung both his fists as hard as he could, smashing two of their skulls, penetrating and terminating them on impact.

James swung his giant robotic arms into the crowd. Yet, the monsters were too fast. The few hits he landed did not impact enough to cause damage. Within moments, they were swarmed. Both fighting as hard as they could, while being attacked from all around. Karl's legs were swept from beneath him. As the creatures kept biting him, he lay on his back, still fighting hard. He looked over to James to see he was also down on the ground. *This can't be my undoing*, Karl thought.

Moments before the two of them were taken to the other side, a light appeared in the darkness, granting them sight. They heard automatic gunshots firing rapidly but could not see where they were coming from. Karl located the sound and looked in that direction. He saw a man in a trench coat wielding an automatic handgun in each hand. The man rained fire into the crowd. He reloaded quicker than the eye could catch. The gunslinger threw two flash grenades just a few feet from Karl and James. They exploded, disorienting the pile of monsters, leading them away from the two companions. Karl and James quickly rose to their feet, fighting off their attackers.

The gunslinger unloaded three clips in each gun. He then tossed them to the side and pulled out two Desert Eagles. He fired headshot after headshot. Not a single one of his shots missed his target's head. After he'd unloaded all his ammunition, the three of them met in the center where they once were, realizing all hundred or so of their enemies were defeated.

"Follow me," the gunslinger told them as they left the area with haste. They ran to where the light was coming from. The gunslinger turned off his spotlight and packed it into a bag. He tossed the bag on his shoulder, and they proceeded on their journey. The night was a little brighter. Dawn wasn't far away. They all stopped abruptly at the noise of intense buzzing. So loud it sounded like a thousand insects wings. They looked at the sky to see it was full of swarms of giant insects.

"Locusts!" the gunslinger yelled at the two of them. They started flying down, swarming by the hundreds, biting with their pinchers. The locusts must have been six inches to a foot long. Insects straight out of hell.

"Get behind me!" the gunslinger directed his company. He pulled two long, chained whips from his bag. Raising them in front of him, he began to swing them back and forth. Quickening the speed progressively, he created a horizontal figure-eight between the swarming insects and his companions. The ends of his whips trailed behind, forming an impassable wall of death. The swarms of locusts poured in, only to be obliterated by the hundreds.

He lifted the whips high above him while circling Karl and James. Continuing his form, he deterred the locusts' attacks. Within a few minutes, all the vampiric insects were splattered to bits.

"There's a corridor between the mountains ahead. We will be safe there," he assured the two travelers.

After a few hundred feet of running, they had made it to the path between the mountains. As the sun rose, they could now see their surroundings. They stood in the tight corridor around fifteen feet wide looking up a hundred feet to the top of the rocky hill. Karl studied the gunslinger. He wore a hood with oversized goggles on and a bandana that covered his face. He was a couple of inches shorter than Karl, wearing a large black trench coat, big black boots reaching up to his knees, and a katana-style blade strapped to his back.

"Who are you?" Karl asked the man.

"He's the guardian," James responded.

"This is the only other man I've come across. He saved my life once before."

"I'm assuming you're here for the maze, and you'll need my help if you wish to succeed," the guardian stated. "The temple hasn't had a visitor in over twenty years. The beast may be in a deep slumber. If we can make it past the beast without awakening it, that would be our best bet and maybe our only shot. Your mech is out of the question. You will have to leave it here. Maybe you're helpless without it, but we are certainly doomed with it."

James nodded, opened the door to his Mecha-Unit, climbed out in a sluggish manner and unplugged himself from the suit. He stretched his arms and legs, trying to shake off his atrophy.

The guardian handed him two pills with one hand and a 1911 handgun with the other.

"Wait until a moment of desperation to take the pills. One is adrenaline and the other is anti-anxiety medicine to calm down and focus."

James nodded and told him, "My life is in your hands now."

The three of them headed down the crevice within the mountain toward the entrance of the maze. All of them at a walking pace because of James's physical state. After some time, they arrived at the entrance. The path came to an abrupt stop, and they looked down to see a forty-foot drop. They had reached a canyon in the mountain, which opened to a giant area in the style of an arena. A path wrapped around the wall of the mountain, hugging it all the way down.

At the bottom of the cliff, the beast slumbered. It must have been thirty feet long. Covered in scales with bony spikes protruding from its back. It had six legs and three heads, with long necks, a long tail and a fat belly. Its heads resembled that of a snake. It bore two giant wings that had slashes through them, remnants of an ancient battle.

"Definitely don't want to wake that…" James whispered as Karl gave him a dirty 'shut up' look.

They followed the guardian down the path twisting around the side of the mountain. Heading away from the beast that was directly under the edge of the cliff where they had begun their descent. The path got smaller as they began to scale the last bit of the wall down to the ground. The three of them quietly helped one another down and continued slowly and silently stepping toward the gate of the maze.

"You're not worthy of a new life," a deep, raspy, powerful old voice stated.

All three turned together, revealing the beast had awoken and was standing on all six legs. Its eyes were the same red serpent eyes as the creatures they had seen before.

"Complete the maze. I will find you," the guardian assured Karl and James.

"I can help," Karl offered.

"You must complete your mission. This isn't your fight… It's mine," the guardian answered.

Karl wrapped James's arm over his shoulder and helped him run off into the maze.

The guardian walked toward his enemy at a steady pace. "I've been waiting for this for a hundred years," he told the beast.

"As have I," it answered.

The guardian ran at his foe, leaping ten feet into the air toward it, drawing his sword from his back.

Karl and James entered the maze through a giant arc of a doorway and arrived in a dark stone hallway, unable to see where it ended. There were manmade holes in the ceiling that the light beamed through. They headed down the hall a short distance and then came to a fork in their road. The hall split into two tunnel-like stone halls. In the middle was some writing: *Don't let your eyes deceive, let your heart perceive.* They noticed their shadows but didn't understand how the light above portrayed them on the wall beside them. When their shadows suddenly began to walk away from them toward the right path, they were startled. James, mesmerized by the effect, began following.

Karl grabbed his shoulder. "Don't. Don't let your eyes deceive you," he reminded him.

They turned around and took the left hall. As they moved along the hallway, the walls revealed a story told by old, ancient-looking drawings. Images of men building structures. A man at the peak of a mountain, lifting his hands toward the sky. Further down they saw the same drawing again. But in the second illustration, he had fire burning from his palms. Next, they came across images of a great forest, the trees becoming more and more withered, until eventually there was no forest left.

They arrived at the end of the hall where they were confronted with an image of the beast.

"Wrong turn?" James wondered.

"I don't believe so. We're missing something." Karl inspected the wall. He pressed his hand to it, then knocked his knuckles against it, looking for hollow points. Suddenly, they heard an odd whistling sound that rose and fell in volume. Then, words began to appear on the wall in front of them, written by an unseen hand. Ancient writing became visible in the upper part of the wall. The symbols were of some ancient dialect. The companions couldn't interpret it. The symbols became transparent and turned into English. The passage read:

You feel me but cannot touch me. It takes two to need but not to feed. I come when unexpected. I seep into your mind. I can be your very undoing or your greatest strength. What am I?'

The travelers stood awestruck.

"It's a riddle," James realized.

He read it over and over. His hand scratched his dirty white beard. James pondered the riddle for some time. Karl leaned his back toward the wall and crossed his arms. He stared at the ground in front of him, deep in thought. Both tried to unlock this puzzle.

"Fear," James yelled looking at Karl with a fat grin across his face. They looked around to see nothing had changed. James walked to the wall where the passage had been inscribed. He put his finger to the stone and began etching the word. As he wrote with his finger, the first letter began to appear in the stone with a dark, mysterious ink.

"Wait!" Karl told him.

James pulled his hand back.

Karl stepped to the wall and placed his finger upon it. He traced the word he believed to be the answer. "Love."

The loud whistling suddenly returned as the stone wall opened for them. They continued down, deeper into the maze. The path led them to an open, circular area with a giant scale in the center of the room. No other exits or entrances. A dead end. Karl stepped onto the scale, but nothing happened. James then stepped on the other side of the scale. This caused a door to open, revealing another circular room full of artifacts. They heard another door opening from the other side down the hall they had come from. James looked at Karl as they heard screeching and the sound of footsteps running. Karl stepped forward toward the door, off the scale.

When James stepped off, the door began to close, so James got back on the scale. Karl made eye contact with James.

"Only one of us is getting out of here," James said.

"There has to be another way," Karl pleaded.

"You know there isn't. I was meant for this. You can fix all of this. Save yourself, save Andromeda, save the world." James took the two pills and nodded to Karl.

Karl looked up behind James to see a horde of the red-eyed monsters speedily approaching from the hall they had come from. Karl stepped into the artifact room as James stepped off the scale. The door closed. All Karl could hear were a few gunshots, then silence. His eyes formed tears as he fell to his knees in mourning.

After a few moments, he stood up to see the room he was in was full of schematics and boxes with different varieties of seeds. The Declaration of Independence, partially burned to ash, was mounted on the wall in front of him. He rummaged through the blueprints and schematics until he found the time machine print. He grabbed it and a few select boxes of seeds and packed them into a satchel-like bag he found on a nearby table. On the opposite side of the room from where he had entered was a small door. He noticed a handprint in the top right of the door, faded and hardly visible. He brushed it off to realize there was writing underneath it. It read: *Only the worthy will ascend, blood costs blood.*

Karl grabbed a sharp piece of metal from a table near him. He pressed it into his hand, crushing it into his skin and making a slight cut in his palm. He placed his hand, cut and lightly bleeding into the handprint. Perfect fit. His blood dripped down a hole in the bottom of the print's palm. The door made the sound of gears engaging and began opening. Light shone through, blinding his darkened vision.

He stepped out, and the door closed shut behind him. His vision was blurry but became clear. He realized the door was gone behind him and was now part of the mountainside. He turned back around to see the guardian standing before him. Karl reached out and grabbed him by his coat. He lifted him off the ground and slammed him into the mountain.

"Did you know?" Karl demanded.

The guardian did not respond.

Karl smashed him into the mountain again, continuing to question him. "Did you know only one of us would make it out?"

"Yes," the guardian answered sounding remorseful. "The maze was meant for you and only you, Karl Fassbinder."

Karl paused for a moment. He had never told him his name. "How do you know that name?"

"I know everything about you, Karl. Everything has happened for a reason, leading us to this point in time. Trust me. Trust in your instincts."

Karl loosened his grip and let the guardian down.

The guardian brushed off his coat. "Our next destination, Andromeda."

CHAPTER 8

Andromeda

The guardian led Karl down a path winding along the outer rim of the mountain. Beneath him was a hundred-foot drop down to the sea-level waste of a desert. He hugged the mountainside closely. They soon after arrived at a large flat area with a metal plate in the center, with an odd symbol inscribed on it. It appeared similar to a pentagram and also resembled the star of David.

"What is this?" Karl asked his pathfinder.

"This is the gate of Prometheus. Using the same technology as the portal through time, mankind created a new gateway. This gateway is used to travel through space, harnessing the power of the other dimension."

"The other dimension? What dimension would that be?" Karl asked, his intuition throttling him.

"Focus on the path. You will see many things you don't understand. If you keep your head straight and your spirit clean, you will make it to the other side."

The guardian then began to chant some ancient ritual in Latin. Using his sword, he cut through his hand. He fell to his knees and wiped his blood across the symbol.

"Praying for safe passage," he assured Karl.

He put his middle finger and thumb into two holes on the fixture within the plate they stood upon. He turned the center gear inside the plate with the symbol clockwise until they heard a loud noise, like a great and powerful horn. Karl shivered. He recognized this sound from before. The two of them were standing in broad daylight as darkness overcame them. A storm? Not from this world. Karl looked to the sky to see the familiar red electricity appear above them. It morphed into two perpendicular lines, forming a cross. The mysterious electricity circled around them, broadening its range with each pass. It covered all their surroundings, so they were engulfed in darkness with a red glowing light above a dark sky. The light disappeared.

In the pitch black, Karl noticed the aroma of rotting flesh again. He started to sink where he stood. He could feel the ground was made of a warm liquid mixed with sharp broken-down solids. He felt a hand grab his arm and pull him out to solid ground.

The guardian whispered, "*Et erit lux.*"

The sword he held in front of him was struck by red lightning, setting it ablaze. It miraculously stayed lit.

The guardian led Karl down a narrow path with marshes on both sides.

"If you hear or see anything, do not respond. We don't want him to know you are here," he warned Karl.

"Him?" Karl responded.

They journeyed into the abyss. Karl heard a faint ringing noise in the distance. He looked around to see where it was coming from. The ringing stopped, and he shrugged it off. A few moments later, he heard it again. It was oddly familiar yet foreign to him all at once. He homed in on this mysterious ring. In the darkness he could start to make out a small desk lit with an old dial phone on it. He immediately stopped. He remembered where he knew this. When he was just three years old, the day that Axel woke. He and his father had just gotten home after a long night in the emergency room with his mother, only to get a call with the terrible news that she had passed. His eyes pooled. His fists clenched. How could he see this? What knew his fears better than he did? he wondered.

The guardian stopped, quickly realizing Karl was no longer behind him. Waving his flaming sword back and forth, he searched for Karl, but he was nowhere in sight.

He jogged back down the path and spotted Karl reaching toward the dark nothingness.

"Don't!" he yelled, but it was too late.

Karl lifted the phone as they heard the horn again. This time, louder than ever before. Karl looked at his guide, concerned.

"Hell has awakened," The guardian told him.

They began running as red lightning flashed across a dark sky with neither stars nor moon.

"A white knight approaches in a shroud of darkness," a deep, mysterious, omniscient voice declared from all around them.

With all the flashing from the lightning, Karl finally realized what the marshes were made up of. Human blood and corpses. He saw the marshes moving. The disembodied corpses were coming together. Bodies started standing up out of the marshes walking toward the travelers with no skin, only flesh.

While attempting to run away, Karl nearly ran straight into one of the bodies. A body with a face he recognized. "James?"

Its closed eyes opened, revealing the red serpent eyes from the creatures before. It grinned. "There you are!" it yelled with the same omniscient voice.

Karl pushed the monster back, continuing in his direction. The guardian and Karl could see a light in the distance. A shadowy figure appeared in front of the light. The guardian sprinted ahead so fast Karl hardly saw him. He leapt forward stabbing his fiery sword into the shadowy figure, then lifted it over him, finishing it off by slamming it into the ground.

As the fire from the flaming sword spread around him, Karl followed as fast as he could and jumped into the light. The guardian stepped through behind Karl. They were in a small room lit with manmade lights. The guardian turned toward the portal, slashing through it with his sword. He destroyed the gateway as the sword's flame went out. As the gateway closed, a hand reached through, grabbing Karl's arm. The portal shut and cut the arm off, dismembering him. The arm fell to the ground, twitching. Its fingers were still moving, trying to grab at the air.

"It would have been nice if you gave me a little more warning," Karl remarked.

"If I told you how we were getting here, you wouldn't have come," the guardian replied. "Welcome to Andromeda," he continued.

"Alright, look, I've followed you through hell and back. I lost a friend for you. I'm not going any further until you give me some answers. Who are you? How do you know who I am?" Karl demanded.

The guardian sighed and explained, "I didn't want you to know because I was afraid it would change the events to come."

He took off his black goggles and unwrapped his bandana, revealing a face Karl knew all too well.

"Axel? How? I don't understand… How are you alive?" Karl questioned his brother as he inspected his face. He had aged but only appeared to be in his forties or so.

"My regenerative ability evolved into something else entirely. I don't age like men. My strength and speed have become greater through the years. As others grow old and weak, I stay young and grow stronger," he told his lost brother. "When I watched you vanish into thin air, something sparked in my mind. The idea that anything is possible. A part of me changed that day and… I've already said too much. The more I tell you, the greater chance we have of repeating the past. We need to keep going."

He began to head for the door, but Karl put his hand on his chest. "What is the other dimension?"

The guardian exhaled slowly and looked down. "Time and space work differently there. Distance is shorter, time isn't linear. It is a realm where place and time are relative. Where your worst nightmares come true. And are true," he answered.

"So, mankind played God and unleashed hell," Karl presumed.

"Hell is an understatement. I believe this can be fixed, and you're the only one who can fix it," he told him.

Axel walked over to the door, turning the bar to open it. As the door opened, both their faces fell. The once beautiful utopia of Andromeda was all but beautiful. All the trees and plants were dead and withered.

The two gazed across a giant room the size of a small city, encased in a glass-shaped dome. It looked to be one hundred feet tall and five miles around. Through the glass ceiling they could see a sky full of stars. There was no sign of life anywhere to be seen within the dome.

"What happened here?" Karl asked.

"We're too late. The city has been taken," Axel answered. "We must hurry to the inventions room and hope our presence goes unnoticed."

Karl followed him down a stone pathway about the width of a road. It ran between two lines of buildings. He studied this new world, incredulous that it existed. The buildings were a mix of shops and apartments. After about a mile of walking, they approached a stone courtyard in the center of the city. In the middle, stood a tall, white marble statue of a man.

"Who was he?" Karl asked him.

"Thaddeus Lee. He was the founder of the organization that built this place. He died a few days before the first migrants arrived. He was slain by a great warrior. My successor, so to speak. And this…" He lifted his arms up and turned in a circle, displaying the advanced structural design. "This was the new Times Square. Where all the important events would occur. Last time I saw this place, it was filled with families wearing smiles, full of cheer and celebration."

He knelt and put his hand in the soil surrounding the statue. He cupped his hand and pushed it in, digging up a small handful, shaking it as it fell through the gaps in his fingers.

"How many people lived here?" Karl asked sadly. He could feel Axel's sense of loss.

"The population of Andromeda was over one hundred thousand. No crime, no hate, just doomed men running from fate."

He continued walking down the path, with Karl following. After another mile of walking, they reached an intersection. They heard a snarl from around the corner. Axel lifted his hand in a fist, signaling to stop. He slowly approached the corner where the noise had come from. One of the creatures was on all fours, sniffing the air. It appeared to be tracking something.

Axel unsheathed his sword from his back, dashing at the beast faster than the eye could see, slashing off the creature's head instantly. Immediately they heard screams in the distance from the direction they had come. They started running toward the inventions room. Both traveling over fifty miles per hour.

Karl glanced over his shoulder to see hundreds of the creatures running toward them down the walkway. Karl and Axel ran so fast they arrived at the door to the inventions room within a minute or two. Axel ripped the door open hastily, holding it for Karl. Once Karl was inside, he closed the door behind them. He slid three thick steel bars into their slots to lock it. The room was about thirty feet high and maybe fifty feet wide. In the center was a device Karl recognized.

"Damned mankind repeating its mistakes," Axel told Karl as he closed the device and packed it into a bag he found on a nearby table.

"What happened to them?" Karl questioned.

"They must have been testing the machine and opened the gateway prematurely. This works in our favor. If the machine didn't work, the gateway wouldn't have opened," Axel explained.

"So, the time-travel device opened the other dimension into Andromeda?" Karl asked, trying to understand.

"Goddamn idiots. They must have been trying to undo the past, not realizing what would happen when it turned on," Axel replied.

He headed over to the wall and pressed a combination of buttons on a panel by a door. The door opened, revealing a small pod-type ship. "This is an escape pod to take you back to Earth. If you travel back here, you'll end up in space. When you activate the device, it is fairly simple. You enter in the number of years and press the green button."

Suddenly they were interrupted by pounding on the door.

"You need to go now," Axel declared.

"What do you mean? You're not coming?"

"Only you can complete this task. We've already destroyed the past enough."

He paused for a moment, hesitating. "In case something happens, and you don't make it all the way back to your time, just know I wasn't the same after your disappearance. The bitterness of loss changed my chemistry as a man. I've been through the shadows of death and the valleys of the damned. I was misguided by human inaccuracies and flaws. My life has been a conjunction of missed opportunities and regret. Where those paths meet, that is where my undying discontentment thrives. My regrets are many. My biggest… Well… All I can say is that it only takes one moment to mess everything up. But it could take the rest of your life to try and fix it."

He paused again while exhaling in a slow, painful manner. "There are some lessons that only time can teach… Just remember what Father always told us. The Fassbinders' greatest strength lies in their hearts. No matter what happens, once you land on Earth, travel back as fast as you can."

A louder single knock pounded on the door, interrupting Axel. "Go now, he has arrived."

Karl stepped into the tiny escape pod and sat down. Axel handed him the bag with the time travel device. They nodded to each other in understanding. Axel closed the door and pressed the escape release, sending Karl off to Earth. He turned back toward the wall. The wall began to crack, blood leaking through the fissures. The streams of blood combined to form a big bloody tentacle that slithered through the air toward him. He turned toward a large, pressurized container of flammable gases, used for making the device.

"This is not our end. It's yours," he told the beast as he struck the container.

The room burst into flames, triggering a chain reaction as room after room exploded. All of Andromeda burst into a giant ball of fire and smoke. The glass barrier was obliterated as the city on the moon turned to nothingness. The eruption sent a shock through the moon's core, splitting it in two.

Karl's pod crash-landed on a cliff. The door opened, and he exited it. He looked up to the moon to see it was in pieces, fragments raining into the atmosphere.

"I will make this right, brother," he whispered to himself, activating the device and traveling back to the past.

CHAPTER 9

Gamble Bright

If we valued one another's wellbeing as much as our own, then we would have no reason to fail as a people. Every action indeed manifests an equal or greater reaction. In the year 2033, our technology had come a long way. The first flying car had been manufactured by the technologically advanced automobile company known as Tesla. In addition, new technology designed by the applied science company, Binder-Corp, changed the direction of where modern civilization was heading.

The world was at peace six years after the threat of a world war. In 2027, Binder-Corp invented an anti-nuclear defense mechanism known as the Atom Scrambler. This device targeted the neutrons in the atoms, essentially combusting them from within. This effect dissolved anything in the blast radius instantly. This device could target enemy missiles and turn them to nothingness before they hit the ground.

The United States enemies' reaction after learning of this technology was to make peace with the U.S. The Sovereign Nations Compliance was then formed, bringing a true world peace. However, the question of peace is longevity. As a dog returns to its vomit, mankind's sinful nature continues to breed.

Gamble Bright was a young, ambitious man. Yet compared to the amount of willpower and determination in his heart, he was physically quite small. Between his preppy school uniform and his greased, combed-over hair, he had a rather quaint appearance. He grew up in downtown Manhattan with his mother, attending a private school in a wealthy neighborhood. His father, Thomas Bright, was hardly part of the picture, only showing up for the occasional birthday and holiday. That was, until one fateful day when Gamble was sixteen years old. His mother did not come home from work at half-past six, the time she usually came back.

For three days, Gamble took the bus to school, came home and awaited his mother's return. Every day after school, he sat on the olive-colored linen-textured sofa in the living room of their loft. He sank into the cushions, staring at a blank screen on the television. His dark brown hair was slicked into place, each lock carefully greased. His leafy green eyes sparkled with anticipation.

On the fourth day, he was called into the school's office. His father was waiting for him. Thomas told him that he needed to come live with him immediately. He explained that his belongings were already packed.

Gamble followed his father out to the parking lot. The two got into a black Yukon SUV. Two men sat across from Gamble and his father, both wearing the same black-on-black suits. One of the men was tremendous in size. Far bigger than any man the teenager had ever seen before.

Thomas told his son, "Gamble, this is Maverick. He has been watching over you for the last few years. On your way to and from school. Since then, you have never left his sight. And through that, never left mine. I work for a highly classified division of the government, and it calls for me to live on base 24/7. I am deeply sorry for my absence throughout most of your life, but it's only been for your safety. Your mother is missing, and we fear the worst. Terrible people want to hurt our family. This isn't the life I wanted for you, but unfortunately, we don't always get what we want. Now our worst fears have been realized. This is our time to face them."

They drove for some time, arriving at a private take-off point where a jet was waiting for them. Gamble and his father boarded the jet.

Their destination, the Nevada desert. Forty thousand feet off the ground, Gamble sat near the window gazing down at the world. *What will become of us? Will I ever see my mother again?*

When they landed, American soldiers escorted them off the plane to their bunker. The soldier left them in their room and closed the door.

"So how long do we have to live here?" Gamble questioned.

His father walked over to him and lifted his arm over Gamble. Gamble pushed him away. An awkward silence occurred for just a moment between the long-separated father and son.

Thomas stepped back and sat down. "It may be a while, son; I promise as soon as it's possible, you'll be free."

Gamble's stay lasted longer than he could have expected. During that time, his life was very uneventful. The highlight of his week was playing basketball on the dirt court with a few of the soldiers. Occasionally, he was allowed to join in on the conditioning. Most of his time was spent alone in a small room with just a deck of cards and writing utensils. When he turned eighteen, his father had arranged with the man in charge for his son to be free to leave under strict supervision and guidelines.

The eighteen-year-old boy was taken to San Francisco, California to stay with his cousin. He started working at a café as a dishwasher, his very first job. On his first day, his boss, Rahul, a late middle-aged Middle Eastern man, told him, "I'm gonna be straight with you, kid. Any dickless monkey could do this job. The last guy messed up so bad I had to let him go. If you can keep up with the rush, you got a job."

Gamble nodded. "Understood, sir. I'm confident in my responsibilities and will remain competent enough and able to manage anything."

His boss grinned and nodded back.

Over the next couple of months, Gamble impressed Rahul and eventually moved up into a cooking position. Shortly after his promotion, a new server started working with him. Her name was Tara, young and beautiful. Her sandy blonde, mid-length hair and deep hazel eyes were more beautiful than he could handle.

On a Friday evening, while closing up, Gamble said to Rahul, "Hey, could I ask you for some advice?"

Rahul sat in his beat-up old computer chair in his tiny closet-sized office. "What, kid? I got a lot of paperwork to fake."

"I wanted to ask the new server… Tara? I was trying to figure out a way to ask her out."

Rahul chuckled while looking through receipts. He stopped what he was doing and sat them down on his cluttered desk. "Well, first off, I'd like to tell you good luck. But somehow, I feel like you're already questioning if it's a good idea, so I would say go for it."

Gamble stood there, confused. "I kind of meant like advice on maybe *how* I should ask her?"

His boss sighed. "Look, I ain't your dad or your relationship counselor. I'll tell ya what I tell my kids. At least the younger three that is. If you save your milk for too long because you're scared of not having it anymore, eventually it will spoil."

Gamble scratched his head, then his chin. Then it clicked. "Thank you, sir."

"Yeah, don't mention it. Like literally this conversation didn't happen. Now let me get back to work. Damn kids…"

Gamble approached Tara while she was cleaning one of the tables. She clumsily knocked the sugar off. Gamble dived down onto one knee to catch it. He stood up with a broad smile across his face.

"Thanks," Tara said, smirking slightly.

"No problem… Hey, I was wondering if you wanted to come in early tomorrow and have a coffee on me?"

"Hmm… come into work a couple of hours early with no pay… I mean, it doesn't sound too appealing, but I am trying to be more open to new things. That sounds great."

The following morning, they met at their café as planned.

"So, are you from San Francisco?" Gamble asked her while mixing her cream and sugar for her.

"Um no. Actually, I'm from Queens."

"Queens? No way! I'm from Manhattan. That's crazy. So what brought you here?"

"I guess it was when my parents split. My adopted parents, that is. I never met my real parents, but my family is pretty awesome. They were, at least. My parents just kept working their way up in their careers. Kept focusing on making more and more. They thought that would make them happier, I guess. Over time they had spent so little time with each other it just kind of happened, you know. It was always about that dream car or that dream house. I realize now they call it a dream for a reason. Because once you have it, you're never satisfied. You just spend your whole life chasing that next dream."

"Wow, that's profound. I'm sorry for what led you here, but I'm glad, because if it hadn't happened, then I would never have met you."

He smiled, casually reached his hand over the table, and softly held hers.

The two of them became romantically involved over the following couple of months.

One evening, after watching a horror flick at the movie theatre, the young couple went back to Gamble's apartment. They laughed and flirted in his small kitchen. He popped two bottles of Rolling Rock lager. The landline in his apartment rang.

Tara seemed concerned. "Should we answer it? It's kind of late… it may be an emergency."

Gamble smiled with a buzzed look in his eyes. "I'm sure it can wait."

The phone rang again. It seemed more aggressive than the first ring. Gamble answered.

"Gamble, I'm so sorry. The agency needs you to come in. They will be there at any moment. Take your girl and run as far and as fast as you can." His father's words were distraught.

Gamble hung up the phone and turned to Tara to see two men on either side of her. One of the men held a gun to her head. He declared, "If you care for her life, you'll come with us."

Gamble nodded. He kissed Tara and promised her, "I will see you again, my love."

He left with the men in a black SUV, and they took a jet back to the military base where his father was waiting for him. After exiting the jet, he was expecting to head toward the bunker he and his father had stayed in previously. Instead, they walked toward a large metal box with a door. One of the soldiers beside him scanned their security card to open the door. It was a compact elevator. After filing in, they descended. Twenty-five floors down they arrived at the deepest level of the facility. The doors opened, and Gamble was guided into a room with a display glass. He spotted his father beside a large machine, slaving away programming it, surrounded by armed soldiers.

One of the soldiers beside Gamble yelled at his father. "Is this enough motivation?!" He then pointed his sidearm at Gamble's head. Gamble made eye contact with his father. The sensation in his heart caused a tear to stream down his cheek. His father's eyes told him, *I'm sorry*.

Moments later, the elevator arrived again. It opened to reveal a tall man in a suit, with slicked-back blond hair and sunglasses. The man stepped out of the elevator, demanding. "Are we ready?"

His soldiers stood at attention as the sergeant answered, "Yes, sir, the device is almost ready to bridge."

"Then it is our time," the man in the suit decided.

Thomas began powering up the machine. Gamble was escorted into the room to a pad in front of the machine. His eyes made contact with his father's lips, whispering, "I love you, son." He pulled the lever down, commencing the machine's launch.

Instantly, everyone in the room disintegrated into dust as Gamble disappeared. The power flickered as each individual's atoms collapsed into nothingness. The man in the suit was the only one left. He looked at the machine, then glanced where Gamble once stood. With true sorrow in his voice, he muttered, "I'm sorry, kid."

He turned toward the elevator and rode it back up.

After a few moments of silence in the underground base, Gamble began to materialize where he once stood. His body was transparent. Flashing in and out of the different dimensions. He endured a terrible migraine and felt his body falling apart. He held his hands in front of his face to see they were flickering, changing into many different shades. Every ten seconds or so they would disappear just for a brief second. He stood up and walked toward the exit of the room. As he reached for the doorknob, his hand phased straight through it. He tried to grab the knob a few more times, becoming frustrated. He realized something had happened to him. He pressed his palm to the door to see it phase through. He walked through the door like a ghost.

Am I dead? he thought. He staggered toward the elevator door. Suddenly the lift came crashing down in front of him. This knocked him back through the wall he had phased through. He was thrown to the ground by the impact and rolled over near where the machine once was. He pushed himself up from the ground. A cough startled him from the other side of a large, ruined pillar. Gamble rose to his feet and peeked over to see a man. He had medium-length dark hair and was taller than Gamble. He wore a black shirt with blue jeans. The man stood up and paced around the room confused. When he noticed Gamble, he approached him. He grabbed Gamble aggressively by his shirt and demanded, "Where am I?"

"I don't know," Gamble answered.

The man became furious and demanded again, "Where am I?"

Gamble trembled at the power in the man's voice. "I really don't know. I'm a victim here too. All I know is we are deep underground in some form of covert military base. My father… He disappeared. As well as everyone else. Then you showed up out of nowhere. Who are you?"

The man scrunched his face, looking confused. "I don't remember. I can't remember anything."

"Whatever happened must have given you some kind of amnesia. I think we should focus on getting out of here. The elevator is toast. We may be trapped," Gamble explained.

The two of them walked into the other room where the elevator had crashed down. The man dug into a pile of concrete blocks and cleared the path with ease. Gamble raised a brow at this. He followed the man into the elevator shaft. The area was about five feet by five feet. They looked at each other, clueless as to what they would do next.

At that moment, a rope landed between the two lost companions. They looked up to see a figure descending the rope. He stopped a few meters above them and yelled, "Climb up, quick!" The voice. Gamble oddly recognized it. Together they climbed a whole hundred feet to the surface. Nearing the top, Gamble accidentally phased and his hand lost grip of the rope, moving straight through it. He fell a few feet and was caught by a muscular arm and thrown up over the ledge to solid ground.

The man that saved him, helped him out. It was bright outside. Gamble figured it must have been early in the afternoon.

He turned to the large figure that had saved him. "Maverick?"

"Get in the car now!" Maverick demanded.

They all piled into a black SUV and departed the base with great haste. Once they were a half a mile away, the base was unexpectedly devoured by a giant explosion. Gamble watched the smoke drift from the violent flames as his eyes filled with sorrow. The realization that his father was no longer with him, sank in.

"There's a lot you need to know, Gamble," Maverick said.

"Like why my father is dead and I'm turning into something inhuman? What's happening?" he demanded angrily.

"I'm sorry for everything. We had no part in this. I work for the ADA. The Anarchists of Democratic Associations. The CIA and Binder-Corp are responsible for what happened here. Not us. We had been allied with both agencies in attempts at creating world peace. At some point in the last year, they started working on a new project. A machine that harnesses other dimensions to use them to travel through space or maybe even time. I will bring you to the head of my order. He will know what to do with you."

"What about me? Can you tell me who I am? Or why I'm here?" the forgetful man asked.

"All I can say is that you're in the Nevada desert. You must have come from another place or time. We will find out the truth about everything soon enough," Maverick replied.

They drove for some time until they arrived in Reno, Nevada. They parked in front of a big building downtown. Gamble and the forgetful man followed Maverick through two wide glass doors, and he led them into a room in the center of the building. There were two men and a woman sitting in throne-style chairs side by side, awaiting them.

"Stop right there!" one of the men in the chairs told them.

He stood up and casually strolled over to Gamble. The man wore a black suit and had short, well-cut hair and dark skin. He lifted his hand to Gamble's cheek and pressed into it, until his hand eventually phased straight through Gamble.

"Fascinating. Your body must have bonded to the other dimensions on a molecular level." He turned toward the man with no memory. "As for you, you must have been on the other side of the wormhole.

Considering your body endured the other dimensions so well, I would say it is safe to assume you are no ordinary man." He paused for a moment, noticing the man had a necklace with two rings on it. He carefully advanced to an arm's length distance. He reached for the necklace and read on each ring the two names. "Peter and Carrie. It appears you may have a name after all." He gave his colleague a devious look. "We shall call you Pete, in the meantime. Whether it is your name or not."

"I know that name, but I don't believe it is mine."

"Nonetheless, a name is a name. My name is Miles Palestine. I am the president of the ADA, and it is my honor to meet the both of you. If Binder-Corp or the CIA were ever to discover you survived, and that you exist in this time, your lives would be in grave danger. Because of times like these, we have safe houses spread out across the U.S. You will be staying outside of Los Angeles," Miles explained in his polite manner.

"Sir, if I may ask... I spent my whole life hoping one day I would have my father back. This man in the suit, he took everything from me. I would like nothing more than to avenge my father's death," Gamble pleaded with Mr. Palestine.

Miles laid his hand gently on Gamble's shoulder and reassured him, "Your father will be avenged son. That I can promise you. However, we must be on the defensive. We will show you the power to avenge him, but it will take time. We will show you the power to defeat a god."

"I have one more question. There is someone that means the world to me in San Francisco. A girl... Will I ever see her again?" Gamble asked.

"Tara Smith is missing. We tried to get to her before they did, but regrettably, when my men arrived at the scene she was already gone. We checked her apartment and work. Nothing."

"What do I have to do to get her back? We have to save her. She's all I have left."

"I will personally see to it that if she is alive, we will find her and protect her. At this point, that's all I can guarantee. I'm sorry if that's not the answer you wanted," Miles said as he turned away and headed back to his seat.

He sat on his throne between the others, continuing, "Training will begin tomorrow. Maverick is going to be by your side the whole way. This meeting is adjourned."

Maverick walked up behind Pete and Gamble. He put a hand on each of their shoulders. "That's our cue. We've got a long drive ahead of us, boys. Sooner than later."

They followed him outside and into the same vehicle. The three of them drove for six hours to their safehouse. In the dead of night, they arrived at a small cabin in the woods.

"Nothing feels more like home than an abandoned cabin in the middle of nowhere," Gamble snarked.

Maverick gave him a 'not amused' look.

They made themselves at home as best as they could. Maverick cooked them some potatoes and onions for dinner in a skillet in the tiny mobile-sized kitchen. Gamble and Pete sat on a small picnic bench neighboring the petite kitchen.

"Looks like we have a vegetable lover here," Gamble remarked.

Maverick looked at him with a blank face. "The neighbor farmer drops off a bunch of potatoes and onions once a week. So hopefully you're also a vegetable lover," he replied.

"Potatoes and onions. I don't know if those even count," Gamble said as Mav opened the fridge and pulled out a pack of Budweiser.

"Here, wash it down with that. We've got a long day ahead of us."

Gamble and Pete were shown their room. The cabin was made of logs split in half vertically. It was very old and authentic, with only one small bedroom with two beds against the walls on opposite sides from one another. Gamble and Pete made themselves at home. Neither slept much that first night. Just as sleep overcame them, they were woken up abruptly. A loud alarm startled both of them to their feet.

Mav busted in the door forcefully. "Sun's up, shit birds. Your training begins now."

The two men followed Mav outside to reveal a squad of armed soldiers. "This is your first task. Survive," he declared.

"Wait, what?" Gamble asked.

The soldiers lifted their weapons at Gamble and Pete. They began firing. Gamble's anxiety forced his body into some kind of disfigurement. He rapidly phased as all the bullets went clear through him, causing him no harm. Pete was hit by at least ten bullets before he realized that his skin was impenetrable. He dashed forward, grabbed one soldier by the shoulder, and hurled him powerfully into a tree. He followed it up with a couple of fatal blows to the nearby combatants.

Gamble, in his phantom-like state, was shot at repeatedly, but the bullets went straight through him. He walked up to his assailant, sending a fist through his face. His hit was too weak to knock him down, and the soldier swung back at Gamble. Gamble phased through the punch. A moment later, he grabbed his enemy's gun and knocked him unconscious with the butt of it.

Pete yelled in anger, "What is this? You could have killed us!"

Maverick was nowhere to be seen. Suddenly he dropped down from the roof with a quick fist to Pete's head. Mav picked him up and threw him into a tree ten feet away. He turned toward Gamble and reached for his chest. Gamble phased through his blow and took a step back. Mav attacked again and again. Gamble continued to dodge every attempt Mav made to make contact. Eventually the giant went for a hit to the head and Gamble did not phase through it in time. He was knocked to the ground almost comatose. Mav turned back toward where Pete was lying to see he was gone. Maverick took a hard hit from behind, sending him flying through the air then rolling on the ground into a tree stump. He stood up and turned around to see Pete walking toward him with murder in his step. Mav picked up a hollowed-out log beside him. He swung it like a huge bat into Pete's side, sending him far off into the distance.

"Not bad for your first day," Maverick told them. "Clean yourselves up. Your next course is at noon."

Pete helped Gamble to his feet and inside. They sat at the table, and it started to dawn on them what situation they'd found themselves in.

"Didn't realize we were going to be target practice," Gamble snarled.

"We're not mortal men. I believe that this ADA may have similar interests to our own," the man they called Pete responded.

At noon, they met Mav at a giant cliff overlooking a drop of a few hundred feet. "This is your finish point. You must climb the mountain. The hardest way," Mav instructed while pointing down to the bottom.

"What? That's a straight vertical climb. Not even most professional mountain climbers could do that," Gamble tried to reason with the brute.

Mav grunted in an angry fashion. He slowly walked to Gamble and hunched down to meet him face to face. "When your strength gives, your legs break, and your mind flails. Just when you think you can't go on any longer, that is when you'll be halfway there," he lectured the young man.

Gamble and Pete made their way to the bottom of the cliff. "Here goes nothing," Gamble said.

It took Pete about fifteen minutes to make it all the way to the top with ease. However, his younger teammate struggled over and over. Ten days later, on the tenth attempt, Gamble reached the top.

Maverick trained the two for quite some time. Weeks, then months. Intensive combat exercises for Pete. As well as stealth and assassin-style practice for Gamble.

October 3rd, 2035. Four months after arriving at the cabin, on a pleasant morning during breakfast, an armored vehicle arrived at the doorstep of the cabin's entrance. Miles exited the vehicle. Mav greeted his master pleasantly. "Training has been very effective. I believe he is ready. Not a single soul on the entire planet could overcome him."

"Good. Very good. I need him for a project. Some unforeseen circumstances have come to my attention, and we need to run some tests on Mr. Fassbinder."

Maverick led Miles inside to the two sitting at the bench-like table. "Pete, it's time. We need you to go with Mr. Palestine. There is an important task which may change the outcome of this world."

The man called Pete looked at the coffee mug in his hand like he had seen it before somewhere in a past dream. "Peter... Peter was my son's name. My name is Don Fassbinder, and my allegiance lies with the benefit of humanity. Not your malicious cult."

"So, you have remembered," Miles said. "How long have you known?"

"Long enough. I will not be turned into some kind of weapon."

"If only you knew the events that are soon to transpire. You would be a lot more willing," Miles tried to reason with Don.

Don stood up and ran directly through the wall beside him. He ran as fast as he could away from this doom.

"Get him," Miles directed. Mav looked confused, as if thinking *Me?*

"GET HIM NOW!" Miles commanded.

Maverick ran after him, venturing through the woods.

Not long after, he told Miles on his headset, "I need some air support. He's gone."

Within moments a helicopter flew by with a ladder hanging down to the ground. It brushed through the grass. As it passed Mav who was jogging steadily, he grabbed onto it.

The chopper lifted him up above the trees. He pursued Don's tracks to a deep ledge, fifty feet high. Maverick dropped off the rope. He walked to the drop-off and looked down to see Don at the bottom, standing up from a great fall. Maverick dropped down too, crashing into the ground and making a loud impact.

"FASSBINDER!" he yelled.

Don stopped in his tracks and turned around. "Listen, Maverick, I fight for the American people. I fought for justice. What you're doing here, I want no part in it."

"Our cause is the same as yours. You don't know what we know. Our world is on the verge of destruction. You could save us all," Mav pleaded with Don.

"You knew who I was. You know what I am. How can I trust you after what you've done? I'll take my chances. I would rather die a hero then be brainwashed into being some villain," he replied.

Maverick shook his head, disappointed. "Then I will do whatever is necessary to preserve the peace," Mav declared.

There was a moment of silence as the two giants glared into one another's eyes. Maverick was far bigger than any man Don had ever seen. Standing seven inches taller than him, and about one hundred and fifty pounds larger.

"This is your last chance," Mav threatened as the two approached each other for combat.

"We always get another chance," Don answered with a smirk.

Mav shook his head again and walked up to Don. He violently reached for Don's chest. Don grabbed Mav's hand, twisted it and threw a punch straight into his jaw. Mav fell back briefly, then quickly rose to his feet, displaying a light cut on his chin, hardly noticeable.

Don paused for a moment. *That should have broken his jaw,* he thought.

"You look confused, Fassbinder. Well, I may have had some unnatural upgrades."

Mav charged at Don and wrapped his arms around him, bear-hugging his chest. Continuing his tight grip, he lifted Don over his head and smashed him into the ground behind him. By the time Mav turned around and was on his feet, he realized Don had beat him on his recovery and was already standing.

"You know you can't win this fight, Maverick."

"I don't have to. I'm just keeping you in sight."

Don look confused as the roar of an incoming jet filled the air. Just as he spotted the jet, it fired a ball of energy into his stomach. It sent him into the ground and into a coma. Mav tossed Don over his shoulder and climbed into the helicopter.

Meanwhile, Gamble and Miles were sitting at the table in the cabin, an awkward silence hanging between them.

"What will become of him?" Gamble finally asked, concerned about his friend's wellbeing.

"He is the key to everything. There are dark forces in the making and Mr. Fassbinder may be the answer that we seek. We have our own roles to play in this and he has his."

Gamble nodded in understanding.

"I need you to wait for us here. I promise we are doing everything in our power to find Tara, but we need more time. As well as your cooperation," Miles continued.

He stood up and walked out the door. A moment later, he drove off in the armored vehicle he had arrived in.

Maverick arrived with Don at a familiar base in the desert. He opened a body bag and pulled out Don in his comatose state. He carried him to a small elevator and entered it. The lift went deep within the facility. The door opened. Maverick carried Don in and set him on a surgically purposed table. The procedure began. Two sets of machine-like red eyes appeared in the darkness. They approached Don's body. The humanoids had robotic arms yet were still somewhat human. The two cybernetic surgeons began heating up hundreds of metallic plates. They placed each plate individually on Don's skin. Each one merged with his flesh upon contact. They installed a visor over his eyes, embedding it deep in his corneas. Finally, one of the cybernetics took a micro drill and planted a chip in the back of Don's head.

"The process is complete; his body put up quite the fight. In order for the adaptive camouflage plates to merge properly, we had to burn through the epidermis layer of the skin. This will weaken his invulnerability to almost that of a man," one of the robots told Mav.

"A fair cost," Maverick commented. He turned to Don's counterpart. "Wake up, Agent."

He rose from the surgery bed.

"What is the mission?" the metal man asked his master.

"The past," Maverick answered.

<hr>

Gamble spent the next few weeks in solitude. Waiting for something or someone. He had no calendar or way of tracking time, so Gamble did his best to imagine what day and time it was. One morning, at what he assumed was around nine, he sat at the table eating the usual onion and potatoes, staring blankly into the distance, when he heard a helicopter traveling fast.

BOOM! A loud explosion followed, then another crashing noise right by the house. He ran outside to see a helicopter had crashed on its side and multiple pieces of it were strewn across the ground.

"Gamble…" a weak troubled voice choked out from inside the chopper.

Gamble slowly approached the cockpit to see Miles in critical condition. A piece of the propeller about a foot wide had stabbed through his chest.

"The ADA is compromised. Everyone is dead. You must survive. You must," Miles pleaded.

Gamble looked at the sky to see three Black Hawks en route.

"Run, Gamble, run," Miles commanded.

Within seconds, the downed chopper exploded from missiles fired from the Hawks. When the smoke cleared, Gamble stood his ground with murderous intent. His anger strengthened him. He focused on phasing harder than ever before. He found the perfect balance between destruction and serenity.

Suddenly, he was no longer on the ground. He was in the sky, inside one of the helicopters. A soldier turned toward him, drawing his sidearm. Gamble put his hand through his foe's chest, making it materialize inside of him, killing him instantly. He then stabbed his hand through the pilot's neck and pulled his body to redirect the Hawk. He steered the Hawk into the other two. The propellers hit each other, sending metal pieces shooting everywhere. Gamble faded out of the crash and landed on the ground safely in the distance. All three choppers crashed horrifically. He just stood there, watching them burn. Listening to the screams of terror.

For Gamble, the bloodshed was only the beginning. He realized he could harness his multidimensional power to travel through space in glimpses. He ran in the direction his attackers had come from. He flashed through matter. Teleporting one hundred meters at a time.

Within no time he arrived at the military base. When he arrived, chaos was unleashed. He walked up to the gate in plain sight. The soldiers in the guard towers on each side of him immediately recognized him and opened fire. Gamble phased in place, standing his ground as every bullet went straight through him.

The battle commenced. Gamble teleported into one watch tower, causing those in the other tower to fire upon it. Immediately, he phased to the other side as the soldiers destroyed one another.

Gamble continued down into the underground base. Floor by floor he massacred every single soldier, until he eventually made it to the bottom of the base. He found the captain hiding in his quarters. The captain shot twice at Gamble, but the bullets went straight through him. Gamble disappeared and then reconfigured behind the captain. He smashed his head into the concrete wall.

"I'M GOING TO ASK YOU ONCE. WHERE IS TARA SMITH?!"

The captain quivered in fear. "I don't know who that is."

Gamble smashed his head into the wall again.

"I swear," he continued. The captain closed his eyes, expecting his end. For a moment, he was left confused. When he opened his eyes, Gamble was gone. He had spared him.

The wind gusted through the trees as Gamble walked casually out of the base. On the outskirts, he hijacked a jeep and headed back to find his beloved. He clenched the steering wheel the whole seven-hour drive. His anger bred something unfamiliar in Gamble—hate. He passed a small town. He thought maybe the jeep was a little too high profile. He parked at a pub. A big, hefty biker pulled up and parked.

Gamble approached him. "I need your bike."

"Excuse me? Do you know who I am?"

Gamble walked straight through him and grabbed his key. He got on the bike and drove off.

"What? What just happened?" The biker stood confused, patting his own chest to check he was still real.

When Gamble arrived in San Francisco he drove straight to Rahul's and parked in the alleyway behind it. He walked to the door and when he opened it, he saw Rahul right away. Rahul hurried over to him.

"You shouldn't be here, kid. We thought you were dead."

"What do you mean *we*?" Gamble quietly responded.

"Look I can't help you. If they find out your alive, they'll be looking for you."

"I need to know when you saw Tara last. I need to find her," Gamble said.

Rahul shook his head. "I can't… I'm sorry, man."

Gamble stormed out of the diner. When he turned the corner into the alley, he received a swift kick to his head, disorienting him. The figure dragged him into the alley, lifting back Gamble's hood. "Gamble?"

His attacker was wearing a full, thick leather suit with a helmet. They lifted their helmet off to reveal the face beneath—it was Tara.

Tears came to her eyes and in a sorrowful voice she told him, "I thought you were dead. Why didn't you come?"

"I couldn't. I tried. But I'm here now."

"We can't stay here. I have a room a few blocks away."

Tara helped him up and onto his bike. They quickly drove down the road to a dilapidated apartment complex. Tara led him inside an apartment where the windows were all covered with wood on the inside. They walked down the hall inside the apartment. Gamble had no idea what awaited him. Maverick stepped out from the back room.

"I thought you were dead, Maverick," Gamble muttered in confusion. "Why are you here?"

"Well… not dead yet. When we were ambushed, only Miles and I made it out in a chopper. We were followed and he dropped me off in a river. Hopefully we'll hear from him."

"He died in the chopper," Gamble said. "It crashed by the cabin, but I killed all of the soldiers responsible."

Mav and Tara looked at each other with pained expressions.

"So, he is dead. But he will not die in vain," Tara declared. She walked up to Gamble and grabbed his shoulder, looking him in the eyes.

"I haven't been completely honest with you. I've been working for the ADA the whole time. Originally, I was meant to watch over you for protection. But then… I fell in love. I'm really sorry. I couldn't tell you."

This was a slap in the face. Gamble couldn't fathom how much anger burst through his veins. He turned toward Mav and yelled, "HOW COULD YOU LIE TO ME? I THOUGHT SHE WAS DEAD BECAUSE OF YOU!"

"I was following orders. They wanted you focused and angry. I do apologize. I did what I had to," Mav replied.

Gamble pondered for a moment, desperately wanting to seek vengeance. In a frightful manner, he whispered, "Where is the man in the suit?"

CHAPTER 10

Fire Wagon Blue

Karl grunted in pain as he traveled through time. The machine began tearing apart. His arm, being near the corner, started aging rapidly. He panicked and struggled to stop the machine. He slammed his fist into the center where the controls were. Suddenly, it stopped and started, falling apart. He crawled out of the remains of the box, puking uncontrollably. He rested on his hands and knees for a moment. Once his pain had subsided, he stood up and gazed around him. He could see he was surrounded by farmlands and orchards.

"Last time I'm doing that," he muttered to himself.

Karl walked through the crops until he found a house in the center of one of the fields. A man ran out of the house aggressively wielding a shotgun. He pointed the rifle in Karl's direction. He was an old and brittle fellow, with Latin features.

"Whoa, Whoa wait! I'm not here to hurt you," Karl pleaded.

"*¿Quién eres tu?*" the man demanded while holding the gun toward Karl's head.

Karl realized he may not have crash-landed close to home. He raised his hands in front of him, gesturing 'Don't shoot'.

"English? Do you speak English?" he asked.

"No English," the man answered as he lowered his gun and changed his approach to the situation. He waved for Karl to follow him into his home. Inside was a woman whom Karl assumed was the man's wife. The man told her Karl was foreign, and she needed to translate for him.

"I speak English. Where do you come from?" the lady asked politely.

"Far from here. If it's not too much to ask, could you take me to the city? I can find my way home from there."

The lady agreed to help and told her husband to take Karl into the nearest town. The man and Karl got into the car and headed for the city. As they drove through the beautiful farmlands, Karl glanced out the window. He remembered the future. All of the wildlife was long dead. He had a flashback of the desert of ash and felt a shiver through his core. After some time, they arrived in the nearest city, which turned out to be Madrid. He noticed some of the vehicles were hovering above the ground. Not even touching it. Confused by this, Karl concluded that he was not yet back in his time. The friendly man dropped him off at the airport.

"*Gracias, Amigo,*" Karl said. The man smiled, waved, and drove off.

Karl entered the airport door, acknowledging that he seemed quite out of place. His shirt and pants torn, his boots worn, while he was surrounded by elegantly dressed individuals.

He walked toward the ticket agent. "I need to purchase a ticket to the United States," he told the lady.

"I'm going to need to see a passport and some identification. We have a flight to New York at 3:00 p.m. and Chicago at 5:40 p.m."

"Whatever's cheapest."

"That would be New York, and it will be about seven hundred and thirty euros," she answered.

"Well, I don't have a passport, but I do have my ID card, and I can find a way to come up with however much that is."

He handed the woman his ID. She looked at it closely and then looked back at Karl. She scanned him from head to toe. "Sir, this ID is thirty years expired and says that you're fifty-seven years old."

"Shit," he snarled, while pondering what to do.

"Also, is that blood on your leg?"

Karl looked down to see his right leg was drenched in blood. "Umm, yes, but it's not my blood."

The lady's eyes widened, and she started panicking.

"I mean, it's my dog's. He attacked some coyotes, and I had to take him to the vet."

The lady seemed very concerned.

"Give me a minute, please," Karl told her as he turned away and left the building. He walked down the stairs by the entrance and sat down by a tree on the corner. *How did the immigrants do it?* he thought.

He walked back inside and asked the woman, "Where's the nearest coastline?"

She looked at him in disbelief that he actually came back in. "Probably a hundred miles southwest of here. Now please leave before I call security," she said sharply.

Karl left the building and walked south-west of the airport. He walked through the streets and noticed a sign advertising Madrid's attractions. He was in Spain—he had always wanted to go. Just not under these kinds of circumstances. He walked through the city for some time. Once he had exited the city's perimeters, he broke into a jog. His pace was around forty miles per hour. He ran for hours until he heard the seagulls and felt the crisp ocean breeze. A refreshing reminder of his home. He spotted a small harbor and could see two men standing by a boat there. He approached them and without hesitation, he told them, "I need to get to America."

The two men looked at each other, confused. One of them walked up to Karl and looked him in the eyes. "Don't we all."

He continued, "If I did know someone, well... It would be very expensive."

"I don't have money here. I'm far from home, but if you can get me to America, I promise I'll pay you tenfold," Karl pleaded.

"What's your name, American?"

"Karl. Karl Fassbinder."

"Fassbinder? Like the company Fassbinder?"

Karl, confused, responded, "No, I don't believe so."

"No, that's right. Axel Fassbinder, the creator of Binder-Corp had a brother named Karl. If I remember correctly, he has been dead for over thirty years."

The man pulled out a Glock, pointing it at Karl. Karl slowly pulled out his wallet to show the man his ID. The man looked carefully at Karl's Identification card and then back at Karl. He put away his weapon and said, "I may know someone with the balls to take you across the Atlantic, but we will need two hundred grand for our troubles. My name is Antonio."

"Two hundred thousand? That seems a bit stiff, don't you think?" Karl asked, astonished.

"Well obviously you're not up to date with world affairs. In the last twenty years, the coastline has gone up over a hundred feet and the storms across the ocean have gotten so dangerous people don't travel across on boat anymore. Not to mention the U.S. border surveillance. This was once the border of Portugal. Can you believe it?"

"Where is Portugal?" Karl asked.

Antonio pointed to the vast sea. "It was there." He laughed.

"I'll get you your money, just get me home," Karl responded.

Antonio smiled and waved for Karl to follow. They walked down the dock to a thirty-foot long Motorsailer. Walking onto the ship, Antonio led Karl downstairs to meet the captain.

"Mr. Quinn, I have a business proposition," Antonio said.

Mr. Quinn turned around, revealing his half-scarred face, an eye patch covering one eye. In a scratchy voice, he replied, "And what may that be?"

"This here is the missing brother of Binder-Corp's creator. He promises us a cash cow if we can get him to America."

"I need something upfront. I don't take chances," Quinn responded.

Antonio sighed, looking down. He paused for a moment, then told Quinn, "I'll cover fifty grand till we get there."

Karl's eyes opened wide. He thought this must be a serious situation.

"We part at dawn," Mr. Quinn replied.

Monday, September 24th, 2035, a couple of weeks before the death of Mr. Black and the fall of the agency.

Across the globe. Tara Smith was sitting in her apartment waiting for a call from her superior. The phone rang. She answered it immediately.

"Hello?"

"Tara, this is Mr. Palestine. I need you to come into the office as soon as you can," he said, then hung up.

Tara got dressed and took her bike down main street. She arrived at the office. Entering the building, she scanned her eye to enter. A sliding steel door opened. She walked through the door and proceeded down the hallway to Miles's office. When she walked in, Mr. Palestine was sitting at his desk with one leg crossed over the other and his fingers interlinked.

He sat up straight. "Please sit down," he gestured to her. "I regret to inform you that Gamble Bright did not make it out before the explosion. I'm sincerely sorry. We tried everything we could."

Tara dropped to the ground and screamed in agony. Tears filled her eyes. She clenched her stomach and fists. Miles stood up and walked over to her. He placed his hand on the back of her head, comforting her.

"I promise, dear, things will get better. Justice will be served. You're quite an amazing woman and don't deserve such tragedy. Please let me take you out on Friday night. It will be nice being around a familiar face."

"Of course, sir. May I go home now?" she asked. "I need some time alone to grieve."

"No need to ask, Ms. Smith. You have my condolences, and please, call me Miles."

Tara rode home and mourned day in and day out. On Friday, she got all done up. She wore a bright red dress with sparkling heels.

Miles picked her up in a limousine at around seven in the evening. A man in a suit stepped out to open the door for her.

"You look incredible. Dazzling," Miles told her.

"Thank you," she replied awkwardly.

They drove to a fancy Italian restaurant downtown. After being seated the waiter made haste to their table. "Two glasses of your finest cabernet, please," Miles ordered.

Tara and Miles conversed about common areas of interest while enjoying glass after glass.

The next morning Tara woke up in Miles's bed, unable to remember the previous night. She grabbed her jacket and bolted out the door, heading home barefoot. The guilt and confusion she felt angered her. She started running home and as she arrived, kicked through her door, hurting herself. She flopped onto the couch and tried to relax. Unfortunately, to her surprise, she heard the last noise she could bear to hear in this emotionally terrifying moment.

"Fire wagon blue," a robotic voice repeated.

Duty calls, she thought. She rushed to her hidden closet behind the bookshelf. Once she was suited up, she sped off on her bike. Speeding down the highway going one hundred miles per hour. She arrived at headquarters within minutes. Entering the building, she took the elevator down. She looked at the elevator floor beneath her feet. Flooded with memories of Gamble. She wiped a tear from her eye as the door opened. Miles and Maverick were standing side by side, waiting for her.

"We have an urgent mission, Agent Blue," Miles declared. "Commander Silver and Commander Gold are compromised. Gold is dead and Silver is missing. Because of this, you are now kill squad A. The Spanish government has retrieved the remains of a device that can potentially change the outcome of our world. You and Agent Red will be dispatched immediately. My drones are already en route."

"Yes, sir," Tara and Mav responded simultaneously.

"There is a jet at takeoff point B awaiting you," Miles finished his orders.

Maverick and Tara left the room in the elevator. Once inside, Mav addressed his colleague, "You ready for this?"

"As ready as I'm going to be," Tara responded.

When the elevator arrived at ground level, she stepped out. Maverick grabbed her arm. "You need to be. This is our most vital mission yet."

She ripped her arm out of his grasp and nodded in mutual understanding. They approached a black Yukon. Maverick grabbed her arm and dragged her around the corner.

"What are you doing?!" she demanded.

"What is going on with you?" he questioned.

"I… I spent the night at Miles's house. I don't remember what happened," she confessed in tears.

"Nothing happened, Tara. You were too drunk, so he let you crash on his bed. I came by later and had a glass of wine with him."

"I thought… I was so confused."

"It's not like that with him. You know that, right? He would never take advantage of you like that. Miles is older than your parents." He paused for a moment and smirked at an idea. "He didn't tell you, did he? Miles is a complicated person. Trust me, I have known him the longest out of anyone in his life."

She wiped her tears and looked at him curiously. "What didn't he tell me?"

"Miles had a family once. A wife and a daughter. Shortly after his daughter turned eighteen, she was diagnosed with a rare nerve disorder. Her condition was terminal. They found the best doctors in the field, and they prescribed experimental medicine to treat her condition. It ended up killing her almost instantly. Through the pain of loss, Miles and his wife separated. Miles was determined to find justice for all of the corrupt medical providers that assisted in his daughter's death. It was what led him to the ADA to begin with. You remind him of her, Tara. He sees you as the daughter he lost, in a sense. You mean a great deal to him. But not in the way you implied from last night."

"I… I didn't know. I didn't mean to…"

Mav interrupted her with a hug. "It's okay, Blue. I understand. I got you."

The driver took them to the take-off point, and they boarded the jet headed for Spain. The two of them were suited up for battle and strapped on their chutes. They dropped out of the jet about two miles from the base.

"Impact successful, Agents?" Miles asked on their intercom headsets.

"Yes, sir," Mav assured him.

Tara hid her small sidearm and handed her heavier artillery to Maverick. Moments later, a Spanish military jeep came crashing over the hill.

Tara was standing alone in the open with her hands up, right in front of the oncoming vehicles. Maverick had vanished.

"*Manos arriba! Manos arriba!*" a man yelled as two soldiers wielding automatic weaponry exited the jeep.

"*¿Hablas español?*" the man demanded.

Tara shook her head no. He hit her stomach with the butt of his rifle as another soldier cuffed her hands behind her back. The soldiers loaded her into the jeep and took her back to their base. They drove through a large gate approaching a giant Andalusian villa The building's doors were made of reinforced carbon steel.

The men escorted Tara out of the vehicle to the door and stood awaiting orders. The door slowly opened, and they took her inside. The entrance opened into a high-ceilinged room with a staircase. They proceeded up the stairs and down the hall. The soldiers took her into a room and tied her to a chair. Moments later, a Spanish general walked in and addressed Tara.

"Who are you and where is your troop?" he demanded.

"I have no troop, sir. I was skydiving for my first time and all of these armed soldiers kidnapped me," she explained.

The general laughed. "You were skydiving from a military jet?"

"Agent Blue, Agent Red is ready for entry," Miles told Tara over the intercom hidden in her ear canal.

"A little distraction would be nice," she responded out loud.

"Excuse me?" the general said.

As the words left his lips, a drone fired a rocket into the crowded doorway of the room. The explosion baffled everyone but Tara. She instantly cut off her cuffs with a small carbide saw on her watch. She kicked her chair back behind her and punched the general in the face. In the same fluid motion, she swung her left leg around, using the same momentum to strike the soldier down beside him. While all five men in the room were disoriented, she picked up a rifle and unloaded hell into all of them. After she finished her clip, she spat on the corpse of the general.

"*Pedazo de escoria de mierda,*" she mocked.

Agent Blue opened the door with two automatic rifles and headed down the hallway. She turned right to see three soldiers running in her direction. As their eyes locked with hers, they attempted to lift their weapons to fire. She pushed her trigger fingers down and slammed their bodies into the walls. After dropping her weapons, she entered an elevator door near the top of the stairs. A group of soldiers climbing the stairs fired a few shots as the doors closed. Tara sat on the floor of the elevator and pulled out her hidden sidearm.

During all the havoc, Maverick approached the main gate. In his hands, he gripped a heavy .50-caliber automatic turret. The most destructive gun a man could attempt to carry. Maverick was no ordinary man. As he stepped out from behind the trees near the gate, the few soldiers in the two guard towers noticed him. Before they could fire a shot, Maverick fired up his weapon. Chopper-sized bullets rained down on them, devastating the towers and anything living within them. He continued firing into the hinges that were holding the large steel door together. Once he cut through, he kicked the giant twenty-by-twenty-foot gate down. He received a hard shot to the shoulder. For a moment, he dropped his turret and fell to his knees. Right away, a drone fired a shot directly into the head of the sniper who had shot Maverick, splattering his insides across the roof.

"Agent Blue, he needs entry!" Miles pleaded through the headset in her ear.

The elevator doors opened. At least ten armed soldiers were ready with their guns pointed in her direction. Tara held herself at the top of the elevator, out of sight. Her legs split as she pushed on each side of the walls. She threw a smoke grenade followed by a poison grenade into the room. After putting on a foldable mask, she waited a few moments. Gunshots, screams, then silence.

Tara dropped down and casually walked through the bodies. She grabbed a corpse and dragged it to the front door, lifting the eyelid to allow the eye to be scanned. It was read successfully, and the door opened.

Maverick walked into the building with his own mask on. "Damn, Blue. Did you leave any for me?"

"I think I'm gonna call you terror from now on, Terror Smith," he continued.

"And you can be my trusty side kick," she taunted him.

His smile dropped into a pissed-off smirk. "Mr. Black, where is the item?" he asked into his headset's microphone.

"Second story, third room down. I don't know what lies beyond those doors, but it's out of our drone and satellite visuals."

"Not my ideal scenario," Mav said.

He led them up the stairs, down the same hallway toward a different room. As he slowly approached the door, he turned back to Tara.

"This doesn't feel right, sir." He took one step further and heard a trap engaging. "It's a ruse!" he yelled.

The room exploded while Mav hugged Tara, shielding her from the explosion. He fell to his knees in pain. "Find it," he demanded.

Tara sprinted downstairs and bolted out the door, scanning the area until her eyes locked on a jeep. She hotwired it and headed out.

"I have visuals, Blue," Miles spoke into her headset. "Head northeast. There's a military jeep leaving your location, driving with haste."

As Tara pursued her target, Miles received an unexpected visitor back in headquarters.

"Sir, this is Agent Davis on base floor. Commander Silver is entering the building," Miles heard on the telecom.

His eyes widened in terror. "Arm yourself, Agent!"

The commander scanned his eye at the entrance of the building. He was over six feet with golden locks of hair. As the doors opened, he put on his helmet. He was clad in his full carbide suit.

Agent Davis, with his gun drawn, demanded, "Surrender your heavy artillery now, Commander Silver!"

Silver looked at the ground before him silently. He slowly lifted his helmet to his old friend.

"By all means, Nicolas," Silver responded as he lifted his rifle. He tore down Davis, head to toe.

Silver turned toward a large entryway with maybe fifteen agents drawing weapons. He fired a missile off the bottom of his assault rifle, deterring their response. He unloaded his rifle into the agents faster than the eye could see. Fifteen headshots in under thirty seconds. Most of the bodies dropped at once. A few followed within moments.

After everyone in the room was defeated, he tossed his rifle to the ground and drew out two automatic handguns. A guard door closed off the hallway beyond him. He pressed a button on his arm, triggering a small saw made of diamond. It shot out of his wrist, spinning. He cut a small hole through the door, then tossed a small grenade-like object through the hole. He continued to cut a larger hole in the door. As he was cutting, the grenade exploded in a burst of plasma. He heard a few faint screams from the other side of the door as everyone in the vicinity was obliterated. Silver finished cutting and kicked through the door. The floor was covered in ashes, the remains of the agents.

Silver walked down the corridor toward the elevator. He pulled out a tripod from the scabbard on his back, coated with a gooey substance. He set it before him and pressed a button on his arm, magnetizing the crystals in the goo. The tripod turned into a shield as the elevator arrived. Five agents in full body armor stepped out with armor-piercing weaponry. Silver extended two chained whips out of his armor near his wrists. He spun them around the shield as the men fired at it. Their bullets deflected back at them. All his assailants were knocked back briefly. He kicked the shield to the side and attacked with his whips. In three fluid motions, his chained whips wrapped around the agents' armor. Between the helmets and pauldrons, the whips hit the skin as he ripped back violently—like he was painting a masterpiece. He decapitated all five of them simultaneously.

He continued into the elevator. Ascending upward, the elevator came to an abrupt stop between levels one and two. On level three, Miles, awaiting his fate, watched the cameras. An agent walked into the room.

"Sir, we have agents dropping like flies. We stopped the elevator in an attempt to slow him down."

Miles clenched a small medallion tight within his fingers. "That may buy us a matter of minutes. Agent Wilson, you and everyone left on this floor need to leave now. Your duty is served."

"What about you, sir?" Wilson questioned, looking concerned.

"I'll face Silver and show him why he was the apprentice."

Wilson nodded and retreated with the few agents left on level three.

Commander Silver cut a hole in the ceiling of the elevator. He leapt up on top of it with ease and pressed a few controls on his utility gauntlet. Lifting his arm, he aimed for level two's doors. He fired a grappling hook through the door and retracted the belt, lifting himself up to the level. He grabbed the ledge where the floor began and pulled himself up. He received multiple shots to his suit, but his suit deflected the bullets. He pointed down the hallway, a gun in each hand. He killed two agents and kept up the offensive pressure.

When he stepped out of the hallway, he found himself in a big open room. There were barricades in a half circle with maybe twenty armed and armored agents between him and his prize. Shots were fired. Silver suffered heavy damage as all his foes opened fire on him. He quickly grabbed two plasma grenades and threw them behind each barricade. They exploded, and he unloaded the clips in both guns while continuing to take fire. His guns ran empty. He tossed them toward the remaining group of men. His whips spiraled out of his suit as he swung one, cutting an agent's gun down.

Silver danced with his whips, surrounded by the last eight men. He spiraled them at one enemy, ripping their gun from their grasp and smashing it into another. He dashed toward two more, wrapping his whips around their necks. Then he lunged at another as the whips cut through. Five men left. He threw both whips on each side, severing the trigger fingers of two men at once.

Silver's whips retracted, and he pulled out another plasma grenade. He dashed to the closest, shoving the grenade into his armor. He threw that agent toward the other three and they all disintegrated. The last agent ran away down the hall. Silver picked up one of the fallen agent's rifles and fired a few rounds into his back. After every agent was dead, he continued to a door that led to a fire escape stairway. He walked up two flights of stairs and arrived on the third level. He poked his gun out the door, then glanced around, finding the hallway empty.

Silver crept up to Miles's quarters. He opened the door gently. Miles was standing facing the opposite direction in the center of the room.

"I've been bothered greatly, contemplating the idea of Commander Gold dying on a mission. She was one of the deadliest, most brilliant mercenaries on the planet. It makes sense. You would have been the only one who could fulfill that task."

"She put up a hell of a fight," Silver responded as he raised his weapon toward Miles's head.

"So did you," Miles answered as Silver took his shot.

Silver's bullet went straight through the hologram. Miles revealed himself behind Silver and fired rapidly into the back of his neck. The suit's Achilles' heel. Continuing fire, Miles bent Silver's head forward with one arm and finished the kill with a bullet directly into his brain. Silver's body dropped to the floor.

Miles told Tara on the intercom, "Agent Blue, we are compromised. Regroup at Safehouse Four. This line is dead."

Meanwhile, across the globe, Tara caught up to the jeep. "Agent Red, I'm right on him now," Tara proclaimed on the private line. Half a mile behind, she pursued her target. She kicked out the windshield and fired her weapon at the jeep till she hit their tire. The enemy jeep drifted into the broad side of the vehicle starting to roll. Tara crashed head on into the rolling vehicle, slamming it into a wide tree. She got out and ripped the soldier out, then snapped his neck. She climbed into the bottomed-up vehicle and found a small rectangular device, grabbed it and packed it in a satchel on her side.

"Blue, I'm en route. Hold your ground," Mav said.

Tara held her position and within moments, multiple military jeeps arrived, surrounding her.

"I need help, Red," she begged.

The sun rose on the horizon, shining upon Blue. She realized this might be her last dawn.

The soldiers from the jeeps stepped out and prepared for gunfire. At that moment, Maverick crashed over the hill in another jeep. He drove straight into an enemy vehicle and rolled out of his. He rolled a bit, then stood up, revealing his turret. He opened fire on the other two vehicles backed by soldiers. They fired a few shots back; they missed, and Mav devastated each and every one of them.

"You alright, Blue?" he asked his partner.

"As okay as I can be... what now?" she responded.

"Vengeance," Red answered.

The two agents headed back to the U.S. on a jet. Their destination was the Nevada desert. The jet dropped them off in chutes near Safehouse Four. It was a few miles to the safehouse from their landing point, and after traversing thick forest, they finally arrived at a small cabin.

Maverick slowly opened the door with his sidearm facing in front of him.

"No need for that, Maverick," Miles said. Maverick sighed in relief and lowered his weapon. "Wasn't too sure what to expect, sir. What happened?"

Miles stepped out of the shadows with a face full of sorrow. "The ADA has fallen. Commander Silver betrayed us. He is responsible for Gold's death. While you were on your mission, he invaded headquarters, killing nearly all of our agents," he explained. "I have reason to believe he was working with Binder-Corp. His timing was too coincidental. Did you retrieve the item?"

"That we did," Mav responded while turning toward Tara.

She pulled out the rectangular device. Miles smiled in appreciation.

"There is still hope," Miles said. "Maverick, you and I will rally the remaining agents. We have a mission regarding Mr. Fassbinder."

Mav nodded in confirmation.

"Tara, I need you to head back to California and keep a low profile."

"But sir, I would like to accompany you on the mission."

"I understand, dear, but things are far too dangerous as of right now. I can't let anything happen to you. Your fate lies beyond this agency."

"Understood, sir."

Miles gestured to them to follow him further into the cabin. Down the hallway they entered a garage. There was a black Escalade and a small Kawasaki parked there. Miles tossed Tara the keys to the bike. "Be safe, Tara."

The garage door opened as Tara mounted the bike and rode off. Miles got into the driver's seat of the SUV. Maverick slid into the passenger side, and they departed.

"Are you gonna tell her about Gold?" Mav asked.

"It's too late for it to matter now."

They drove for some time, heading for the other safehouse. They parked out front.

"Continue training until further instructed," Miles directed Mav.

"Will do, sir."

Before stepping out, Mav said, "And Miles, be safe."

Miles smiled and nodded. The black Escalade drove off as Mav entered the safehouse.

"Long night?" Gamble asked. "You look rough."

"Something like that. You know one day that sense of humor is gonna get you in some trouble," Mav lectured.

"Training will start where we left off tomorrow. Everything is falling into place."

Miles drove for two hours to an old run-down military base. He made three calls, summoning the remaining five ADA agents. One of the agents was a molecular engineer/technological expert.

The five agents arrived at the base by the next morning. The last of the ADA stood at attention as Miles walked out of the bunker to greet them.

"Agents, friends, we have come to an unforeseen end. All of your duties have been served. If any of you want to go back to your normal lives, you are free to leave now." Miles paused for a minute or two. None of the agents even hesitated. They all wanted to stay.

"You are all admirable men. We have an opportunity to change everything. To bring justice. To change the tides. Christoph Hammond, I need you to follow me. The rest of you, prepare the bases' defenses. Quickly."

Miles led Christoph into a small box with a door. They entered an elevator and descended. On their way down, he explained to Chris the situation and the device.

"I need you to take everything apart and reverse engineer it. Create blueprints for every part in case we need to make it again. Afterwards, I need you to fix the machine. I have full faith and confidence in you. Your grandfather was part of the creation of this mechanism. If anyone can accomplish this, it's you."

"If it can be done, it will be, sir," Hammond proclaimed.

Agent Hammond worked on the device for five days until he was confident that he had perfected it. He approached Miles. "Sir, I believe I have reconstructed the device and have designed all the blueprints necessary to rebuild it."

"Fantastic. I will retrieve the man meant for the machine."

October 3rd, 2035, the final gathering of the ADA.

At the deepest floor of the base, the sequence began. Don's counterpart entered a small room with agent Hammond.

"Begin the gap!" Miles instructed Hammond.

They were accompanied by Maverick and the other four agents. Hammond set the device for the year 2000. He executed the machine's launch and ran away to safety in the other room.

Don was instantly surrounded by a large metal box. Flashes of red lightning burst throughout the room as the lights and power flickered. The floor shook, and after a moment, the box disappeared.

"It works," Miles whispered to himself in disbelief.

The power surge came up on a nearby radar.

Thaddeus Lee was sitting on his throne in his private chambers when an armored soldier walked into the room.

"Sir, I believe we have found them."

Thaddeus Lee dispatched his top mercenaries to the ADA's base, led by Lars Grossman, the world's deadliest criminal. They headed off in three Black Hawk choppers.

Miles, Maverick, and the other five remaining agents ascended to ground level and prepared themselves for war.

"Arm the guard towers!" Miles directed his company. The mercenaries arrived at the base. Their choppers lowered below the tree level, flying between the tall redwoods.

Agent Wilson grabbed a belt of bullets and armed his turret, aiming it toward the wall of trees. The ADA quietly awaited their attack. They could hear the approaching propellers in the distance. The agents shook with anticipation. The vibrations from the propellers radiated through the neighboring trees in the wood. Some of the withered hollowed-out remains of wood thumped, like a war drum.

Suddenly, the first Hawk appeared. Wilson opened fire, but before he could hit the pilot, the hawk fired a missile into the tower. It burst into flames and threw Wilson's corpse down fifteen feet to the ground. The other two Hawks flew over the open area above the base, circling and unloading heavy artillery. Another agent in a guard tower was annihilated.

One of the Hawks landed, and Grossman and two mercenaries jumped out. Agent Randall appeared around the corner of the building and fired his clip at them. He landed a few shots at one mercenary, who dropped to the ground. Grossman dashed at Randall and fired his sidearm into his head. Maverick revealed himself from behind a sandbag barricade, wielding a bazooka. He fired it into the Hawk that the mercenaries had landed in, exploding it into oblivion. He knelt down and grabbed a pre-loaded secondary rocket and fired an accurate successful shot into one of the Hawks circling the base. The rocket contacted the tail as the second Hawk spun down, crashing. Fire spread everywhere. The base was burning down in ten-foot-tall flames. Explosions left and right.

Maverick stood Miles by his side.

Hammond made a shot for the military Hummer hidden behind one of the fallen guard towers. Grossman appeared between Hammond and the hummer with his gun drawn. He shot through his neck and grabbed the blueprints from his hand as Hammond bled out.

Maverick tackled Grossman out of nowhere and threw him into the wall, following his attack with a charge and a right hook. Grossman dodged his punch, and Maverick's fist dug a foot into the wall behind him. Grossman lifted his knuckles, which were wrapped with an electric brass amplifier. He swung his fist into Mav's face. When it hit, it sent Mav through the air, shocked with electricity. For a moment, he couldn't move.

Grossman put the blueprints in a capsule. He fired it into the air as a drone sped by and caught it. "Get the prints to safety. Burn the base."

Grossman was picked up by the remaining Black Hawk.

A jet flew by with a napalm strike. Miles helped Mav up and entered a hidden chopper within the remaining segment of the base. They ascended quickly as the napalm strike hit the base. The last two ADA agents were killed instantly. As Maverick and Miles flew off in an attempt to escape, they realized there were more Hawks en route. Two more appeared out of the thick forest, firing at the survivors' chopper. Miles was negating all the bullets with his steering.

"Get out of here, Maverick!" Miles demanded. Moments later they flew over a small canal and Mav jumped out, diving into the shallow water. He swam to the bottom and underneath a bridge. He peeked out to see Miles's chopper heading off in the distance, followed by the two Hawks.

About forty minutes later, Lars Grossman approached Castle Lee. He stood leaning out the cabin door of the helicopter, holding the handlebar with one hand. He watched the dirt road in the desert drop beneath him into a beautiful, forested canyon.

In the center was the great castle-fortress, surrounded by a twenty-foot-tall stone wall with five guard towers evenly spaced around it. The castle's stone was a darkish gray that reflected the mysterious glow of red and blue energy emanating from within.

The chopper touched down on a landing pad with three black merlons wrapped around it, connected by stone crenels.

Grossman walked through a wooden door and down a spiral staircase to Mr. Lee's quarters. He was welcomed in through the steel doors by a spherical android hovering above the ground.

As he entered the circular room, Thaddeus stood from his throne.

"I'm pleased to see that you and the blueprints made it here unharmed. The lab has already received the prints and developed mechanical drawings for the manufacturing of the device. They have given me an estimated completion time of thirty-six hours."

"That was fast" Grossman commented.

"They are the best. So you are sure about all of the details? The time and location?"

"Positive. My source wouldn't shut up about it."

Thaddeus grinned sinisterly. "Then let us begin preparations."

Meanwhile, Maverick waited for an hour or so submerged in the nasty water. He was patient and focused. When he thought it was safe, he found the nearest road, flagged a car down and told the driver he was a police officer, commandeering their vehicle. He drove for some hours to San Francisco. When he arrived, he used a payphone to call the only line he could. Tara answered.

"Hello?"

"Blue, it's Maverick, meet me where the office once stood."

Maverick waited on the corner, shrouded in an oversized hoodie.

Tara arrived on her bike. "Hop on," she told him.

He gave her bike a disapproving look. As they drove off, they hit a bump and the bottom of the bike sparked from the extra weight.

Tara took him to a beat-up apartment in the ghetto. Parking the bike, they walked inside.

"Everything went to shit. Everyone is dead, except maybe Miles," he explained. "We barely escaped and now Binder-Corp has the blueprints needed to recreate the time machine."

"Where is Miles?" she asked, attempting to stay calm and collected.

"We escaped in a chopper and were followed. I jumped out into a canal. I fear he didn't make it." He paused to give her a chance to take it all in.

"Tara, there's something I need to tell you. Miles saved my life by curing my gigantism. I would be dead without him. But you, Tara, he didn't save your life. He condemned it. Your mother was Commander Gold. Miles never wanted either of you to know. When you turned eighteen, he had an opportunity to recruit you and he took it. In his mind, it was justified, because he was saving you from your prison sentence. But you would have been better off without his deal. Gold never wanted this life for you."

"What? What do you mean? How couldn't you have told me?" she demanded.

"I was bound by my loyalty to the agency. Bound by oath. There's something else. Gamble is alive. Or he was at least."

Tara slapped Maverick across the face aggressively. "Where is he?" she yelled.

"He is at a safehouse, but if you go there, you'll risk both of your lives. Your best bet is to keep an eye out here. I reckon if Miles doesn't make it to him, or we never show up, he won't wait for long. He was very persistent about finding you. He will come. I'm sure of it."

For the next couple of days, Tara rode around town. Driving back and forth between the diner and Gamble's old apartment. On the second day, a few hours passed dusk, her luck turned and while driving by the diner she spotted a man who looked like Gamble. She parked her bike in the alleyway and waited for him to come out. She sent a swift kick to his head and dragged him into the shadows. Realizing it was him, she took off her helmet and revealed her face.

"I thought you were dead. Why didn't you come?"

"I couldn't. I tried. But I'm here now."

"We can't stay here. I have a room a few blocks away.

She helped him onto her bike, and they drove off. Soon after they arrived at the complex. Tara led them through the door and down the hallway. Mav stepped out from the back room.

I thought you were dead, Maverick," Gamble muttered in confusion. "Why are you here?"

"Well... not dead yet. When we were ambushed, only Miles and I made it out in a chopper. We were followed and he dropped me off in a river. Hopefully we'll hear from him."

"He died in the chopper," Gamble said. "It crashed by the cabin, but I killed all of the soldiers responsible."

Mav and Tara looked at each other with pained expressions.

"So, he is dead. But he will not die in vain," Tara declared. She walked up to Gamble and grabbed his shoulder, looking him in the eyes. "I haven't been completely honest with you. I've been working for the ADA the whole time. Originally, I was meant to watch over you for protection. But then… I fell in love. I'm really sorry. I couldn't tell you."

This was a slap in the face. Gamble couldn't fathom how much anger burst through his veins. He turned toward Mav and yelled, "HOW COULD YOU LIE TO ME? I THOUGHT SHE WAS DEAD BECAUSE OF YOU!"

"I was following orders. They wanted you focused and angry. I do apologize. I did what I had to," Mav replied.

Gamble pondered for a moment, desperately wanting to seek vengeance. In a frightful manner, he whispered, "Where is the man in the suit?"

"The man in the suit is the creator of Binder-Corp. Axel Fassbinder is his name, and he is no mortal man," Mav told his colleagues. "He is the most powerful man on the planet."

"I don't care who he is or what he is. I will avenge my mother and father. And Miles…"

"I respect your urge for vengeance, but he is not our biggest threat. Thaddeus Lee, his right-hand man, has been working on a project for the last three years. He's building a utopia on the moon that he calls Andromeda. A small city for Binder-Corp executives and their families to survive the apocalypse. We fear that when he finishes the city, Binder-Corp plans on destroying any possibility of us interfering by destroying the planet."

Mav continued, "Mr. Lee is now in possession of the time-machine prints. We're not sure what he wants them for, but those prints may be our last hope."

Gamble and Tara stared at each other.

"If there's one thing I can do to redeem myself in both your eyes, it's to urge you both to give up this life. Go start a family. Live your lives," Mav pleaded.

"We're in this together. My whole life has been dedicated to the cause. I will finish my duty," Tara stated in a firm manner.

"Gamble?" Mav asked, looking toward him.

"I've always wanted to make a difference. If what you're saying is true, we won't have a place to live our lives soon. I'm with you," Gamble answered as he grabbed Tara's hand and looked into her eyes with a smile.

"Then it is decided… Heroes aren't born. They're made. The agency is no more. If we're doing this, it's as free men. Maybe we can be the heroes the world needs. Maybe with a fool's hope, we can make a difference," Maverick stated.

CHAPTER 11

In the Eye of the Storm

On the coastline of what remained of Spain, Karl lay down to rest. In a small house at the shore, he contemplated his journey.

"Get some sleep. You're gonna need it. It's hard to sleep at sea," Antonio said.

"I'll do what I can," he responded in a pessimistic tone.

The two of them slept until morning. Antonio went to wake Karl with his hand on his shoulder. Karl grabbed his hand right before he touched him. "I'm up."

Antonio smiled. "It's time to go, my friend."

Antonio packed a bag full, and they left the house, headed for the ship. Mr. Quinn was on the deck waiting for them. The ship was a mid-sized motorsailer. Its hull was painted navy blue, with a gray trim running along the rail. The deck was a weathered beige and had a tall white mast spouting in the center before the matching cockpit. The whole boat looked rundown.

We're crossing the Atlantic in this piece of junk? Karl thought.

"Are we going or not?" Quinn questioned them.

"Yes, yes we're ready," Antonio answered.

They settled down on the ship. Moments later, they departed on their journey across the Atlantic. Five thousand miles to their destination.

"Hopefully you don't get seasick. Depending on the weather, it could take us up to three weeks," Antonio told his lost passenger.

"There's only one way to find out," Karl remarked.

A few days into the trip, Antonio and Karl were up above deck leaning on the railing near the front of the ship, observing the sea.

"So, I gotta ask. What happened to you?" Antonio turned toward Karl and peered into his eyes.

Karl seemed confused. "What do you mean exactly?"

"Like you know, why did you disappear for thirty years and come back the same age?"

Karl chuckled and looked at Antonio. He was surprised to see his serious expression.

Karl looked back at the sea. "You wouldn't believe me if I told you."

"Try me," Antonio replied with a smirk.

"In the year 2000 I was with my brother on a mission when two mercenaries… from the future… I'm assuming, showed up out of nowhere. They sent me through a machine. Far into our future. All the way to hell."

"What was it like?" Karl's new companion asked.

"What do you mean? You believe me?"

"Let's just say if I did, what would you tell me about our future?"

"All I can say is that you don't want to know," Karl stated firmly as he turned and walked toward the hatch. "I think that's enough story time for one day."

A week passed at sea. So far so good. Karl and Antonio met in the small dining area within the cabin below the deck. Mr. Quinn was wearing an apron over his torn-up clothes while he cooked their breakfast. They all sat down cross-legged on the floor for breakfast at a small table a couple feet off the ground.

"Mackerel again, man? Can't you fish for something bigger?" Antonio complained to Quinn.

"You catch your own damn fish," he remarked.

"I actually love mackerel," Karl interjected, trying to cheer them up.

They looked at each other and both laughed.

"It could definitely be worse," Antonio commented. "Maybe we can catch some of those mutant fish they talked about on the TV."

Quinn laughed and turned toward Karl who was looking concerned. "What mutant fish?" Karl asked.

"Apparently all these technology companies have been dumping some crazy toxic shit into the ocean. So people have been claiming to see giant deformed sea creatures."

"That's very comforting. Thank you," Karl remarked sarcastically.

Antonio laughed harder and told him, "Don't you worry, man. No one believes that bullshit."

"Sometimes what seems impossible is more possible than what's right before your eyes," Karl lectured.

"Wow that's pretty heavy. Let's hope you aren't right about that one."

The next day in the afternoon Karl leant on the mast, staring deep into the water, inspecting every ripple from the tides.

Antonio approached him from behind. "So, what's your play in all of this?"

Antonio paused for a moment and continued. "What does the stronger brother of the Army of Two have to do with our undoing?"

Karl's eyes widened and he turned almost aggressively toward his companion. "What did you say? How do you know about the Army of Two?"

"Well, it's a well-known story. Two brothers with superpowers fighting crime. It hasn't been that long."

Karl took a long deep breath. "I haven't heard that name in years. I'm afraid the Army of Two will never again be what it was. Circumstances changed us both. Likely and unfortunately for the worse."

"That's a true tragedy. The world could really use them nowadays."

Later that night, Mr. Quinn popped open an old bottle of tequila. "This here is Spain's best agave. Not quite what they've got in Mexico, but it gets the job done."

"Bottoms up," Antonio said as they all took a shot. Five shots later they were all fairly drunk.

"How you liking the sea?" Antonio asked Karl, attempting not to slur his words.

Karl was still relatively collected. "You know, not my cup of tea, but I've seen worse."

"Yeah, you never really get used to it unless your like Quinn over here."

"The ocean is the only woman for me," Quinn said. "She doesn't say a word. Just lets me ride her waves."

Karl and Antonio burst out laughing. They drank late into the night until all of them fell asleep. A couple of hours later, Karl was startled awake by Quinn yelling, "All men on deck!"

Karl and Antonio stumbled to get up and hurried to climb the ladder to the deck. When they peeked out, heavy rain hit their heads. Karl saw they had sailed into a huge storm. He looked upwards to see the clear sky surrounded by dark clouds.

"We're in the eye of the storm!" Quinn yelled.

"Karl, help me get the sail down," Antonio demanded.

The ship shook, making it difficult to move. Karl crawled toward the mast and began climbing it. He climbed to the top, releasing the sails. The ship rocked harder than before. The waves got bigger and bigger, crashing onto the deck.

"Close the hatch!" Quinn shouted.

Antonio slammed the hatch shut and locked it. Lightning crackled and hit the tip of the mast, breaking it in half. Quinn was in the pilot room attempting to steer the ship. The top of the mast swung perpendicularly at a hundred miles an hour into the pilot room where Quinn stood.

"Quinn!" Antonio yelled in agony.

Karl grabbed his shoulder and turned him toward their imminent demise. The two survivors looked up at a giant tidal wave maybe thirty feet tall.

"Hold on!" Antonio screamed as the wave crashed down on the ship, knocking it under water for a minute or so. When the ship had surfaced, Karl and Antonio were both holding tightly to its side rail. They gasped for air.

"Mr. Quinn?" Antonio shouted, running over toward the pilot room. He could see Quinn's body, his head was caved in. "Quinn, wake up, wake up!" Antonio yelled, violently shaking Quinn's chest.

Karl grabbed his shoulder. "He's gone, Antonio."

"Then it's all damned. Our task has failed."

"We haven't failed anything. We're still here. Do you know how to drive this thing?"

"I don't, but it seems like I'm about to learn."

Karl walked over to the mast and lifted it up, then tossed it off the boat. Antonio approached Quinn's body. A tear streamed down his face as he looked down at him.

"The storm's not over yet. We need to get below deck," Karl recommended.

"We can't leave him like this. He deserves a proper burial."

"If we don't get under now, then our fate will be the same as his," Karl advised him.

"The captain becomes one with the ship. Help me bring him down," Antonio stated firmly.

Karl nodded and they carried Quinn's body down below deck. They sat him down on his bed and locked the hatch. The two of them lay down and attempted to sleep. The next day, the companions got up and met at the table.

Karl told Antonio, "I feel like I've failed. I don't know if I'll ever see my brother again. After everything I've been through to get back to him, I've ended up right where I began, lost."

"I need to show you something," Antonio said. He left for his room and rummaged through the bag he had brought. Grabbing a thin paperback, he sat by Karl and handed it to him. It was a comic book titled *Army of Two*.

"What's this?" Karl asked as a smile grew on his face.

"The heroic journey of the Army of Two. When I was young, I had little hope. Saw things as half empty. My father was a drunk, my mother a pill popper. Between the two, the fights got pretty serious. I found solace in these comics. They taught me that there is good in this world. Men who fight for justice and righteousness. One day, after reading the final volume when you disappeared, I finally stood up to my father. And well, he kicked my ass. But my mother and I never heard from him again. If I can push forward, so can the notorious Karl Fassbinder."

Antonio rested his hand on Karl's shoulder. "Sometimes you just need to believe. And know that someone believes in you, my friend."

Karl smiled with his eyes full of tears. Another wave pushed the ship under.

"Are you sure this won't sink?" Karl asked.

"It's not supposed to. The ship is filled with syntactic foam to help improve its buoyancy. Let's just pray that's enough."

The storm lasted another night as the two companions remained below deck.

On the third day, when the ocean calmed, Antonio opened up the hatch. Karl followed him up the ladder to see the blue sky above them.

"We made it," Antonio shouted.

"Where are we?" Karl asked.

Antonio hurried over to the cockpit.

"Looks as if everything is still working properly, surprisingly. The maps are going haywire, but it looks like we're just eighty miles off the coast of Florida."

They both paused for a moment. "Which direction from Florida?" Karl asked with trepidation.

"Southeastern."

"Just my luck," Karl muttered.

"The storm must've carried us pretty far south. Directly into the most dangerous part of the ocean," Antonio said.

Suddenly they felt something hit the bottom of the ship.

"Do you see land in the distance?" Karl hesitated to ask.

They heard another thud against the bottom of the ship.

"That's not land!"

The ocean roared as a giant head full of teeth violently flopped onto the ship. A Jurassic-sized beast. The mouth was at least six feet in diameter. Its teeth were twice the size of a great white's. The creature appeared to only be showing its head. It slithered across the center of the ship and back into the water, wrapping its long, whitish-green snake-like body around the ship.

"Holy shit!" Antonio screamed. "A fucking sea monster!"

Karl grabbed a long fishing spear and stabbed it into the creature's side. The monster sent an electric shock through its body, knocking Karl onto his back. The beast tightened its grip, breaking the ship in half. Antonio grabbed his machete and hacked into its side repeatedly. The beast sent an electric shock, knocking him to the ground unconscious. The bow and stern lifted up as the monster squeezed the ship. The center was submerged, with the monster in the water. Karl came to as he slid down the deck toward the water. The beast was gone. Antonio's body slid down past Karl, and he grabbed him right before he fell into the submerged trench. Karl threw Antonio over his shoulder and climbed up to the ship's bow. The farthest point from the water. Karl shook him awake.

"Where'd it go?" Antonio asked his savior.

"It knocked me out for a second and when I came to, it was gone," Karl explained.

"Screw this, man. If we can't kill it, I know what will," Antonio said as he took a knife from his side. He cut deep into his hand and lifted it over the side of the ship, letting his blood pour into the water.

"What the hell are you doing?" Karl demanded angrily.

"Sharks love eels."

The giant monstrous eel-like creature pulled the ship down again, leaving the two survivors only a few feet above the water.

"Alright, I need you to do me a huge solid. Dive into the ship and find the lifeboat," Antonio directed Karl.

"What? Are you kidding me? Why didn't we grab that sooner?" Karl remarked.

He paused for a moment and realized that it wasn't time to argue.

"Where is it?"

"Below deck, next to the table near Quinn's cabin. You'll see it."

Karl took off his jacket and looked around to try and spot the beast. He dived into the dark, murky water. Under the surface he could only see about twenty feet in each direction. The monster was nowhere to be seen. He swam over to the hatch. As he twisted the latch open, the ship instantly dropped further into the ocean. The wall of teeth appeared behind Karl, biting at the entrance, just missing his foot. Karl looked out of the hatch to see the beast flaring its electricity furiously. He swam into Quinn's quarters, past his floating body. He grabbed a small, yellow, oblong device, then turned toward the hatch to see the sea monster had been ambushed by a shiver of tiger sharks.

The monster screeched and fled away from the boat. Karl swam to the exit and as he left, he was attacked from behind. Something bit his leg. He looked back to see it was what had once been a tiger shark, its deformed face now nothing but an oval ball of teeth. He swiftly kicked the beast away and climbed out of the water.

The shark's teeth had no effect on the great Fassbinder's skin.

"That was close, man," Antonio told him.

Karl exhaled slowly. "You're telling me…" Karl handed Antonio the lifeboat.

Antonio pressed a few buttons on the side and set it in the water next to them. Just as the survivors' feet were submerged by the ocean, they climbed into the emergency boat and escaped the wreckage. Antonio looked back and watched the ship sink.

He muttered, "The captain goes down with the ship."

"Any idea on what that thing was?" Karl asked.

"If I'm not mistaken, I think that was a giant moray eel. Giant as in like a hundred times the size. I took marine biology in college. And also, I watched *The Little Mermaid*," Antonio explained.

Karl gave him a confused look. "Aren't you a little young for that?"

"Hey man, classics never die." They both had a good laugh.

"Damn it," Antonio said suddenly.

Karl looked where Antonio was focused to see hundreds of fins pursuing their boat.

"Still think that was a good idea? Bold, not smart," Karl remarked.

The fins caught up and surrounded the lifeboat. The survivors heard an old familiar noise. A helicopter. Machine guns fired at the sharks. A military Black Hawk centered above the raft, and a ladder descended.

"Get on!" a soldier yelled.

Karl and Antonio climbed up the ladder into the chopper as the raft was devastated by hundreds of mutated sharks. A soldier directed them to sit at the back. He cuffed both survivors.

"Who are you and why are you traveling across this ocean?"

Antonio looked at Karl and shook his head.

"I'm Karl Fassbinder and I've been trying—"

Antonio interrupted him, "We are mere merchants from Spain, and we lost our ship," he corrected.

Antonio whispered to Karl, "Don't let them know who you are."

"What was that?" the soldier asked.

Antonio headbutted the soldier and wrestled for his gun. A shot fired off directly into Karl's chest. They all paused for a moment, looking at Karl. Karl looked down at the wound and then back up. He broke his cuffs with ease, quickly knocking out the soldier. Another soldier in the front pulled out his sidearm. Karl grabbed it and threw it back, knocking him unconscious. He tossed the soldier into the back and sat up front with the pilot.

"What's your name, soldier?" Karl asked him.

"Brad Poller."

"Listen, Brad, we are no enemies of this country. My task determines the fate of this world. I need you to take us to the mainland so that I can get to the West Coast."

The pilot's face was pale as he considered his decision very carefully. His intuition told him that Karl was telling the truth, and he decided to cooperate. "Understood," he replied.

"Take us to Miami or wherever the nearest city is to here."

"Miami has been below sea level for five years. But I can drop you off at the beach north of there."

The pilot flew them over Miami beach. The city was abandoned. Most of the buildings still sat above the water line. The first to second stories were flooded. Occasional homeless people could be spotted on the rooftops. Karl looked down and then back at Antonio. Antonio nodded, confirming Karl's concerns.

"Atlantis," Antonio commented with a grin.

The pilot flew them to the closest stretch of U.S. coastline.

As the chopper landed, Karl told him, "Listen, I know your duty, and I'm not asking you not to report this to your superiors. All I can ask is that you give us a running start, in return for us sparing your life."

"I can give you twenty minutes," the pilot declared.

"That will do. Thank you."

Karl and Antonio jumped out of the chopper and ran into the nearby forest. They sprinted as fast as Antonio's legs could carry him. Fifteen minutes later they arrived at a small town. When they came out of the thick forest, Antonio stopped.

"Karl!"

Karl stopped and turned toward his companion.

"I believe this is where our paths part," Antonio told him.

"What do you mean? What about the money?" Karl asked in surprise.

"It was never about the money. When I saw you, I knew who you were. I thought maybe you were here for a reason. Maybe my life purpose was to get you across the Atlantic. The greatest gift you can give me is to finish your task. Our world is dying. Maybe you're the means to fix it. I lost all my money in the ship, but I want you to take this." He handed Karl a gold watch. "It's made out of real solid gold. I'm sure that will buy you a trip to California."

Antonio placed the watch in Karl's hand and looked him in the eye.

Karl looked at the watch and then back up at him. "Thank you, Antonio."

"God speed, my friend." Antonio ran north toward the city.

Karl clenched the watch in his hand. He continued west into the small town and found a general store there.

"I'm looking to sell this watch," he told the shopkeeper.

"Is it stolen? What kind of sketchy shit is this? The pawn shop's a few towns over."

"That's out of my way. Look, it's a family heirloom and I'm in a time of crisis."

"Okay. Well, what do you want for it? I'll give you fifty bucks," the shopkeeper said, downplaying its worth.

"This watch isn't only gold-plated, it's solid. Worth at least two thousand. However, I could get rid of it for five hundred, cash."

"I'll buy it."

"Where is the nearest Greyhound?" Karl asked the man.

"Greyhound? I haven't heard that name since I was a kid. The Google Cobra will take you wherever you need to go," the clerk explained.

"Like all the way to Los Angeles?"

"Yes, sir. It's almost as fast as flying. Only a six-hour trip from here."

"Six hours? How is that possible?"

"It's similar to the old subways but with new technology they can safely run up to three hundred miles per hour. It's pretty well known. You must be one of those anti-smart-phone people."

"Yes. Whatever that means. Where can I find this Cobra?"

The clerk gave Karl directions to the train station. Karl jogged for an hour until he saw it. A wide, covered area with stairs leading downward. He walked down the stairs to a subway-style station. He looked to see a small, lit-up booth with a teller next to three electronic boxes with screens and number pads. He approached the booth and addressed the attendant.

"I need one ticket to Los Angeles."

The attendant pressed his keypad a few times and looked back up at Karl. "That will be five hundred and three dollars."

"What? Why is it so expensive?" Karl demanded.

"Five hundred isn't so much." The attendant chuckled and continued. "Minimum wage pays more than that in a day."

Karl shook his head at this revelation. "Listen, I've come a long way. I'm a few bucks short. I'll give you the shirt off my back for Christ's sake. Just get me on that goddamn train!" Karl yelled, scaring the poor man.

"Five hundred is perfect. Do you have Google pay?"

He paused for a moment, gauging Karl's face.

Karl handed him his cash.

"I'm technically not allowed to take cash."

Karl gave him a death glare.

"Thank you, sir. Your train will be arriving soon."

Karl tore the ticket from him and sat down on the bench near the stop. A robotic voice stated overhead, "The Cobra is approaching. Step back and hold onto your seat or safety handle."

The tunnel shook as a long glass-plated train arrived.

"Please board safely," a voice repeated as the doors opened. Karl walked in and sat down. Two seat belts strapped around him automatically harnessing him in. The Cobra departed throwing all of the passengers back and giving unexpected whiplash. After about two hours, the Cobra made its first stop, coming to an abrupt halt.

A businessman with a peacoat stood up, leaving his pen and notepad on the seat next to him. Karl tried to get his attention, "Sir! Sir, you left this!"

The man ignored Karl and continued out of the train. Karl grabbed the pen and notepad. To his surprise, all the pages were blank. He pondered for a moment. He decided to write about his journey throughout the timelines. After three more stops and another four hours had passed, Karl arrived in Los Angeles.

'Please exit safely. Thank you for riding," the robotic voice told Karl as he exited the train.

He walked up the stairs and entered Los Angeles. All around him giant skyscrapers were lit up. He grabbed a random man's shoulder and asked, "Excuse me, do you know where to find the Binder-Corp building?"

The random civilian gave him a scared look, then proceeded to run away, terrified.

Karl stood there, confused. He slowly turned around to see the tallest building he had ever laid eyes on. Down its side, the name glowed in neon lights. Binder-Corp Tower. He had made it. Astonished by the sight of it, Karl quickly approached the door. The ground floor was comprised of glass walls separated every ten feet horizontally and twenty feet vertically. He attempted to reach for some form of handle near the entrance. It seemed to be locked. He banged his fist on the glass door. "Hello?!"

Three men in black suits came out immediately. One of them questioned Karl. "Who are you? Why are you here?"

Karl stepped back defensively. "I'm looking for my brother. Axel Fassbinder."

"We got another one," one of the agents whispered on his microphone.

Karl heard the message and shook his head. He walked to the nearest parked car and lifted it up off the ground, over his head. The three agents stood, awestruck. The confused agent corrected his transmission.

"Scratch that. Alert Mr. Fassbinder immediately: his brother has been found."

"Sorry, sir, we get a lot of Karl Fassbinders."

Karl followed the men into the building. In the middle of an important meeting, Axel received a call. "Sir, we may have found your brother finally," an agent told him on his headset.

Axel was sitting at an oblong table in a nearby building. He interrupted the board member who was speaking. "My apologies, I need to postpone our meeting. Some unforeseen circumstances have suddenly revealed themselves," he told the board.

He left the room and climbed the staircase heading to the roof. He took a chopper back to Binder-Corp Tower. As he arrived, his domestic agent met him on the helipad.

"Sir, we believe your real brother has finally arrived. He is in your quarters awaiting you."

"Thank you, Leon. Continue with your duties."

Axel entered the elevator heading for his private chambers on the forty-third floor. When the door opened, he saw a familiar face. Karl stood in his ragged clothes in the center of the large living room studying his surroundings. Axel's living quarters were tremendous in size. They were at least four thousand square feet. To the right was a large kitchen with Nero oak cabinetry that stood ten feet tall. Adjacent to the kitchen was a long dining table made of marble with a chandelier hanging above it. Across the room was a small, gray L-shaped couch near the hallway leading to the bedrooms.

Karl heard the elevator door and turned. He watched Axel step out wearing a full tailored suit with his hair combed back.

"Brother!" Karl yelled as he saw Axel.

The brothers both ran toward each other throwing their arms around one another. After a minute of holding each other, they studied each other's faces.

"You... you look exactly the same," Axel told his brother.

"So do you..." Karl realized that Axel hadn't aged a day.

"What happened to you?" Axel asked.

"Oh man, where to begin..." Karl commented and then paused, reflecting. "Last thing I remember is those two mercenaries. Then pain. Then I arrived here."

Axel could tell he was lying but didn't understand why.

"The important part is that you're here now," he told his lost brother.

"And look at you, man! You're a big hot shot, I see. Your name's all across the globe!" Karl shook Axel's shoulder.

"Yeah, you could say that. I've definitely lived many lives since the one we spent together."

"Many lives?... Yeah, I can relate to that."

"Are you hungry? It's about dinner time."

"Starving man. I've hardly eaten."

Axel smiled. "I have multiple private chefs. Do you want Italian or Japanese? Maybe some prawns and pasta? Or shrimp tempura?"

"Some prawns and pasta sounds good to me," Karl replied ecstatically.

Axel whispered the order into his headset.

"Come with me outside." Axel put his arm over Karl's shoulder and led him through the large living room section to a balcony. The glass patio extended fifteen feet and wrapped around the building. There were two wicker chairs near a table and a bar.

"Please sit," Axel gestured.

The brothers sat on the balcony two thousand feet above the ground, looking over the city of Los Angeles.

"Little breezy up here," Karl remarked.

"Yeah. I wanted something higher up. The further from people the better. Sorry about the guards. A few years after I started the company, I made a public announcement stating I would pay anyone ten million dollars to find my brother. As you can imagine, I had a lot of people pretending to be you."

Karl laughed and responded, "Well, that makes a lot of sense. I'm sorry I didn't come back sooner."

Axel didn't respond. He stood up and walked over to the bar, pouring a glass of scotch on the rocks. "Would you like a drink?"

"Um… yes please?" Karl answered.

Axel waited a moment for clarification. "Do you have a preference?"

"Whatever you're having."

Axel dumped a few ice cubes into a glass and poured a few shots of his finest scotch. He handed the glass to Karl. He took a sip.

"So, where's Dad?" the lost brother asked.

Axel walked over and gripped the railing of the balcony with his left hand while he tilted his glass of scotch down with his right. "He died a few years back. Leukemia." Karl looked down in grief. "He lived a good life. An honest life. He died past eighty. That's more than most come to see."

Karl finished his drink. "How was he in the later days?" he asked, his eyes pooling. Axel paused, taking a moment to contemplate his response. "I didn't actually see him much in his later days."

Karl stood up abruptly. "What?! What do you mean? Why?" Karl demanded, upset.

"There's something I need to tell you, Karl," Axel spoke in a calculated tone.

"I'm listening."

"I'm not a Fassbinder."

"What? What do you mean?" Karl responded angrily.

"I'm a product of infidelity. The reason I exist, why I was born, why mother died. It is all because my father is not your father."

"How do you know for sure?" Karl questioned.

"Father told me. About five years after your disappearance. I'm not like you, Karl."

Karl walked over to the railing adjacent to Axel. He gripped it tight and looked far down to the city. "Why do you run a company named Fassbinder if you aren't one?"

"I found out after I started the company. I wasn't going to change it then. My biological father could never be found. I have no surname."

Karl looked down at the city, clenching his fists. "Well... look at you with your private chefs and your own personal skyscraper." He paused and turned toward his younger brother. "Have you forgotten the blood, sweat, and tears that got you to where you are?!"

Axel stood still for a moment. He slowly turned toward his brother. "I may have forgotten about the blood and sweat. But I haven't forgotten the tears."

Karl and Axel stared at each other.

Karl's anger faded when he saw the sincerity in Axel's eyes.

"What about Russ?" Karl asked.

Axel looked off in the distance. "I haven't spoken with him since before you disappeared."

Karl asked his brother, "What happened when I disappeared, brother?"

Axel exhaled and looked back over the railing, down at the city.

Two hours previously, a few hundred miles away, the last of the ADA planned their attack. Tara, Maverick, and Gamble waited patiently in a small apartment for something to happen. Sitting without knowing what to do, they waited for some form of sign or direction. Tara was at her computer desk in the corner when she received a random notification.

"Guys, I have something." She paused while reading. "A random ghost agent just became active to send us two separate transmissions."

Maverick dashed over and rested his hand on the back of Tara's chair. "What? Who?"

Gamble walked up behind them to see the screen.

"I don't know who, but they sent two attachments," she continued.

"One is a transcript and the other a video." She clicked on the video attachment. An image of Miles appeared on the screen. "If you're watching this video, unfortunately I am no longer among the living. Maverick, you were the best right-hand man anyone could ask for. Your duty was served a long time ago. The agency can ask no more of you. As for you, Tara, I'm sorry I never told you about your mother. I always knew your life was meant for something more. I wanted you to aspire to different goals. I didn't want you to believe that killing was in your blood or your nature. When someone validates your deepest fears, you tend to feel a certain kind of something. I didn't want you to believe that this life is what you're meant for. We are a nation built on the idea that everything we are told is true. That is the world you seek. You may think what I did was wrong. But if only you understood. Things are not so black and white. The ADA was never meant to become what it was. All we were meant to do was keep the peace. I believe you and Maverick are the sole soldiers to enforce that. Soldiers who fight for the good of mankind. Not for a number on a piece of paper. I am childless, wifeless, and nameless but I have certain individuals that I confide in. You two were my family. Now you must decide what to do next on your own." The screen turned black.

The three of them paused, deep in thought.

Tara sat back in her chair.

"Well, that was a hell of a goodbye," Gamble remarked.

"I guess he wasn't as much of a piece of shit as I thought," Tara commented, then stood up and stormed into the back room of the apartment.

Mav gave Gamble a 'go talk to her' look. Gamble went down the hall and knocked on the room's door.

"You okay?"

Tara opened the door immediately and stormed back past him. "No… I'm ready." She sat back down and looked at the computer screen. She clicked on the other attachment. "It's specific coordinates and directions. I can't make much sense of it."

At that moment, Maverick, who was standing behind Tara, received a random call on his burner phone. Tara and Gamble slowly turned toward Maverick in shock.

"No one has this number yet," Mav assured them. He gradually pulled the phone out and answered it, lifting it to his head with caution.

A deep modulated voice told him over the call, "This is the last of the ADA. Meet me at the designated address in your directions. One of you must head to Binder-Corp Tower. Mr. Fassbinder will aid the strike. Someone has to be there to detour him. This is Mr. Black. Transmission over."

They gaped, shocked. "Mr. Black? After Miles, Gold and Silver, I should be the new Black," Maverick stated, completely unaware of the caller's identity.

"It could be a trap, but I'll take that risk," Tara declared.

"Axel Fassbinder…" Gamble muttered. He continued, "I will distract Mr. Fassbinder."

Tara's eyes opened wide. She rushed to him and grabbed his shoulders. "No! Not you, Gamble. I can't lose you again," she pleaded. "Maverick can go to Binder-Corp Tower. I want you by my side."

"He's right, Tara," Mav interjected. "Postponing his response is debatably more important than the primary task. Gamble is the only one of us who stands a chance. His power may equate to that of Mr. Fassbinder."

Tara stepped back confused. "Powers? What powers?"

Gamble walked up to her and phased his hand through her face. She looked at him in a manner that she never had before. Confused and unsettled.

"Whatever the machine my father built did, it caused my body to change on a molecular level," Gamble explained to his lover.

"If anything goes wrong, you have to leave. This man, he isn't like anything you can imagine," she warned.

"I know, baby, I promise we will succeed. I'll see you again. Whatever means necessary." Gamble brushed her bangs out of her eyes.

She looked at the ground, her eyes full of tears. He lightly bumped her chin up. She looked up with a half-smile and muttered, "Whatever means necessary."

"Sooner the better, lovebirds," Mav joked.

"Take my bike. We will find other means of transportation," Tara said to Gamble. She hugged him tight and kissed him. "Come back safe."

She strode away.

Maverick gave Gamble a hug. "No hard feelings, little man. I'll take care of her. Worry about yourself."

"That's a hell of a goodbye, Mav, very sentimental."

Gamble hopped on the bike and headed toward Los Angeles to confront Mr. Fassbinder.

Tara and Mav—Agents Red and Blue—left in a black sedan, heading toward the northern Nevada desert on their last mission for the ADA.

They drove for five hours into the Nevada desert. The landscape transformed into a barren, unsteady pile of rocks.

"We are five miles from the destination on the map, and I see nothing," Maverick said pessimistically.

"I know it's here," Tara responded.

Within a minute of Mav's comment, he realized the dirt road they traveled on was about to end at a giant drop-off. He slammed on the brakes, skidding right to the edge of the cliff. The car stopped with the left tire inches from the edge. Mav and Tara exited the vehicle carefully. They looked down into the canyon and saw a giant castle, a quarter mile wide. It looked like an old crenellated medieval-style castle surrounded by a giant wall. Five guard towers sat at every possible entrance. The base seemed well armed and defended.

"Great. Another impossible task," Mav mumbled to himself.

Maverick and Tara were standing side by side, looking down at the two-hundred-foot drop into the forest in front of the base. As they were contemplating the drop, two jets crashed into the front two guard towers. Great explosions flared throughout the canyon. An army of drones flew over the agents' heads down into the drift.

Mav and Tara watched the lit drones fly over and looked to see where they came from. A larger drone flew to them carrying a man in a metal suit. He dropped down right in front of the remaining agents, making a loud impact. Tara and Mav looked to see Commander Silver in his armor before them. In a chopped-up raspy voice, the armored man said. "G-g-glad you made it."

Within a split second, both Tara and Mav pulled out multiple guns and aimed them in his direction. Silver raised his arms defensively. "Easy now, Agents. I'm the ghost agent. Things aren't how they seem."

"You killed all of our fellow agents. How could they not be as they seem?" Tara declared aggressively, holding her trigger fingers back.

"My body killed those agents. I had a spine worm. The same piece of tech you used on Don Fassbinder was originally Binder-Corp tech. They used it on me after I was captured. My gut tells me that Miles knew. His shot went straight through the worm and barely missed my spinal nerves," he explained.

Tara responded quickly with her finger gripping the trigger. "How was the notorious Commander Silver compromised?"

"We did have a rat. But it wasn't me." Silver paused for a moment in regret. "Commander Gold, out of her hate for Mr. Palestine. She betrayed the agency. I found out after it was too late. I fought her to the death. Her death."

"You think I would believe a…" Tara started to respond as Maverick interrupted her. "I believe him, Tara. If he were lying, we would be dead already."

The three agents stood in a dangerous silence for a few moments. Tara shook her head and looked down the cliff. Then back to Silver. "What is our next move, Mr. Black?" she asked her new superior.

"The drones have taken down their perimeter. We'll enter the main gate. Once we're inside, I'll take care of the militia. Agent Red, you'll distract Mr. Lee. Agent Blue, you'll find the lab. You must retrieve the machine and blueprints. We'll handle the rest."

Tara and Mav looked at one another and nodded. "Understood, sir," they responded simultaneously.

Silver nodded as a drone dropped down. "You'll get your own," he directed them as the drone lifted Silver up quickly and dashed down into the canyon. Two more drones dropped down, and Maverick and Tara grabbed onto them and were pulled up into the air. The drones spun through the air, dodging backfire from the guard towers. They dropped the agents down in the forest a few hundred feet from the main gate, and they thudded to the ground. Tara and Maverick found each other in the thick forest. Mav put his finger to his lips, reminding her to be silent. They crouched and steadily approached the main gate. Between two big trees, they could see a large gate with a few soldiers standing before it. One of the guards dropped suddenly. The other two started firing into the woods near the agents. Within seconds, another one was shot down, then the other.

Silver emerged to their right, about thirty feet away with his sniper in hand.

"That seemed a little too easy," Mav commented.

Silver called down a strike as the gate was obliterated. A giant cloud of smoke billowed before the companions. As the smoke cleared, they realized they were in for a rude awakening. The three of them were greeted by an unexpected army. Maybe fifty armored soldiers stood in formation beginning to open fire.

"Take cover!" Silver yelled.

Tara and Maverick dived into a trench nearby, covering their heads. Silver faced the army head on. Hundreds of bullets hit his suit and were deflected. He quickly threw up a flash grenade, blinding his assailants. It exploded, blinding them all. His whips extended out of his gauntlets. He gradually approached the wall of enemies with a limp from his previous injuries. Twenty feet away, he took his steps as quickly as he could. One of the solders in the front line regained his sight as he saw his worst nightmare just ten feet away. He lifted his weapon, but it was too late. Silver threw his right-handed whip into a line of three soldiers. He sliced through them diagonally, cutting them in half. He spun a full one-eighty, his left-hand striking backhanded into the crowd. He waved his whip up and down, so it sat on ten soldiers' shoulders. He ripped his arm back with full force, decapitating ten men at once. The angel of death couldn't have managed such destruction.

After his first dozen kills, the remaining army regained their sight. Silver dashed ten feet ahead, into the crowd. His whips spiraled out around him. He danced with his chains of death, cutting them down by the dozen. Silver retrieved his whips and threw two plasma grenades forward, and another twenty men disintegrated. The last few soldiers turned away and retreated.

Silver took his sniper rifle off his back and finished them off with a few shots to their backs. Mav and Tara peeked out of the trench to see a bloody massacre. They ran to catch up with Silver.

"Holy shit, Silver. You really are as the legends say," Mav remarked respectfully.

Silver turned slowly toward his companions. Through his helmet he stared at them. "I am no legend. Only a message to be spoken," he corrected.

The three of them continued toward the enemy base. The main entrance stood about fifteen feet tall and twenty feet wide. Two round doors blocked the aggressors. Silver stood for a moment, scratching his helmet. He looked at each of the door's hinges, trying to identify the proper approach. He decided he was thinking too far in. He readied his plasma cannon on his shoulder.

"You're just gonna fire through?" Mav asked.

"Those hinges are unbreakable without it." Silver fired his cannon. It shot a beam of bright blue plasma following the ridges of the door. The plasma beam cut through each hinge on both sides.

"Step back," he told his companions as he finished off the last hinge. The large doors fell forward making a loud thud. The three of them quietly continued into the giant castle-like construct. Standing before them was a statue of Mr. Lee.

"Self-absorbed asshole," Mav commented.

"Security droids!" Silver yelled as three hovering spherical robots flew into the room. The droids prepared for fire just as Tara dropped an EMP. The electrical blast shut them all down instantly. Silver fell to the ground for a moment. Maverick ran to his aid. Silver indicated a stop gesture with his hand and stood up on his own.

"Agent Red, this is your time," Silver directed Maverick.

Mav nodded and followed the directions on the piece of paper Silver previously gave him. Maverick headed up the stairs with regret, toward Mr. Lee's headquarters.

Tara followed her new superior into the neighboring room. There was a long hallway before them. The hall was round and made of gray steel. It was almost like a tunnel, big enough for a tank to fit through.

"Have you been here before?" she asked.

"Unfortunately, yes," Silver answered.

They continued until they arrived at the end of the giant hallway maybe half a mile along. There was a large door shaped like a pentagon that was just slightly smaller than the hallway. Silver looked at Tara. "Take cover until I disarm the majority of them."

He proceeded to pick the lock on the door panel. They heard a loud sound like gears were disengaging. The door slowly opened vertically. Tara ran to the side behind some metallic crates. Silver stood in the center of the large hallway. When the door rose to eye level, Silver saw two tanks and hundreds of soldiers prepared for battle. An army stood before the angel of death. A cannon fired into Silver's chest, sending him back a hundred feet. He landed on his back, unconscious for a moment. Tara turned around the corner and threw two poison grenades into the room. Moments later, unaffected, a tank drove toward Silver, through the long wide hallway.

Tara hid in a crevice by some supplies. She peeked out to see the giant tank run by her a few feet away. Not knowing what state Silver was in, she hid behind the utility box. Silver awoke, lifting his chin up to see a tank twenty feet away. He looked around for Tara and realized she was nowhere to be seen. Commander Silver was reignited. He jumped to his feet, arming his plasma cannon. He fired it into the tank, destroying it. The tank exploded into thousands of shards. The second tank headed down the tunnel behind the first. Silver bolted toward the remains of the first tank. He used it as a ramp and ran off the top, jumping ten feet in the air to face the second tank. He fired his plasma cannon through the second, obliterating it.

The army watched the explosions form a huge cloud of smoke. They stood silent with their guns drawn. As the smoke cleared, all they could see was a silhouette of a humanoid. Silver dropped the plasma cannon due to the heat. He unsheathed his sniper. The front line of men started to make out the man and began to fire. Silver took his last six grenades and threw them into the crowd.

The room was a large dome around four hundred feet in diameter full of armed soldiers. The grenades blew up. Two were flash grenades, the rest were plasma. The bright explosions blinded almost everyone for a minute. He strategically fired his last five rounds on his rifle into the few soldiers that weren't deterred by the flash. He threw his rifle toward a wall of twenty men, then pressed a button on his gauntlet, exploding his sniper, killing at least ten soldiers.

The remaining soldiers regained their sight and fired their weapons directly at Silver while taking hundreds of bullets every few seconds. Silver's armor began to fail him. Tara revealed herself, returning fire on them with a handgun. Silver extended his whips. He dashed into the center of the crowd, slashing his whips around him. His form started flawless. Within a few seconds, he began to toss them around. He had lost his accuracy. A fallen wounded soldier put a lock mine on his leg.

"Go to hell bastard," the soldier proclaimed as it exploded.

Silver flew into the air and then slammed into a wall as the remaining fifty soldiers or so fired at his body. Tara ran up and picked up a rifle and fired an AR-15 into them. She killed a few before the rifle ran empty. She pulled out her sidearm and sprinted at her foes. A group of surviving solders turned to return fire. Leaning back, she slid on her knees while firing headshot after headshot into her assailants. The friction from her knees only gave her about a ten-foot slick when she stopped. Arriving at the dead pile of bodies, she grabbed two automatic rifles and fired back and forth into the last line of men. Two shots hit Tara. Her shoulder, then her leg. She dropped as the last few living soldiers approached her.

One soldier walked to her and pressed his sidearm to her head. "Good riddance."

As the words left his mouth, Silver's remaining whip wrapped around the soldier's neck, removing his mouth and the rest of his head from his body. The head rolled across the ground as Silver appeared above Tara. He helped her to her feet, then dropped to the ground with a grunt. His leg was destroyed.

"Can I help?" Tara asked while Silver tampered with his leg.

"No… I just need some support to keep it straight. Hand me that piece of the rifle's barrel." He pointed at a gun near an enemy corpse. Tara grabbed it and handed it to him. Silver pulled back his armor, revealing a mechanical leg beneath. Tara stepped back in awe.

"You're part robotic?"

"Not by my doing. If it were up to me, I would be dead."

Tara paused and gave him a blank look. She hesitated before asking, "What do you mean?"

Silver sighed. "The agency I was with before the ADA was training the best of the best. I was better than that. Every mission I failed I lost something. They brought me back and fixed it. I fear I'm more machine than human nowadays."

"No machine could have done what you did today. For us and for this world," she reassured him with a smile.

She helped him to his feet, then put his arm over her shoulder. "What's next, sir?" she asked him.

"Red may need help. I need you to continue down the left wing. I will accompany Red and Mr. Lee."

Tara nodded as she turned to walk toward the left wing.

Silver grabbed her shoulder. "Wait, Tara. I have to tell you something. Do you remember anything from your adolescence?"

Tara paused, confused for a moment. "I don't remember anything before the adoption. The youngest memory I have I was maybe four."

Silver looked around to see if the coast was clear. He looked back and carefully told her, "I don't really know how to put this, but this is likely to be the last time we see each other. So here goes… I'm your brother, Tara."

Tara's eyes opened wide. "What? That's not possible."

"Just like Gold being your mother was impossible?"

A moment of silence occurred between the two. "We were Irish immigrants born in Sweden. Our family wasn't always what it is now. We used to be good people. Innocent people. When you were an infant, maybe a year old, our father was a gambling man. He made a bet that his wallet couldn't cash. The mob isn't a very forgiving loan system. They broke into our home, assaulted Mother, beat Father half to death. Then finished off our father with a bullet through his head. Mother didn't take that too well. I was maybe thirteen when she came running out to the tree house, a bruise on her cheek and blood running down her lip. She stumbled close enough to shout, fell to her knees and screamed the news, horrified. Watching the person you love and respect above all else in that much pain is a sight you will never forget.

"We packed up and left immediately. She sent us on a plane to the U.S. to stay with extended family. She had business to take care of. Mother trained herself in the wilderness to hunt bears using only a sharpened stick. She practiced for a few weeks and then took care of the business. Those poor sons of bitches had no idea what was coming. She hunted them down one by one, every single member. She massacred maybe fifty men.

"Unfortunately for her, she didn't realize they were associates of GIL—Gentlemen's Intelligence Liberated, basically the ADA for Europe. When they found her and surrounded her, they gave her an option. Either die or work for them as their top assassin."

Silver was interrupted by a soldier running out. He quickly sent a bullet through them. "Sorry about that. As I was saying, Mother became what she was because of these people. A few years passed and we hadn't heard anything. I decided to put you up for adoption, stating both our parents were deceased. It was for your safety, because of what came next. I stole our distant relatives 1911 he had in his safe. I say distant because I don't even remember how we were related, maybe second cousins or something. I snuck my way on a plane to Sweden, hiding in luggage. I was a thirteen-year-old boy wielding a powerful handgun.

"After asking multiple people, I found someone who knew where she might be. The man disarmed me and took me to the headquarters, where I was regrettably reacquainted with our mother. I discovered both my and her identities no longer existed, and the rest is history, as they say."

"Why the fuck would you wait until now to tell me this?" she demanded angrily.

"I just know how it feels not knowing. I couldn't die without telling you that I love you, sister."

"That's very deep and sentimental, Silver. But as you know we aren't people. We are weapons. I've been done caring about who I was long before I became who I am now."

"Well… I have paid my dues. Now we have lost the war. The world will die. We can't beat him now, but we may be able to beat him in the past. Here is a list of coordinates for the time and place he will be. I wrote down notes in case he flees."

Silver handed Tara a rolled-up transcript.

"Good luck, Agent Blue."

She nodded with teary eyes. They both limped off in separate directions.

Meanwhile Maverick climbed the staircase of doom, spiraling up hundreds of feet. "Can afford robotic guards but not a damn elevator," he muttered to himself.

After climbing for quite a bit, Mav stepped out to flat ground. Two guards ran out blazing fire into him. Mav received a few shots into his bulletproof vest. He then quickly unsheathed his pistol, snapping off two shots into their heads.

He walked up to Mr. Lee's quarters. The doors wouldn't open. Maverick used his extraordinary strength to pull open the security door by hand. The seam ran vertically through the center of the door. He pushed his fingers into the gap, grunting in pain as he ripped it open. His arms slammed out from his sides into the door frame, fully extended in a cross-like stance. When he looked inside the room he saw a wide circular area with a throne in the center. Mr. Lee sat calmly upon it, gripping the side of his golden chair.

"Agent Red, it is a pleasure for you to join me. This may be the most monumental event in history."

"You seem pretty positive about killing billions of people."

"I'm not killing anybody. That is my associate's job. I'm merely saving what's left."

"Where is Lars Grossman? What time have you sent him to?" Maverick demanded.

"Why on earth would I tell you that? That would be giving up my queen for a pawn. I won't tell you when or where, but I will tell you why. I have a bit of information that the ADA does not. I sent him to ensure a happening that may turn out to be detrimental to my operation."

"And you're telling me this why?" Mav asked confused.

"Because neither of us is making it out of here."

"Speak for yourself," Mav responded while drawing his gun, aiming it at Thaddeus Lee.

"Bold move. Let's see if your trigger finger is fast enough."

Mav instantly fired a few shots in Thaddeus's direction. Mr. Lee moved faster than the eye could see, dashing out of each bullet's path. He then punched Mav. His fist went through Maverick's shoulder, dislocating it. He then sent a blow with his left fist into Mav's chest, sending him ten feet back into the wall behind him. Maverick crashed into the wall and landed on the ground face down. He pressed his arms into the ground and lifted his chin up.

"What… are you?" he questioned his attacker.

"I am only a man of science. The flame should not be your concern. It is what the fire has already burned that should be your worry."

Maverick slowly stood up and pressed his shoulder back into place. "You didn't answer my question."

"Mr. Fassbinder… his blood carries superhuman qualities. A brief taste of the apex of evolution. Immortality runs through my veins. I didn't acquire enough to mass produce, but it was enough to make myself a God amongst men. As well as Mr. Grossman."

"Did you ever think to use your technological capabilities to save the planet instead of condemning it?" Mav suggested.

"I did at one point… Once upon a time." Thaddeus paused, looking off in the distance. He walked toward Maverick at a steady pace. "Times have changed quite a bit since then."

A raspy distorted voice startled them from the entrance. "Take a step back…"

Mr. Lee turned to see Commander Silver standing in the entrance. Silver lifted his hands to his helmet and removed it. He revealed his face with his jaw partially blown off and bandages almost holding it together.

"So, it is you… You're one resilient bastard, aren't you?"

Silver revealed his plasma cannon on his shoulder and shot its beam into Thaddeus. Thaddeus flew into the wall of the dome-like room. Silver hurried to Maverick's aid and helped him to his feet. "Get out of here. Take this, you'll need it." Silver handed Mav the plasma cannon.

"Follow Tara. She'll know what to do."

Thaddeus Lee stood up from the blast, hardly wounded. "START THE LAUNCH NOW!" he yelled on his headset. The castle-like construct began shaking intensely, almost as if an earthquake had hit.

"This must be the ship!" Silver yelled. "Hurry, Red. Get out!" he continued.

Mav took the cannon and ran down the stairs as fast as he could. Silver faced Mr. Lee.

"At last, I'm face to face with the notorious Commander Silver," Mr. Lee provoked.

Silver slowly turned his nightmarish face toward his foe. "And that was a grave mistake. The greatest mistake of your life," Silver commented as Thaddeus crashed into him.

Silver grabbed his foe and pressed a button on his gauntlet, triggering his suit's self-destruct feature. They both exploded in a large ball of blue flame. The only remains were dark ashes.

Maverick ran down the spiraled stairs. On the other side of the ship, moments before, Tara had arrived in the engineering room. She gazed upon two iterations of the time machine beside one another, displayed atop glass stands, each at different stages of development. The device on the left was just an empty frame, as the device on the right appeared to be completed. The blueprint lay on a nearby table. A thought crossed her mind… *What if?* She grabbed the completed machine and left the blueprint.

Tara felt the building shake intensely. She started jogging back to the entrance as fast as she could in her injured state. Through the big open area, down the giant hallway. She arrived in the front room where the droids had attacked. Abruptly, she received a shot to the back and collapsed, dropping the machine in front of her. All she could think about was what would happen to Gamble.

"Gamble, I know you can't hear me, but I'm sorry. I'm sorry about everything. Words cannot express. You were the most passionate man I've ever met. So full of life. Please, please forgive me," she finished as two soldiers walked up to her body.

Suddenly a blue beam blasted through them both, cutting them in half. A giant hand reached down to her. Tara looked up to see Maverick. "I got you, Blue. I got you."

He picked her up and threw her over his shoulder, then ran out of the castle as it began its launch. The jets fired as Mav leaped out with Tara on his shoulder. They were sent flying into the scorched wood.

The castle's exterior folded into a triangular-shaped ship. The ship headed for the atmosphere. Maverick and Tara crawled toward each other.

"Silver?" Tara asked.

Mav shook his head.

"Let's finish this," Tara said as Mav entered 'minus thirty-two' into the rectangular device. "We got one way there and one way back. Let's make it count."

CHAPTER 12

Cloak and Dagger

September 13th, 2010, in rural Sweden, a lower-class family prepared their children for bed. The thirty-year-old parents laid down their thirteen-year-old son and their two-year-old daughter.

The father, Nicolas, stepped outside of the small hut in the white forest. He lit a rolled-up cigarette as the snow fell before him. A snowflake hit the cherry of his cigarette, sparking it brighter. His wife opened the wooden round door behind him.

"Ya goin' out tonight again?" she asked him with her Irish accent.

"What do ya think, woman? We need the money," he responded aggressively.

"You never win nothin'. Luck ain't gonna fix our problems, dear."

The man shook his shoulders, trying to shake off the cold.

"Our day will come. Not much point in farming when it snows most of the year."

He grabbed his keys from his pocket and walked toward the old pickup in the driveway. His wife looked down, distraught. She closed the door and headed inside.

Nicolas drove off in his old Volkswagen truck. He headed into the little town with five small, rounded hut-style buildings set close together. After shutting off the truck, he walked through the thick snow into the local bar and casino. He approached the barkeep, who greeted his regular.

"Big timers here tonight, mate. Some hot shots from down south." The bartender had a British accent.

"Thanks for the heads up. I'll take my regular well whisky. Put it on my tab."

"Your tab is getting pretty high, mate," the friendly bartender reminded him.

"It's my lucky day, Joey."

The bartender shook his head. "If you say so…"

He poured the drink and handed it to Nicolas. Nicolas walked over to the sharks. Three high rollers dressed in peacoats sat around a table in the corner.

"What are we bettin' on?" he asked.

The three well-dressed men looked at each other and then back at him.

"No offense, but you couldn't afford our buy in," one of the men commented.

Nicolas, out of desperation, slapped his savings on the table. "I'll go all in if I need to."

The men looked at one another and chuckled. "Are you willing to bet your life on it?"

Nicolas thought about his family for a moment. They didn't have enough money or supplies to survive the winter. "Yes, I am. What game are we playing?"

"Blackjack," a different well-dressed gentleman answered.

"What do you have to offer? This is a high-stakes game."

"I offer my home and truck," Nicolas responded.

The three men sat back in surprise.

"You really are a desperate man."

"Yes… unfortunately I am."

The leader of the three looked at his subordinate to the right. "Deal him in."

Nicolas received an eight and a nine. A great hand right off the bat.

One of his opponents was dealt a nine and a queen.

There was a moment of awkward silence around the table.

"Hit me," Nicolas stated.

The dealer handed him a card. It was the seven of hearts. Nicolas's heart melted. He had lost. The three men immediately stood up and grabbed him by his shoulders.

"Where is this house you speak of? You owe us a pretty penny."

They dragged him outside. One of the men pulled out a compact six-shooter revolver.

"I… I don't know."

The man with the gun struck Nicolas in the back of his head.

"Take us there now."

Nicolas looked into the small glass window to see Joey the barkeep looking out. He nodded.

Joey called the house to warn Nicolas's wife. The men led Nicolas into his truck and followed in a Mercedes Jeep. After traversing the thick snow and forest, they arrived at his home. The lead man road with Nicolas and pushed him out to the ground when they arrived at his house.

"This is your house? This is of no value to me."

He punched the back of his head. He proceeded to grab his coat and drag him through the front door. They kicked the door in and were greeted by Nicolas's wife.

"Please! We are peaceful farmers who are struggling in the harsh winter."

"Step aside, woman!" one of the men shouted.

He kicked her out of the way. They scoured the room to see nothing else.

"No children, aye? I guess your wife is the best gift you could give us."

She stood up and knocked one of the men out unconscious. The other punched her across her face, knocking her down. The main thug put a gun to Nicolas's head.

"I guess you punched your last ticket." He pulled the trigger.

The wife screamed in agony.

"We'll be back tomorrow for the place. You're lucky I feel gracious today."

The three men left with Nicolas's wife sobbing on her knees by his corpse, holding it tight. Her son William had previously taken their daughter Rachael into the woods to hide. She held her husband for an hour or so. She finally came to. Her fists tightened. She ran out into the woods to find her children. William and Rachael were in the treehouse a few hundred feet away, awaiting their mother.

"William? William?"

He peeked out of the wooden box in the tree. His mother dropped to her knees and screamed in anguish. William left his sister in her crib and ran to his mother's aid.

"Mother, it's okay. What happened?"

She gently placed her hand to his cheek. "Your father is gone, my son. I need you to stay strong."

The next day she walked into town. A long, cold journey through the snow. She arrived at the law office.

After she explained what had happened, the local lawman said to her, "Our hands are tied. We don't have enough evidence to convict them. These are powerful men with strong attorneys and ties to the law. I'm sorry."

She walked across the street to the banker. "Mr. Peterson, I need my family's savings," she told the banker.

"I'm sorry, dear, but there isn't much left. I heard about what happened. Everyone has pitched in to help you all get out of town. There is a plane waiting for you to take you to the United States."

She smiled briefly and then looked out the window toward a familiar truck. "Will you take my children? I have unfinished business."

The old man wore a curly wig of white hair with a matching curled mustache. "Madame, you don't have to do this."

She grabbed his upper garments. "If Darcy was murdered, what would you do?"

He nodded. "I'll have Charles take them to the airport right away. As for you, here are five hundred Krona to help you with your endeavor."

She took the envelope. "Thank you."

She kissed her children goodbye briefly.

William asked his mother, "Will you be joining us soon, Mama?"

She paused in deep pain. She squeezed his cheek. "I'll be right behind you, bug. Take care of your sister. No matter what. You need to stay with some extended family for now. I will see you again. I swear it."

His frown lifted for a moment. He held her hand tight and let go as the car pulled up. Charles helped the kids into the car. He tipped his hat at the mother for reassurance. She was ready to pursue her mission.

She walked for miles to find the outsider. On the outskirts of their village lived an old Japanese fighter. People said he was once a killer and found refuge in the snowy mountains of Sweden. Akira Riku sat in his small hut on the top of Wolf Mountain. As she approached, she felt a heaviness behind her. As if she was being hunted. Every time she looked over her shoulder it seemed like she could almost catch a glimpse of something. Her instincts told her there was something out there.

As she continued on her walk, her eyes darted around, looking for some form of weapon. She spotted a stick about an inch thick and grabbed it with haste. She split it in a way that would keep the point very sharp. Just as she found her weapon, a large wolf crossed her path. It was white as snow with deep green eyes. She realized the wolf was not alone. Four other wolves revealed themselves and circled her. She jabbed at the air in front of her.

"You have but two options," a voice spoke from the darkness. "Kill or be killed."

She focused on the beast before her. It paced back and forth. Suddenly, it pounced unexpectedly. She jumped into the attack and stabbed the stick into the bottom of the beast's neck. The wolf, which was considerably heavier than her, fell on her body, dead. The rest of the pack howled and readied their attack.

"Begone!" the voice yelled as Akira revealed himself with a spear. The wolf pack departed.

"You seem to be lost. There must be a reason why you traveled to Wolf Mountain alone."

She looked up in disbelief. "I was looking for you."

He grinned in a sinister manner and reached his hand down to help her up.

The woman paid Akira her five hundred Krona to teach her how to fight and survive in the wilderness. He taught her multiple martial arts and how to kill anyone in any environment. After three months of training, he explained to her, "There is a great beast that the wolves fear. A giant grizzly bear. You must fight it with weapons you have crafted from the earth."

She sharpened about ten sticks, burrowed a deep hole into the earth and dug the spears into it, pointing upward. When the beast arrived, she wielded a torch in one hand and a hand-crafted spear in the other. The beast must have weighed a ton. It approached steadily, wagging its body back and forth.

"I'm all yours!" she yelled like a battle cry.

She ran at the grizzly. It ran toward her. She jumped in the air and stabbed it in the eye with her spear, then spun, dodging it.

The grizzly tumbled into the snow. It quickly retaliated with a sturdy roar. It charged again as she led it into her trap. She grabbed a log off the ground and pressed the end of it into the snow before her. As she leapt into it, she launched herself ten feet over the gap in the snow using immense strength to clear the trap. The grizzly fell into the hole and was stabbed by all ten stakes.

She looked down at her foe. Taking her spear, she stabbed it through its mouth as it roared one last time.

"It's finished," Akira told her. "You are ready."

The woman made her way back into town and found out where the three men came from. The first was easy. He was a few towns over, running a gambling community. She walked through the door wearing ragged fur for clothes. She had used as many resources from the corpse of the grizzly as she could—even cutting it up and creating weapons with the bones.

Her target was at a table dealing cards. When he looked at her it took him a second to recognize her.

"What do you want, woman?" he asked as he realized.

"Wait!" She took the skull of the bear from her back satchel and carved it into his head.

One of his guards stood up as she ripped it out and slit his throat. She casually walked out of the brothel like nothing had happened. This was only the beginning of her hunt.

She hunted down the next two men who were found in towns that neighbored the first. When she killed the last target, there were four men involved. She approached the bar and slammed his face into it. He stood up and swung at her. She ducked and tripped him, following up with a fatal blow. His body guards all stepped in. She revealed a crossbow made of bear bone and shot all three men dead on the spot.

Unfortunately, she didn't realize that two of those four men were actually informants for GIL. This was where vengeance crossed the bridge to madness. As she exited the vicinity, three men in suits greeted her. She sprung for her weapon as one grabbed her arm, and another man put a gun to her chest.

"I would advise that you cooperate."

She realized there was no way to avoid this reckoning. The men took her in a Mercedes limousine a few towns over. The door opened at a great Slavic-style mansion. The men walked her inside. The inside walls were white with flamboyant bright-colored furs decorating them.

"Tie her up," a deep voice spoke from up the stairway.

One of the men in suits grabbed her by the hair as another grabbed her arms and the last man brought a chair to her. They tied her up. She thought this was it. They would torture her to death, she was sure.

The man in charge was bald with round glasses and wore a tuxedo. He walked down the stairs and scanned the woman head to toe.

"You?" He looked at his henchmen. "She killed multiple GIL agents?"

They nodded, confirming. He began laughing hysterically.

"What is your name, woman?" he asked her.

"You don't deserve to speak it."

"I'm not what you think of me. I am no mobster. I would like to get to know you. My name is Remi."

She paused. "My name is Rachael."

"Do you know why you are here, Rachael?"

"Because I killed those scumbags at the brothels."

He looked at his men, then back at her. "Not exactly. Two of the men you killed weren't gangsters. They were informants. Do you know what an informant is?"

"Please explain…" she responded.

"These informants work for me and the British government to keep an eye on greater Europe. The men you brutally executed were undercover working with other mob bosses that are our mutual enemy."

She looked at the ground and backed up. "I was only seeking revenge. They killed my husband and attempted to kill my family. I meant no injustice."

He smiled reassuringly. "I figured as much. I hate to put you in this predicament but… you have two options. We can dispose of you for your wrongful doings, or you can work for us to make up for our losses."

"Working for you how? As a mercenary? I'm only willing if they are people that deserve death. I won't kill the innocent."

He tilted his glasses down. "We only kill the guilty. We are cleansing our country and our greater nation."

She signed her deal with a handshake.

A year passed before her son William decided it was time to intervene. Across the Atlantic, in the state of Wisconsin, William took his three-and-a-half-year-old sister to the social office. He told them that she had no birth certificate and that they must change her name whenever she was adopted. That way it would be impossible for the wrong people to find her.

He stole a handgun from the distant family he had stayed with as well as a few hundred dollars. He used the man's ID card to purchase a ticket. When he entered the airport, he found the line where people were checking bags to go in the baggage compartment. He jumped in someone's big suitcase that was meant for animal food. He hid in there the whole plane ride. He snuck out on arrival and sprinted out of the airport. He headed for his hometown.

The banker told him to find the man at Wolf Mountain. When he reached Akira, he told him she had been compromised down south. William headed to the last place his mother had been seen. After asking some questions, he left the brothel. Two men arrived. William pulled his gun on the men. They backed off and pulled their guns as well.

"Be careful, kid. If you really want to do this, be ready."

He clenched his finger and let go. "I'm looking for my mother."

"We are here about your mother."

His eyes widened.

They took him to her.

The newly respected agent walked into the unexpected meeting to see her long-lost fourteen-year-old son sitting on a chair in the center of the room.

"No! William!" She ran to him. "You shouldn't have come, dear."

He threw his arms around her. "I couldn't have gone on without knowing you were okay, Mama."

A tear dripped down her cheek. "Are you alone?" she asked carefully.

"She is well taken care of, Mother."

"These circumstances are not ideal by the slightest means."

The man in charge commented, "I hate to do this to you, but because you are both here now, you must stay here. You will join your mother in her endeavors. There is no other life for either of you now. I'm sorry. This is how it must be."

The man in the round glasses left no room for argument.

William began training with his mother immediately. She left sometimes, on different missions. As William progressed, the leader of GIL realized that there was something special about him. He held a meeting with the top GIL agents.

After about six months of William training with his mother and other top agents, eleven men sat around a long table in the agency's conference room.

"I'm attempting to build a division of elite agents. I have decided that my top two assassins will be Rachael and William. They will now be known as Cloak and Dagger. William has shown himself to be a powerful attacker. He will be the cloak. Rachael is slick and fast, she will slip around corners as he deters our foe."

One of the more experienced agents stood up and declared, "The boy is only fifteen years old! How will you risk everything on an infant?"

"Do you question the decision of the agency?!"

The agent sat down and tilted his head downward in shame.

The unfortunate mother and son earned a reputation in the years to come. By the time William, also known as the Cloak, was eighteen, he was battered in an assassination attempt. His arm was nearly blown clean off. The agency had their robotics expert use experimental technology to replace it. He was the guinea pig. Over the next three years the Cloak endured multiple losses to appendages. Each time they were fixed by the robotics team. Eventually almost all of his appendages were fully mechanical. His precision was lost every surgery, but his endurance increased. Eventually he was able to maintain the same precision without his natural arms.

About eight years after Nicolas's death, Cloak and Dagger were tasked on a mission to kill an innocent woman. When they arrived, they realized she wasn't who the agency was looking for. Dagger conveyed this over the intercom headset. "Sir, she isn't the leak. I can tell. She is a genuinely scared civilian."

"Kill her now. We can't risk anything."

Dagger looked at her and put a blade to her throat. "Please... I have children."

Dagger's blade quivered. She looked at the Cloak behind her. Then at the other agent. She darted toward her fellow agent and cut his throat.

"Run!" she yelled.

Her son sprinted as fast as he could with his mother. Once they were out of the building, they stole a vehicle. They drove to an airport and stole two tickets to enter the plane. They casually sat on the plane side by side, acting like nothing had happened. The plane lifted off. It landed in New York City, U.S.A. Waiting for them were multiple U.S. agents. The mother nodded at William, confirming that it would be okay.

"Ma'am and sir, we need you to come with us."

They followed the agents to a little room with white walls, three chairs, and a table in the middle. The airport agent gestured for them to sit. "Apparently you entered this plane illegally. Have you ever heard of the association named GIL?"

William and his mother looked at each other, then back at the agents. They responded simultaneously, "No."

"That's what we thought," the airport agents stated as they exited the room.

William looked toward his mother and whispered, "What's our play?"

She readied her response as a Black man wearing a black suit walked into the room. "Greetings! I am your best friend and your worst nightmare."

They looked at each other again. William cut his cuffs using a small diamond pencil-saw that he pried out of his wristwatch and pulled a sharp corner to the man's throat. "Be careful with the next word you say, officer," he told the man.

"Impressive. Very impressive." The man looked at him and said, "Act like you're still in your cuffs."

William looked at his mother for approval. She nodded, and he obeyed.

"I'm not with the airport or the FBI or any other government agency. I know who you are."

The two assassins continued their silence.

"My name is Miles Palestine. I'm the director of the ADA. The Anarchists of Democratic Associations. We are comparable to Gentlemen's Intelligence Liberated."

Agent Dagger kicked her chair back revealing her cuffs were split. She flipped onto her feet, hands free. "Should I kill you now?"

Miles grinned, impressed again. "I'm here to save you, not condemn you. I can offer you protection. They tasked you with killing an innocent person, didn't they? I am not the same. You will be under my protection. You're both very admirable professionals, excellent at what you do. I understand you have morals. So do I... We are not here to kill any innocent individuals. You would be doing the same as you did with GIL, but only for the most horrific beings known to man."

"Doesn't look like we have much of a choice," The Cloak commented.

"On the contrary, I have already organized your pardon. If you two would like to leave, you can. I won't follow you."

They both stood up, contemplating their move, hesitant to leave.

"I can't promise your protection from GIL, however. Only if you join us."

Dagger nodded at Cloak. They followed Miles out of the airport into a Hummer limo. A large man, standing over 6'7" with a muscular build, awaited them.

Demetrius greeted his new company. "It is a pleasure to finally meet you both," he said in his thick Slavic accent.

When they arrived at the ADA agency, they were given new operative names. Agents Gold and Silver. The second generation of agents honored with this rank in the history of the agency.

March 21st, 2021, the ADA became involved in a civil war within a non-disclosed country in central America.

A terrorist organization known as the Mara Implacable ruled over their government with tyranny. The other governments in the world were afraid to get involved, fearing it may escalate the situation. This was not the first time the ADA had been involved with other countries' affairs; however, it would mark the first full-fledged war involving the agency. Mr. Black arranged a meeting with his two top agents and the chief of weapon technology.

On the top floor of the agency's downtown building, Agents Silver and Gold, dressed in elegant civilian garments, were welcomed to the meeting. In a rectangular conference room Mr. Black stood in front of a whiteboard filled with battle plans.

"Agents, welcome," he greeted. "Please sit."

Silver and Gold sat side by side at the head of the oval table facing the presentation.

A man with slicked-back blond hair, wearing a suit, opened the door of the meeting room.

"Welcome, old friend," Miles greeted his equal." Agents, this is…"

The agents both stood. Silver stumbled clumsily to his feet, starstruck. "Mr. Fassbinder, this is quite the pleasure. I have used and witnessed the effectiveness of your technology for some time."

Axel smiled and shook his hand. "I wish I could say I'm proud of that."

Agent Gold was too proud to flatter Mr. Fassbinder, but she smiled and shook his hand.

"We have narrowed the required targets down to four individuals. On March 25th they will all be in the same building celebrating a victory in the south. There will be heavy artillery, and the hired gun count is estimated at around two thousand soldiers within the city."

Gold stood abruptly. "With all due respect, sir, the agency consists of spies and assassins. We are not soldiers. We are no army."

"We are nothing until we become something. We have gathered eighty-five agents that all have at least a year of combat experience under their belt. You two will be at the helm of the army as my commanders. Mr. Fassbinder will be providing you with cutting-edge equipment for your endeavor."

Two drones, each attached to a tall cast-iron chest, flew steadily into the room. Mr. Fassbinder pressed a button on the tablet in his hand, and the chests opened, revealing two sets of armor. The set on the left consisted of a silver-plated carbide helmet, pauldrons, chest plate and thigh plates all seamed together by a black aramid fiber containing grains of carbide to improve deflection. The armor on the right was identical, but with gold plating.

"These suits are lightweight, flexible, and practically impenetrable. Suit up and meet me in my training room in Glendale at 4:00 p.m. Mr. Black will provide you with the address."

Later that day, Commanders Silver and Gold met Mr. Fassbinder alone in his private training facility in southern California. They were guided by his security into a large, two-hundred-foot-long, hundred-foot-wide, thirty-foot-tall white room with a pillar in the northwest corner. Mr. Fassbinder stepped out from behind the pillar. He was wearing a black short-sleeve V-neck shirt with dark brown cargo pants. In his right hand, he held two long chained whips that dragged on the ground behind him for twelve feet. In his left hand, he wielded a novel cannon-like weapon.

"Welcome to my training room," Axel said.

"It's nice. Very white," Silver joked.

"*Anata*, Everest."

Mr. Fassbinder spoke and suddenly their surroundings changed to snowy blue sky. Beneath them was the summit of Mount Everest. A cold breeze blew the two agents back.

"What the…?" Silver remarked, confused.

"Turbine-generated wind simulators. It's best to practice in all elements."

Gold hid a smirk of appreciation under her helmet.

Axel set down the whips gently and approached Gold with the plasma cannon held before him with both arms, perpendicularly, palms up. The cylindrical-shaped weapon had a platinum coating along its thirty-two-inch barrel. Running parallel to it was a thin channel of glass, revealing the light blue plasma energy radiating from within. He handed the weapon to Gold. She grabbed the black handle on the side with her right hand and faced her left-hand palm up to steady it.

"The safety is the gray thermal sensor by your thumb. Fire it into the pillar," Axel directed.

Gold aimed her weapon as the cannon fired up. A loud humming rang as it burst out blue energy firing in a straight unbroken line into the pillar. The pillar glowed orange and absorbed the shock entirely.

"That pillar is invincible, but that weapon is capable of destroying a tank instantly. Its beam doesn't begin to dissipate until around three miles and will continue to fire past that. Never fire it for more than ten consecutive seconds. That being said, be mindful of your surroundings."

"Sir… this is a very formidable weapon. It would be my honor to accept it."

Axel smiled and slowly nodded his head toward her in a sign of mutual respect. He then approached Silver who was standing near the pillar and picked up the whips from the now-frosted floor. From Axel's hand hung the deadly whip, composed of small black chain links with hundreds of carbide razor blades shaped like half-full ellipses. The blades ran along its ten-foot length and one-inch girth up until the last foot that connected around the wielder's wrists.

"This is the *Yaiba no Arashi*. A weapon that has proven its effectiveness in combat time and time again. You see, bullets will run empty, can't fire around corners, and are more likely to hit the wrong target."

He flicked the whip forward so it would rest before him. Then he pulled his arm back and threw it forward quickly. The whip lifted, and as it started to fall, he circled his wrist clockwise at a calculated, rhythmic speed before flicking it violently to the left. The whip followed the motion, spiraling into a strike around the blind corner of the pillar.

"Here, you try," Axel suggested as he removed the whip and attached it to Silver's armor.

"Pretty light on the wrist." Silver paused, contemplating his next question. He looked at Gold for reassurance. "Why are you doing all of this?"

Axel paused and looked at the ground as if he had remembered that he forgot something. "I was your predecessor. And you're going to need it."

On March 25th, there was a great battle between the Mara Implacable and the ADA, Operation desolation. The ADA was successful. Mara Implacable's casualties were high, over fifteen hundred. Only a handful of the ADA agents survived. The survivors were promoted in rank as a reward. Commander Gold was then ranked the second in command proceeded by Mr. Black and followed by Commander Silver.

April 12th, 2026, the hall outside Mr. Black's office echoed with raised voices, "Have you not enough power? You have already forged the key to the future, now you must decide the past? I was there for you when you lost everything and your mind turned to madness. Listen to me, old friend, you cannot meddle with the past. These are lines that we as men do not walk. I cannot and will not follow you in this endeavor," Miles pleaded

"Then I believe this is goodbye." Mr. Fassbinder stood, fixed his coat and put his hand out for a shake. "Mr. Lee is awaiting me."

Miles gave a smug look. "Ah yes, Thaddeus Lee, the business partner."

"He is my employee," Axel responded angrily.

"No matter, Axel. Please. He does not have your best interests in mind."

"I'm sorry, old friend. If our paths do cross again, the outcome may be different."

This was the last time Miles would ever see Axel and marked the beginning of a long and spiteful feud.

February 8th, 2027, Miles sat peacefully at a coffee shop located on a busy corner in downtown San Francisco. A large brute of a man wearing a police officer's uniform squeezed into the seat across from him.

"Busy day?" Miles addressed his friend.

Maverick stared out the window to the street stoically. "Every day is busy for me now. It used to mean something when I felt like I was making a difference. Nowadays half the cops are corrupt. And the judicial system's so twisted even when we're able to convict someone they end up back in the streets in a matter of weeks or months. Starting to make me actually miss the marines. At least then it was easier to know friend from foe."

Miles took a sip off of his coffee. "Corruption spreads like silverfish in a wood shop, feeding on the materials used to build society." He paused for another sip and continued, "How are your symptoms?"

"No abnormal beats in over a year. Doctors can't detect any evidence of the disorder lingering. I think it's safe to say your serum worked. I'm in your debt."

"That is quite the relief. Sadly, the man who created it is no longer with the agency. He would have been thrilled to hear of its success."

"That's unfortunate. You two were close, right?" Maverick leaned forward, pressing his elbows into the table.

"You could say that. He was someone I could trust. A rare quality these days. Which brings me to the purpose of our meeting. I have an opening for a combat operative and would like you to fill it. My list of allies spans thinner and thinner. I need someone who I can trust."

The barista set a cappuccino on the table before Maverick. He casually lifted it and took a sip, setting it back down. "When do I start?"

March 2028. Commander Silver and Commander Gold became the novelty items of the ADA. Gold had asked Miles to find her long-lost daughter and to keep her safe. This was no challenge for a man of his stature. He discovered that Commander Gold's daughter resided in a little town in Michigan with a nice family. Her name had been changed to Tara Smith. Although he hadn't met her, Miles had connected with Tara over the span of a few years. Whenever she was in trouble, he would come to her aid indirectly. Like a guardian angel.

Tara Smith went to a traditional high school where she played varsity soccer. Her team had managed to win state the year before. She had a natural ability in athletics, and any form of competition, for that matter. When she was sixteen her parents told her that she was adopted. This caused a lot of confusion and anger in Tara. She quit her soccer team and joined an MMA club. She practiced fighting to let the anger out. Her grades began dropping from a 3.5 GPA to failing almost every class. Things continued to get worse for Tara. One day while walking through the hall in her high school, one of her old teammates made a remark to her about her being a lesbian as fighting was so masculine. Tara snapped and grabbed the girl by her hair and continued to beat her down to the ground.

When she arrived at the courtroom for her trial, she was troubled to discover the girl had been in the hospital since the incident. The verdict was that she would serve two years in a correctional facility. She had two weeks before she would serve her time. She left the court room and headed for her vehicle. Clicking her key, she unlocked her Prius.

Standing outside was a man in a suit. "How did it go?"

"Um, excuse me?" she told him as she made her way to the driver's side.

"The car won't start," the man informed her. She panicked looking for her pepper spray. She couldn't find it.

"Look, dude, I don't want to have to get physical with you."

Miles raised his hands in a defensive manner. "Ma'am, it isn't like that. I'm here to protect you. I've been watching you for a very long time."

"Are you like a stalker? The police department is right there. I would watch yourself if I were you."

He smiled. "I knew your mother. She asked me to look after you."

"What do you mean you knew my mother? ... She lives two miles away," she snarked.

"I knew your real mother."

Her eyes opened wide.

"Is she..."

"She is no longer with us unfortunately. The same for your biological father. Have you ever wondered what you were meant to be? What your fate has in store for you?"

She looked at the courtroom and at the keys in her hands. "This isn't a trick, is it? Because that would be really fucked up."

Miles smirked in a welcoming manner. "Not at all, dear."

"Well, I'm about to serve two years in prison as an attractive eighteen-year-old, so if you got anything to stop that, I'm in."

"I work for a superior class of government. Your transgressions are already forgotten."

She became an agent of the ADA. As the years progressed, she looked more and more like Commander Gold.

Five years passed. Tara and Maverick had come to be known as Agents Blue and Red. Over time, Gold came to realize that this was her lost daughter. One day she took Silver aside while at headquarters. She made sure the room she had taken him to was secure and private.

"Son... I mean, Silver. Do you notice anything familiar about Tara? Like does she resemble anyone to you?"

Silver shook his head in a confused fashion.

"It's Rachael. She's the spitting image of me."

"Mother, that's impossible... I see the resemblance but that isn't enough proof to think..."

"I know it's her... a mother knows her baby when she looks into their eyes."

"You believe that Miles would betray us like that?" Silver asked.

"No, I... I'm not sure what to believe. I asked him to watch over her a while back. Maybe that thought was misconstrued in his corrupted mind."

"If you truly believe this. Just ask him. I couldn't imagine him lying about that," Silver said, hugging Gold. He left the room. Gold fell back against the wall and slid down to the ground, exhaling painfully.

The next morning, after a long night of reflection, she decided to confront Miles. She knocked politely on his office door.

"Come in," Miles said.

Gold opened the door and sat in a chair across from Miles at his desk. "I need to ask you something. You need to be completely honest with me," she told him.

"Of course, dear. I always am."

"Did you find my daughter?"

Miles's facial expression changed dramatically. "Yes, I have. She lives in Wisconsin with a beautiful family named the Andersons."

Gold didn't like that answer. "So, it's just a coincidence that Tara Smith resembles me so much and appears to be around the same age as my daughter would be...?"

"Easy now, Agent. Tara Smith has no relation to you or anyone else in the agency. Coincidences occur quite often."

Gold put her head in her hands.

"Let me ask you something. If you were to be reacquainted with your daughter, would you want her to know who you are? Or rather *what* you are?"

Gold shook her head. "You're right. My apologies, sir. I meant nothing by it."

"You are perfectly fine, Agent. Now please, I'm very busy," Miles said, gesturing toward the door.

Gold left. Feeling confused and unwell, Commander Gold reached out to Thaddeus Lee. A great and powerful man who opposed the ADA above all else. Her intention was to give Thaddeus any information he requested about the agency's operations in exchange for his protection of her family. This would allow her children, William and Tara, as well as herself, to give up this life. To be able to live a normal life once again.

She arranged a meeting at a nontraceable location in southern Arizona. Silver had been keeping a close eye on her due to her suspicious behavior and picked up her conversation using his radiofrequency interference technology. When he attempted to let Miles know, he was nowhere to be found. Silver left Miles a message that included their intent and destination then proceeded to track Gold on his own, unaware of how extreme the feud between Thaddeus and the agency truly was.

They met near a giant turbine in the earth. A nuclear reactor dwelled within a gray cylindrical building surrounded by the dry desert of Arizona. The engine room was roughly a hundred feet in diameter. It was very dark, slightly lit by blue energy emanating from beneath. There were eight bridges evenly spaced apart in a circular pattern above the turbine reactor. In the center was a wide bore that led down past the turbine and deep into the earth. On opposite sides of the room were two possible entrances.

Wearing her full suit of golden armor, Gold entered the engine room on the north side and walked onto one of the bridges. To her surprise, she looked across to the southern entrance to see Commander Silver fully armored enter the engine room.

"You don't have to do this!" Silver yelled at his mother.

She looked around to see there was no audience. She steadily placed one foot onto the bridge, beginning to cross. About halfway across, she screamed, "It *is* Rachael! They found my baby! He lied to us!"

Silver looked behind him to see fellow soldiers arriving in the engine room. "You have nothing to worry about! We can talk about it. If it is her, we will figure it out together. Please just surrender. Miles is a reasonable man."

Gold was in tears and frozen, standing halfway on the bridge. Her helmet's visor fogged up, her breathing became heavy, she tore it off and dropped it down the cone-shaped tunnel beneath her. She watched it fall down into a bottomless crevice of darkness. As she looked back at Silver, the supposed ally soldiers lifted their weapons. They opened fire at her. Silver realized these were not his men. She fell backwards. He cried violently and ran in her direction as fast as he could. He leapt toward her, landing on his chest on the bridge as her body dropped. One of his whips streamed from his wrist down after her, but it was too late. She was gone. He screamed fiercely and rolled over onto his back to see Lars Grossman approaching him.

Before Silver could stand or retaliate, Lars knocked him unconscious. The next thing he knew, he was on the third floor of the ADA's building. He looked around to see he was in Miles's office. He had blood gushing down his chest. His jaw was partially blown off. He took off his chest plate, ripped off part of his shirt and wrapped it around the remainder of his jaw. He walked over to Miles's desk. He remembered where Miles kept his hidden key to the ADA reserve. Silver grabbed it and disappeared. When he arrived at the safehouse he hurried toward the repairing console. He didn't have much time before he bled out. As his vision started to blur, he saw the circular glass room. Stumbling in, he fell onto a gray seat.

A robotic voice spoke, "Commander Silver, what can I assist you with?"

"Aw lown off, Doctor," he attempted to speak.

"I don't understand."

Silver pressed a few keys on the table near him. Three robotic arms descended from the ceiling of the room, mending his wound. They used a calcium-based epoxy to repair the bone. Silver fainted in his seat. The robotics doctor attached an IV to him. A few minutes later he came to. He changed his clothes, cleaned his armor, and geared up.

Silver walked through a narrow hallway and flipped on the lights. He paced around in an underground base the size of an outlet center. Before him were thousands of drones and weapons. He planned his retaliation, sitting at a desk and gathering everything he needed. He launched the file explorer on the desktop computer and delved deep into the mission database until he found some encrypted files relating to Mr. Fassbinder's last missions as Agent Silver. By the time he was able to hack the encryption he realized all but one file had already been wiped clean. He opened the file and found a known time and location where Mr. Fassbinder would be. He devised a contingency plan: if they couldn't beat him here, he would utilize the last of the ADA to defeat him in the past.

Silver spent the next twenty-four hours planning his attack on Castle Lee and the void in time to defeat the Fassbinder legacy once and for all. When he was ready, he called a line he knew would answer.

"This is the last of the ADA, meet me at the designated address," he said, using a voice modulator.

He walked into the great room with all the drones. He activated the drones A.I. and programmed them to destroy Castle Lee. A giant thirty-by-thirty-foot hatch opened within the earth. Hundreds of drones activated and launched, flying out. Silver caught hold of one. He traveled to the canyon surrounding Castle Lee. Later that day, Silver met his fate. His sister survived.

Tara crawled toward the device. She looked at Maverick. He nodded. Maverick activated the device as Agents Blue and Red crawled into the perimeter of the device's reach. They were sent back to the past. Both agents felt intense pain. Mav grabbed Tara's hand when they felt like they couldn't make it. Suddenly the box opened up, and the sun was shining above them. The agents slowly rose to their feet. Gazing around them there was nothing but forest. Tara dropped unconscious, bleeding out from her previous wounds.

"Blue!" Mav yelled. He was losing her. He slung her body over his shoulder and carried her for about five miles until he found an old ranch-style home. An old couple sat on the porch in rocking chairs.

"Help! Please!" Maverick yelled.

They welcomed the agents in. Pulling out the three bullets in Tara. One from her shoulder, one from her leg, and one from her back. Fortunately, none of the shots were critical. They stitched the wounds and nursed her back to life.

Later that evening, the agents thanked the elderly couple and made their way to their destination.

After hotwiring a little blue Pontiac coupe, they headed back to northern California. Both stayed silent the whole drive. They arrived at the tunnel and entered the city. Their first move was to ditch the vehicle they arrived in. They parked it in an alleyway and continued on foot. Walking through a large metropolis looking for their target. The city looked different than before. A cleaner, brighter city.

"Is it just me or does part of you want to just give up and live a life here?" Maverick suggested after hours of silence.

Tara looked at her companion. "You've never been the one to take the easy way out, Mav. This isn't our life."

"Do you ever wonder? What if?" he asked his younger colleague.

She looked around and saw a man with a hood jump on his bike and ride off. "I finally know what I had. It's worth fighting for."

"Is it worth dying for?" Maverick questioned.

"If it's true," she answered with a smirk.

"Let's get this bastard. And maybe we can live our lives again."

Mav pulled out the notes from Silver. He looked at his watch. "He will be a few blocks from old town on J street in about twenty minutes."

Tara looked around to see a semi-truck unhitched. "Perfect."

She walked over casually and hotwired the vehicle. Mav jumped in the passenger seat, and they drove to J street. They hit a red light as Mav was trying to make out what Silver's directions meant.

"I'm not sure what he means when he says north. He didn't tell us the intersecting street."

Tara looked in front of them. She saw two men in a small sedan and thought she recognized the passenger.

"Is that?" Maverick verified. "That's him! Axel Fassbinder."

Mav grabbed two Uzis out of his bag and handed one to Tara. Tara slammed her foot to the pedal and drove through two red lights directly into the target sedan. They crashed into the side of the car, disorienting the Fassbinder brothers. She lifted up her Uzi and fired blindly at the wreckage, grabbing the other Uzi and kicking the door open. She dropped out of the truck firing at the car that was now bent in half, to her surprise. She saw the driver of the car stand up with the door of the car in his hand. Before she could react, he threw it into her, knocking her back into the semi onto the street. She was incapacitated for a moment. Maverick advanced on his foe from around the corner and fired the plasma cannon. It fired directly into the Fassbinder brother, sending him through multiple parked cars.

Axel Fassbinder attacked Maverick. He grabbed the cannon and turned it against Mav's trigger arm. Due to his previous injuries, Maverick dropped his gun in pain. Mav punched Axel in the head twice and picked him up, smashing him into the car next to them. Mav looked around to see if Tara was okay. Just as he saw her, he was tackled by Karl Fassbinder. Karl threw him through the air. Tara pulled a knife from her belt and threw a kick into Axel. She pressed the knife to his throat. Karl dashed at her and sent his fist into her head. He tossed her to the side, semi-conscious.

The Fassbinders fled in another vehicle while Mav and Tara were recovering. A minute after the brothers had fled, Maverick helped his partner up. "What the hell was that?" he asked Tara. "He didn't say anything about a superhuman bodyguard."

"It doesn't matter what he is. We have a mission. The fate of our world is in our hands. If we can't overpower him, we will outthink him. How do you kill a bulletproof man?"

Mav looked confused and then concerned. "Time... if we do this we will be stuck here forever." "Whatever means necessary? The benefit outweighs the cost, Maverick."

"Us being the cost... Alright, Tara I'm with you. Show them why we call you Terror Smith."

They got back in the truck and headed in the Fassbinders' direction. Tara drove the truck straight into the car when they caught up. The brother swerved off to the right into a covered bus stop. Mav took out the time-travel device and placed it before them. They fired at the vehicle as the older brother dashed at them. He stepped over the device and was sent to the future. Just when Mav and Tara were confident in their kill, something unexpected happened. They steadily approached the wreckage of the vehicle. It seemed like Axel was hiding behind the ruined car. Maverick noticed a blurry movement to his right.

"Something's not right."

Out of nowhere, a being knocked Tara back twenty feet. It grabbed Maverick by the throat, carrying him over and smashing him into the vehicle behind them.

"You forgot about me," the invisible man stated.

"Fassbinder," Mav whispered while being choked out.

Tara stood up and ran for the plasma cannon as the invisible man lifted Maverick off the ground by his throat.

Axel hid behind the car but heard bits and pieces of what was going on. "Not only did you try to kill me, you tried to kill my legacy."

"You d-d-don't understand," Maverick tried to reason while losing consciousness.

Tara appeared with the plasma cannon. The invisible man hurled Mav and dashed away. Tara focused on trying to spot the blur. The cannon was ripped from her hand and tossed away.

"Leave now if you want to live," the voice said to Tara.

She was too close to give up.

"Don't make me kill you both."

Maverick gave Tara a look. Mav spotted his foe and charged Don. He grabbed him and threw his invisible body into the car beside them. After the impact, Don's body became more visible. Just the outline of a metallic humanoid glitching in and out of visibility. Tara grabbed the cannon and pointed it at Don.

"Don't!" Don dashed at Tara and reached his hand to her neck. He crushed it in his palm, ending her life.

"Nooo!!!" Mav screamed.

He ran at Don and grabbed the plasma cannon. This marked the end of her bloodline. In the end, Gold's need for vengeance caused far more loss than she could have imagined.

The two brutes wrestled with the cannon. Mav tried desperately to point it at Don. Don let go and spun around, sending the back of his left knuckle into Maverick's legs, breaking them both, shattering his knees.

Just before he killed Mav, Maverick fired the cannon from the ground into the bottom of Don's neck. He continued firing, pushing the cannon past its limits, until Don's head finally gave. Don's body fell to the ground, headless. The plasma cannon exploded in Maverick's hands.

Maverick lay on the ground with no legs or hands.

Axel Fassbinder walked over and casually picked up a gun off the ground. "What did you do to my brother?"

Maverick chuckled in an insane manner. "You'll never see him again. If I were you…" Axel fired a few shots into his head before he could finish his sentence.

CHAPTER 13

A Recipe for Disaster

Axel's spine shivered. He shook his head, standing back up after looking over the railing. "And that was it. I'll never stop wondering… what if… The man who saved me seemed to know me. It doesn't make sense, but nothing that has happened in my life has."

Karl let go of the railing and faced his brother. "Do you think?"

Axel nodded. "I think I know… I'm almost certain it was him."

Axel walked over to the bar and poured himself another drink. He placed his hand on Karl's shoulder. "On a better note, our food will arrive soon."

He led Karl inside. To the right of the living room ensemble was a glass case displaying some kind of technology.

"What's this?" Karl questioned.

Axel smiled and opened the display case pulling out two different complex parts. One piece was handheld with a switch and a few buttons, the other looked like a compact, carbon-gray rectangular prism.

"This is the peak of my accomplishments. A few years back we were on the verge of world war. I created a mechanism that is able to utilize the electrons within a single atom to dissolve anything out of existence within its blast radius."

Karl's eyes widened. "Anything?" he asked.

"Yes, anything. I designed it as an anti-nuclear defense system. I have many iterations of the same design for different applications. This one is a replica of my prototype. It will only abolish what is within an eight-foot diameter. My largest variation will reach a mile radius."

"Wow! You created this? Couldn't that change how the world works? With other nations knowing you have invented such technologies… I can't imagine their response."

"They made peace with us immediately. I forced all of the United States' enemies to sign an agreement that they will also comply with all of our trade demands, if reasonable."

Karl nodded, feeling undecided about this level of power belonging to anyone.

Axel grabbed both parts of the device and set them on the island in the kitchen. The elevator arrived.

"At last, our dinner is served."

His private chef walked in with a tray on wheels. The brothers sat at the elegant dining room table in the living quarters. The chef set three dishes on the table.

"Thank you, Julian."

"It's very good, sir. Please let me know if you need anything else."

Julian left in the elevator.

"*Bon appétit.*" Axel lifted his glass to Karl.

Just as the brothers dug their forks into their pasta, the elevator unexpectedly arrived again. "We are good, Julian," Axel commented.

At the head of the table, he sat facing the elevator doors. When the doors opened, Axel looked upon a face that he knew all too well. A face his nightmares had unremittingly reminded him of. Gamble Bright stepped out of the elevator with a gun in each hand.

Axel stood immediately. "I thought you were dead…"

Karl finished his bite and stood up with his brother.

"You should have prayed that I was," Gamble snarked. He lifted his guns toward Axel. Right before he fired, Axel yelled, "Wait!"

The shots fired. Axel dashed twenty feet diagonally and another ten feet landing behind Gamble within a split second. He threw a fist to the back of Gamble's head just as Gamble faded out of existence. Karl's eyes dashed around the room. He had never seen Axel, or anyone, move that fast for that matter. Including himself.

Gamble's body appeared behind Karl. Karl's instincts led him to swing his left fist counterclockwise behind him. Before he made contact, Gamble had disappeared. His foe reappeared in front of Axel. Axel sent a powerful blow into his opponent's head. Gamble phased flashing in an out of existence as Axel's fist ran straight through him. Gamble unloaded a quick clip into Axel's chest as Karl dashed behind him and sent a horizontal kick toward the attacker's head. Gamble teleported fifteen feet away.

The Fassbinder brothers became enraged.

"Follow my lead!" Axel directed his brother. Axel dashed toward his enemy as Gamble teleported behind him. Karl dashed behind Gamble in an attempt to punch him. Gamble phased Karl's fist as Axel swung his foot around to the back of the head. He made contact, sending Gamble into the table near them. The attacker smashed into the table and teleported away again.

"Where did he go?" Karl yelled, astounded and confused. The bullets retracted out of Axel's chest, falling to the ground.

"He's still here. I can feel him," Axel whispered.

Suddenly, Gamble appeared behind Axel as Axel leaned his left shoulder downward. His right leg lifted up behind him and swung a kick into Gamble. His foe teleported again as Karl threw a fist at his disappearing body. The punch went straight through him. Finally, Axel saw an algorithm.

He directed Karl, "Try to hit him as fast as you can."

Karl followed him, dashing forward, swinging just a second too late each hit. Eventually Gamble teleported where Axel wanted him to go. Axel threw his arm where Gamble was about to materialize. When Gamble appeared, he was standing with Axel's arm through his chest. Unfortunately for Gamble, he saw that Axel's regenerative trait outpowered his abilities. As Gamble materialized, Axel's arm remained inside his chest. Gamble felt extreme pain. Axel looked him in the eye. Gamble's pupils widened as Axel retrieved his arm. The assailant fell to the ground with a ten-inch hole in his chest. His body twitched on the floor. Karl ran to his side out of empathy.

"It's okay, friend. It will all be okay. Die in peace." Karl grabbed his hand.

"He…" Gamble choked on his blood, trying to communicate. "He killed my father."

The words left Gamble's lips just a moment before he drew his final breath. Karl stood up now, questioning who his foe really was. Axel walked to his sink and washed the blood off his arm.

Karl's demeanor slowly changed. "Is it true?" he demanded angrily. "Did you kill his father?"

Axel walked away and clenched his fists. "Not directly, or intentionally. It was a necessary evil," he explained.

Karl turned gradually and looked at his brother in a way he never had before. "No evil is ever necessary."

He walked toward the sliding glass door and looked out at the city. "What have you become, brother?"

"I became what was necessary to survive in this world."

Karl jerked his head back toward him. "What are you talking about? How much blood is on your hands?"

"On my hands? How much was on his? We had to kill him. His powers came from the other dimensions. You saw him phase and teleport. What comes next, time travel? What if we didn't kill him and he caused even more death?" Axel pleaded.

Karl was quiet for a moment, looking at Axel's invention atop the kitchen island. He closed his eyes and tilted his head down before carefully responding. "How do you know about the other dimensions?"

Axel realized he may have misspoken. He walked to the bar in his kitchen and poured himself another drink. "Do you remember the graveyard that I regrettably sought out? What began all of this?"

Karl nodded. "Yes…"

"It wasn't a real graveyard. Every single grave was empty," Axel explained.

"What does this have to do with the other dimensions?"

"Because somebody put it there to hide something else. I delved deep into top secret government files and discovered there was an experimental base underground, about one hundred feet below that location. However, the entrance conveniently was over a mile west of the actual base. I believe they put the graveyard there because of the supernatural anomalies. Everyone believes graveyards are haunted. Through my research, I discovered that the machine the government had been experimenting with could be of use to my plan. The device manipulated atoms to open reality into another dimension, utilizing that wormhole to travel through time. In those files I learned that the experiment was unsuccessful. I spent years learning about the experiment and the device, inside and out. Eventually I came to the realization that the missing piece wasn't a bad equation or a missing variable. It was much simpler than that. A wormhole needs both sides to work properly. They created the entrance but not the exit."

Karl sighed in an upset manner. He hesitated to ask his next question. "You created the gateway?"

"When you disappeared… My mind began evolving with my body. A new concept spawned in my mind. The idea that anything is possible. I started to learn and know things. Some things that had yet to come. Mankind becoming futile, volatile beings. Destroying each other inside and out." He paused for a moment, wiping a tear from his face. "After everything I lost… Yes. I opened the gateway. Only in an attempt to undo the past. A failed attempt, which has led me to more drastic measures."

"And what measures might they be?"

"The planet is dying. The water level has risen fifty feet in ten years. Storms are destroying cities left and right. The civilians have all become savages. Looting stores, raiding homes, killing with no repercussions. My associate and I have devised a plan to recuperate. Randomly selected good and disease-free citizens will embark on a new world on the moon that we call Andromeda. My device will take care of the remains of mankind."

Karl approached Axel aggressively, getting close, face to face. "Take care of mankind? You're just gonna blow everyone up? It's scary to think that you hold the key to mankind's destiny."

"Have you watched the news recently? Now that is a scary thing."

"You can't just wipe out the whole planet!"

"Only the unworthy…"

Karl awkwardly chuckled and walked away, showing his dissent.

Axel became angered by his brother's lack of understanding. "You think I just changed overnight? I didn't change! People changed, brother… You don't understand how things are. They're not the same. Free will was a recipe for disaster and mankind was the perfect ingredient."

"How could you even think that killing everyone is what is good for mankind?"

"The world is dying. They won't make it either way. I'm giving them an easy relief. The end justifies the means."

Karl walked into the kitchen and washed his face. Axel looked away for a moment.

Karl continued back toward his brother. "It doesn't have to be this way, brother. I know people are flawed, but there is still good in every single one of them. I've seen it. The best people have done wrong, and the worst people have done right. That's just part of being human. We are merely in the darkest part of the night, but I promise the sun will shine again. It will shine brighter than ever amongst the horizons. Life could be free and beautiful again."

"I wish that to be true, brother. But I must do what I must."

Karl raised his voice. "Where is the humility in that? We're not Gods to tamper with the destiny of man!"

Axel became enraged. "Then what are we, brother? We're not men. We have a greater purpose."

"Not to destroy but to create. This isn't salvation, Axel. It's genocide!"

"I respect that you're my brother, but I cannot let you interfere with fate."

"You wanna know something?" Karl said. "You win! You destroy all of it! And do you know who the last poor soul is alive after all of the death? It's you. Alone, waiting for a way to undo what you've done."

Axel set down his scotch and nodded at his brother. "I look at you and see nothing but an obstacle in my way."

It finally registered with Karl. What the guardian had said.

"I was his greatest mistake…" Karl whispered to himself.

Axel heard. "What are you talking about?"

Karl's eyes pooled. "I have fought through time, great beasts and oceans to get back to you, Axel. But I don't see my brother before me. Please remember the family. Remember who you are. Who you were."

Karl's statement confused Axel. Karl revealed the atom scrambler in his hands. "This is supposed to be the part where we fight… deep down you are still my brother. I won't fight you. I won't give the man you've become that satisfaction. I won't be a pawn in the fulfilling of your undoing. This is where my king dies. Now it's your move," he stated as he pressed the trigger.

"Karl!!!!" Axel screamed, falling to his knees in agony as his brother disintegrated into thin air before him. Axel knelt on the foundation of his accomplishments, remaining like that with a blank stare.

He lifted his hands before him. Out of anger he walked over to Gamble's dead body. He picked it up, yelling, "You did this!" He threw the body out of his glass sliding door, shattering it. The body flew off the balcony down into the city. Axel walked outside the broken glass doors and looked down a thousand feet at where the body had landed. Hundreds of civilians were surrounding the victim. He could see law officials looking up at his balcony, pointing at it. It finally hit. He had become the villain of his own story. He turned back toward the broken doors. In the top left corner, a portion of the glass remained. He could see a shadowy face in the reflection.

"You did the right thing. He deserved it," a woman's voice lectured.

"Shut up!" he screamed as he grabbed the scotch glass next to him and threw it into the remaining glass. Silence. He placed his hand over his eyes for a moment. Meditating for a couple of minutes. He bolted out of his room and up the emergency flight of stairs to his helipad. A moment later, he was piloting his private chopper, leaving Binder-Corp Tower for the last time.

He flew out of the greater Los Angeles area. His destination was the only place that ever truly felt like home. A small town up country that was once called Sonora. He glanced over his shoulder to see the beautiful sunset. "Where did I go wrong?" he asked himself.

After some time, he arrived near his childhood home. It used to be difficult to land a chopper in that part of the woods. Disappointingly, there weren't many trees left to avoid. He set down a hundred feet from the house. Before he left the chopper he sat in the pilot's seat grieving for a moment. *How could this happen? I waited thirty-five years for Karl's return and when I finally found him…* He leaned his head downward, and tears poured into his lap. He drew upon his father's words from memory: "No one ever said it was going to be easy."

The memory of his father inspired Axel as his last tear arced upward to drip down a newfound smile. He jumped out of the chopper and approached a familiar house, a log cabin that used to be surrounded by forest. The cabin stood just as when he had left it, but it was surrounded by dry dirt. His eyes dazzled with the reflection of his younger self playing with Karl in the field. He watched his younger self trip on the stairs running into the house and sprain his ankle. He couldn't walk. He was home alone with his brother. Karl heard his cries and came to his brother's aid. Axel was embarrassed thinking his brother would certainly ridicule him for being clumsy. But Karl picked his brother up and told him, "It's okay, brother. We all fall from time to time."

Axel snapped out of his memory and observed the front deck. It was aged and weathered with its share of creaks and cracks. Something odd caught his eye. There was one single letter in the mailbox. He was interrupted by some rustling in the distance. He turned quickly.

"You won't find peace in there," a familiar voice spoke to him again. He regretfully turned around to see Azrael's corpse standing behind him a few feet away. Her body was bullet-ridden and rotten.

"Get out of my head!"

"How could you do this to me? You never listen to me!" she cried.

"You're not real!" he pleaded.

"You don't know what real is anymore, my love."

Axel turned away from his nightmare. As he stepped onto the porch his vision of Azrael disappeared. He looked around him to be sure. He was alone. He reached for the letter in the mailbox. It seemed to be a returned letter that the sender had declined. The letter was addressed to Axel Fassbinder. His eyes filled with tears as his heart dropped. The sender was Peter Fassbinder, his father. He had become so obsessed with the loss of Azrael and Karl that he had forsaken the last loved one he had left. He gathered his courage and reached for the doorknob.

When he opened the door, he looked into the two-story cabin. It was identical to his childhood. Aside from a few cobwebs and missing furniture. The cabin consisted of a mid-size living room at the entrance with a hallway down past the kitchen to two bedrooms and a bathroom, across from a staircase leading up to the third bedroom and loft. As he crept down the hallway, he peeked into his old room to see his and Karl's bunkbed still in the corner as it used to be. The memories hit him hard. He stumbled back and made his way back to the parlor. His father's old desk sat in the corner full of unfinished letters. As he approached the desk, he realized that every letter was an unfinished draft of what he held in his hand. He sat in his father's old chair and opened the returned letter that was addressed to him.

The letter read:

Greetings, my son.

I am sorry it's been so long since we last spoke. The doctor told me today that I only have a matter of weeks left. The only thing I fear more than death is to leave my children in this corrupt world without me. I'm sorry that I waited too long to tell you about your birth. I didn't want you to feel any different about our relationship. I have always loved you as my son. In fact, you were my favorite. In my old dying years, I think about you boys daily. Well, more like every moment of every day. Do you remember when I told you that it wasn't going to be easy? I myself didn't fully understand those words until the last few years. I hope you can understand why things were how they were. There is nothing more a father can ask for than to watch his sons grow up and get married. To bear children of their own. You should never have lost what you did, but all of our journeys are different. You will find your way. I have no doubt about that. Remember to not be ashamed of your scars. They're what makes you stronger. What makes you different. Your scars are what make you, you.

In case these are the last words you hear from me, I just need you to know that nothing was your fault. You are the most brilliant man a father could ask for. God bless.

Sincerely, your father.

Axel held the desk with his left hand, while his right hand, clutching the letter, trembled. He closed his eyes and calmed himself. He folded up the letter and kissed it, gently placing it on his father's desk. At this point, he knew he could no longer go on with his plan.

He left the woods in the helicopter he had arrived in, heading to his laboratory in San Francisco. After about ten minutes of flying, he was startled by a clatter behind him. He heard choking in the back of the helicopter. He looked back to see a body under a blanket. He let go of the controls and went back to assist. When he lifted the blanket there was no one there. He looked back to the pilot's seat to see Azrael's corpse flying the chopper into the ground. It crashed into some orchards, sending Axel to the back of the cabin. The chopper leaned sideways as the propellors hit the ground. Dirt filled the air, blinding him. He awoke and ripped the side door open. The chopper was burning. It burned through the surrounding orchards.

Axel ran to a nearby house yelling, "Help!" hoping the owner was home. An old man came out and panicked when he saw all the almond trees burning. He ran to his sprinkler setup and turned all of the faucets on. After fifteen minutes or so, the fire was out.

Axel disappeared into the orchards. He walked for some time and arrived in another small town. He saw a sign saying welcome to Jamestown. He remembered his mother growing up here. This was the town where his parents had met. A nice little town. It still felt like the nineties, forty-five years later. Approaching a few buildings in town he noticed a diner that seemed busy. Henry's Café was the name. It seemed oddly familiar.

He walked in the crowded entrance. As he waited to be seated, he looked around at the walls. The pictures told a story. A story he knew. It dawned on him that this was the diner his mother worked at before he was born. A chill shivered down his spine. It seemed like he was meant to walk into this café.

The waitress addressed him, "What can I get you, sir?"

"I just wanted some coffee and needed to use your phone."

The waitress walked him to the coffee bar. An older lady came out to serve him. She placed her hand on his shoulder. He jumped.

"Oh my god! I'm sorry, dear. I didn't mean to scare ya. What are ya having?" the weathered waitress asked him.

"My apologies, I'll take a coffee. Black. Sorry, I realized at the last minute that my mother used to work here back in the day," Axel explained.

The waitress walked over and grabbed the hot coffee pot and placed the coffee mug before him, pouring in the coffee.

"What was her name, dear?"

He smiled. "No offense, but you are far too young to have known her."

The waitress matched his smile. "What a polite young man you are. I've been going to this diner since I was a little girl. In fact, my folks used to own this place back in the day. You must be Sarah's boy. It couldn't be though. You're far too young. You must be her grandson's age."

Axel gasped in confusion. "How did you know that?"

The lady set the coffee pot back on the other countertop and turned back, responding, "You look like her… same nose. Same deep passion in your eyes. Like you're always thinking three moves ahead."

Axel grabbed her hand. "You knew Sarah? Sarah Fassbinder?"

"I knew her before she was married and after. She was Sarah Hunter to me. I was with her for both pregnancies. The first was expected. She named her son Karl after her grandfather. Peter was always pretty open about names. I'll never forget when she told me she was pregnant with you. I was only sixteen. Your mother must have been twenty-three or twenty-four. She was as scared as she was excited. She had told me that it wasn't expected and there were early complications. Something had told

her that this child was meant to change the world. For better or worse…"
She paused to tend to another customer.

When she came back to Axel, she continued, "I would imagine you
have had a long road, dear."

Axel drank his coffee while picturing his mother.

"I think I may still have a picture of her in the back." The old
waitress walked around the corner to the back and brought out an old
5 X 8 photograph of Sarah and the other waitresses posing in front of
the coffee bar. Axel slowly placed his hand on the photo, fixating on a
picture of his mother he had never seen. He had only seen her face in a
handful of photos.

"Give me your hand," the waitress told Axel. He reached out his
hand, palm up. She gently grabbed his wrist with one hand and pulled
something out of her pocket with the other. She placed an object in his
open hand as his fingers closed on it. She let go, and he brought his hand
near his chest to look upon the gift. As he opened his hand, he saw a
necklace with a gold cross attached.

"Your mother was a woman of faith. She would always remind me
that we are not alone."

He held the necklace tight. "Thank you," he told the lady.

"Sarah was such a delightful woman. It was a tragedy what happened,
but I suppose it's not tragic to die for someone you love. You're here
now, aren't you? Not many bright people nowadays. Seems like the new
generations act like we have already lost in life. They don't have any fight
left in 'em, ya know?"

Axel's eyes were now open. He realized that he couldn't give up yet.
He had one last Hail Mary.

"Could I use your phone?"

The lady handed him an old landline phone. He dialed the line he
meant to reach. "This is Mr. Fassbinder. I'm stranded in Jamestown,
California at the main diner in town. I need an escort asap."

"Sir, we were worried we hadn't heard anything since the attack on
Binder-Corp Tower. Are you okay?"

"I will be when you get here," he answered and hung up the phone. He hung his mother's necklace around his neck, placing the cross on his chest. Within thirty minutes, a black Lincoln sedan rolled up in front of the diner with two agents in the front seats.

Axel walked up to the back door and entered the vehicle, sitting in a clean leather seat behind the driver. The car drove off out of town into the orchards. About ten minutes into the drive, Axel spoke.

"I need you to contact all of our launch stations immediately," he told his men.

"Unfortunately, sir, we have strict orders from Mr. Lee not to let you interfere. You may not be thinking straight," the driver told him.

"I think I'm finally seeing through my true eyes again," Axel responded as he stabbed his arm through the driver's chest from behind. Through their body he grabbed the steering wheel and ripped it to the left. The car swerved and began to roll on its side for hundreds of feet. When the wreckage came to a stop, Axel kicked the door out and stepped onto solid ground. He looked to see the passenger had died during the roll over.

My own empire has betrayed me, he thought. *I built this organization from the ground up. Harnessing my lost dreams to drive me. I created my own undoing.*

Admitting his defeat when it came to obtaining transportation, he jogged the final hundred miles or so toward his old lab. The fastest he could run was around forty miles per hour. With the exception of a short sprint accelerated by a powerful dash, that he rarely utilized in combat situations. His speed and strength had continued to progress over the years, but he had yet to reach the physical might of Karl.

However, his true power was yet to be unveiled. The power to dream.

After three hours of running without breaking a sweat, he finally entered the city limits.

In an attempt to keep a low profile, he found a thrift store to purchase a hoodie. While inside he looked behind the cash register at a medieval dagger on the wall.

"How much for the dagger?" he asked the clerk.

"Umm, ten bucks."

Axel purchased the sub-par weapon. Not an ideal weapon to break into a high security base but it would suffice. The lab was located between two government buildings with a significant amount of security guards. The irony was that he had been so adamant about keeping people out with his security measures, but now he wasn't able to get back in.

He climbed the neighboring buildings and the fire escape, all the way to the roof. Fortunately, he had also designed the architecture for the building. He climbed down an air duct into the ventilation system. On the fifth floor, he dropped down into the hall. Just out of the perimeter of the motion sensors.

His goal was to make it to the lab with as minimal bloodshed as possible. These weren't Thaddeus's men. They were his own. He crept through a few motion sensors avoiding them by a hair's breadth.

He approached a security guard who was sitting in a computer chair on his phone. If it mattered anymore, Axel would have let him go for such laxity. He took his dagger silently to the guard's throat, startling him.

"Whoa, please don't… I'll do whatever you ask," he begged.

"This isn't exactly your expertise, is it?" Axel lectured him.

The guard looked at his assailant. "Mr. Fassbinder… I'm sorry. They ordered us to detain you immediately."

"I am aware. Your allegiance is to you and your family. However, you will take me where I tell you… Take me down to the basement level Z. As discreetly as possible."

"I'm sorry, I don't have that clearance level."

"You will. I just need you to escort me there. All I ask is you walk me down and scan your eye when needed. Otherwise, I'll just need the eye."

The guard trembled in fear. "Yes, sir, tell me where you need to go."

Axel directed him to the elevator. They descended into the basement level of the facility. There were four armed guards standing, awaiting their arrival. As they exited the elevator, the four guards pointed their weapons at Axel and his captive. Axel held the knife to his hostage's neck.

"Drop the knife or we'll shoot," one of the guards demanded.

Axel removed his hood, displaying a face they would recognize.

"Mr. Fassbinder?" the lead guard questioned. He knelt on one knee and placed his gun before him. "You are not my enemy."

A guard beside him corrected his fault. "Mr. Lee gave us direct orders to keep him away from any base."

The lead guard spun around with his taser baton, striking the side of the contender's head. The guard fell to the ground, shocked. The other two guards laid down their weapons.

"Go, sir, I will hold them off while I can."

Axel nodded. "Thank you, Armon."

The soldier smiled at the thought of Mr. Fassbinder remembering his name. Axel led his hostage down a long and narrow hall toward a gray steel door with a window. At about his shoulder height there was an oval pocket for eye recognition.

"Place your eye on the pocket," Axel directed.

The hostage did as he was told.

The door opened, revealing a square room with steel walls painted yellow.

"Go now. Get home to your family."

The hostage ran off.

Axel walked into the room. Before him there was a keypad with an optical scanner that was taught for his and only his biometrics. As the doors behind him closed, he heard the main elevator arrive in the distance. Abruptly, gunfire sparked. He heard the sound of terror projected from the dying screams of his loyal soldiers. After quickly entering his pin, he scanned his finger. He opened the circular door and stepped in swiftly, closing it and locking it behind him. He was in a dark area with only a ladder near his feet. He climbed down thirty feet and fumbled around the wall looking for the last keypad. He entered the pin and opened the final door revealing his lab.

Once inside, he shut the door behind him, locked it and pressed his back to it. He gradually slid on his back to the ground and sat for a moment, catching his breath. His heart was pained at the thought of his faithful soldiers dying on his behalf. He stood up and inspected his lab. The room glowed with blue plasma lights. It was about seven feet high and ten feet deep and wide. A multitude of inventions lay across the walls of the room. Including the plasma cannon. He had all of the elements and components needed to create his final invention.

Axel delved deep within his thoughts. He thought harder than ever before. Every equation. Every algorithm in time and space crossed his mind.

He walked to his turning lathe and grabbed some titanium blanks, turning them to his desired features. Then he fired up his urn, pressing carbon fiber plates under one foot. He took them to his milling machine and machined the bolt patterns.

Next, he placed magnetic bases inside every hinge of the mechanism. When he had completed his project, it took up half of the room he stood in. He placed the screen on one side accompanied by a few button controls. He connected the electrical cables finishing the controller. When he pressed a button on the control, the machine folded from a large box into a small handheld device. Axel lifted it before his eyes.

"It is finished," he proclaimed.

The first and last time machine was born.

Worried about the basement's age, he didn't want to test the device underground. He waited patiently for his foes to breach. He knew what they would send. He invented them. Axel packed the device into a satchel and waited, sitting cross-legged on his inventions table.

After about an hour, he heard grinding noises. Something or someone was cutting through. Axel waited patiently. At that very moment he could see the grinding wheel peeking through with sparks; a robotic arm burst through the hole. An android's body smashed through the wall, charging Axel. It had a humanoid appearance and stood taller than most men. Axel jumped over the machine, performing a calculated front flip, just as the machine charged the table he was sitting on.

Axel turned back and threw a punch so fast a bullet couldn't catch it. The impact sounded like a great explosion. He obliterated the droid into thousands of pieces. As he turned back around, another droid grabbed him from behind and smashed his face into the wall beside him. It stabbed its other arm through his chest and into the wall. Axel was stuck with the android's arm, stabbed through him diagonally into the upper corner of the wall and the ceiling of the room. Axel lifted his hand to the droid's square head. He smashed it with ease. It froze and continued to hold him where he was. He grabbed the pointed arm from his chest. Ripping it out, he threw the droid back at the wall with a few punches, moving thousands of miles per hour. Upon each impact, the pieces of the droid turned to dust in the air.

Axel ran over to the exit and leapt up the thirty feet, grabbing on to the ledge. Ten human soldiers were standing casually waiting to hear back from the droids. One of the soldiers noticed Axel, and startled, dropped his drink. As the drink fell to the ground, Axel swung back and forth with his fists, stabbing through each enemy in sight. As the half empty paper soda cup hit the floor, so did the corpses of the ten soldiers.

The remainder of the Army of Three continued to the surface. On his way he annihilated another five men in his way. By the time he hit the surface, everyone was dead. The swat team arrived accompanied by Binder-Corp men and five androids. He raised his arms for a moment and slowly walked out to the street. A small army surrounded Axel.

"I would rather do this without killing every single one of you."

A police sergeant called out to him. "Sir, we know you murdered Gamble Bright. There were hundreds of witnesses."

"What happened to self-defense?" Axel muttered.

He shook his head, then dashed into a wall of police officers, tossing them in each direction. He dashed back at an android and ripped it in half. He then jumped thirty feet onto a building and began running from the remaining men, jumping from rooftop to rooftop. When he felt like he was ahead, he dropped down to ground level. He knelt down and pressed the controls on his new device. He remembered the date Azrael had told him. The machine expanded into a rectangular box. He stepped in, commencing the most fateful event of all time. The machine closed above him. Instantly he was dropped to the ground in the dark box. He began puking uncontrollably while bleeding from his eyes. Axel gripped his fists and held his head throughout the inconceivable pain. The box shook. Through the cracks that sealed it, dark, shadowy claws crept in. The beast tried to pull the device apart.

"You cannot undo what is already done," the beast spoke to Axel while its claws ripped at the machine.

Axel looked between the cracks at time reversing outside the box.

"Don't leave me again… Please," Azrael's voice spoke.

Axel grabbed the cross on his chest. "I'm going to save you, my love."

The beast shook the machine again as the claws ripped into Axel's shoulders. He screamed in pain. He closed his eyes. He opened them to see his father and Karl in their Sunday best, walking down the red carpet in their well-lit childhood church's chapel. They sat at the third pew on the left. Peter looked at his sons and smiled. The preacher spoke. Now we will read Psalms 23:4. "Even though I walk through the shadow of the valley of death, I shall fear no evil, for you are with me. Your rod and your staff, they comfort me."

Axel opened his eyes. "Though I walk through the valley of the shadows of death, I shall fear no EVIL!" he yelled.

Suddenly the beast was gone. The machine fell apart. Axel lay on a broken piece of metal in the middle of the road. The remainder of the machine was clawed to pieces.

"For you are with me…" he muttered while blankly staring at the sky above.

After a few moments, he snapped out of it. He looked around him confused, then stepped to his feet and gazed around him. He could tell by the parked cars and the local shops that he had made it.

September 13th, 1989. Axel had arrived back in the golden days. The night her parents were… He observed his surroundings. The night was quiet. It was nostalgic being in these suburbs in 1989. A '72 Camero drove by casually as if it weren't a classic. He realized he had quite the distance to travel and wanted to keep a low profile. To be safe, he decided to find a different means of transportation. He found the highway north and popped his thumb out. Within half of an hour, two young men in a beat-up Honda Civic pulled over to his aid.

As the passenger opened the door, smoke poured out.

"Need a ride, broski?" the passenger asked.

Axel hesitated for a moment. *A ride is a ride*, he figured.

"If you don't mind. Which way are you headed?"

"We're on our way back from Santa Cruz and gonna head up to the Oregon Country Fair. We hear there's plenty of ganja up there. You know what I mean?"

Axel knew what he meant but didn't want to encourage such recklessness. "No, I don't. But it seems like you may pass through Sacramento, if I'm not mistaken?"

"'Course, brah. We can get you there," the kid responded. "My name's Seth and this is my lifelong buddy, Jason," the driver stated while the passenger nodded with a fat grin on his face.

"Okay... how old are you guys?"

"Well... that has no straightforward answer, man. You see, age is just a number. We're only nineteen but our souls are like immortal, you know," Seth answered, confusing Axel.

His first instinct was to correct his arrogance, but then he thought for a moment. He wasn't wrong.

"Well, nineteen is a great age. I remember when I was a kid," Axel responded.

"You don't look much older than us. How old are you, my dude?"

"Old enough to have forgotten what it feels like to live carefree."

"Dude," the two stoners responded simultaneously.

They drove for miles and miles with the two delinquents hotboxing the old shit box they rode in. He told them the address, and they dropped him off a few blocks down.

"Thanks for the ride, guys. It was quite the pleasure."

They both froze, looking forward. Axel awkwardly waited for a response. About ten seconds later, "Oh yeah, bro. Not a problem, man. Let us know if you can make it to the show."

Jason corrected Seth. "It's not a show, man; it's a hippy fest."

"Oh yeah, man. We'll see you there."

Axel paused for a moment and couldn't help but smile. "I'll see you guys there."

They drove off. He tried to shake off the stupidity. He walked across the street and waited a few houses down the street from Azrael's parents' house. Axel looked at his wristwatch, inspecting the street at each tick of the hand.

Ten minutes before midnight a cab pulled up across the street. A man in a coat and a hat stepped out. Axel's anxiety went off like a metal detector. He immediately walked toward the man aggressively. The man tilted his hat down, trying to shroud his face. When he turned to cross the street, he was abruptly confronted by Axel. Axel grabbed him by his shoulder and dragged him to the alleyway.

"What are you doing?" the man pleaded.

The last brother took him around the corner in the alley and pressed him to the fence.

"What are you doing here? Do you live here?"

The man looked down and didn't respond. Axel grabbed his hat and threw it out in the distance. "What is your purpose here?"

"Look… It isn't what it seems. I was here on personal business that has nothing to do with you."

Axel became angered, now knowing this was the perpetrator. He lifted up the man with one hand and threw him ten feet away. The man landed and rolled in the gravel alleyway. He pressed himself up with his hands on his knees.

"What were you going to do? Tell me!" Axel yelled.

The man was terrified. "Okay. Okay. I was here to take my revenge. Mr. Bloch is a horrible person. He's a criminal defense attorney, and he let the killer of my love go free. I was here to take revenge."

Axel walked toward him and grabbed the side of his coat. He stood him up and patted him down to find the gun, then pulled the six-shooter revolver from the man's coat. Everything played out to this point for Axel until… He rotated the revolvers shell out to see that there was only one bullet in the chamber. He didn't understand. He grabbed the man off the ground and lifted him into the air by his coat.

"How were you gonna kill two people with one bullet, genius?"

The man trembled in fear. "I wouldn't kill two people. I didn't even want to kill him. It was only what was right."

Axel tossed him on his back, deep in thought. He looked at his watch to see he had three minutes left. He looked back at the man.

"I'm not gonna kill you. But I need to make sure you never hurt anyone again."

Axel grabbed both the man's hands and crushed them into bits, ensuring he would never use them again. The man screamed in agony.

"Now, run."

The man stopped screaming and ran down the alleyway. Axel jogged over to Azrael's house. He climbed up to the neighbor's roof to try and find her window. He jumped across two rooftops until he saw her. A young Azrael lying in her bed. So innocent. His eyes scanned the perimeter like a hawk. He was confused. He didn't see any additional attackers in sight. Just as Azrael turned her bedroom light off, Axel caught a glimmer of something. A reflection of something metallic coming out of her closet.

He instantly charged, jumping across the roof, breaking through the window. He tackled a large man in the corner of the room. Azrael turned her bedside lantern on. She screamed violently. Axel picked up the man and beat him down. He hit harder than he had ever hit a man before. He smashed his fist into the attacker's head over and over. He then picked him up with his left hand and stabbed his right hand through his armor and chest.

"Enough," the assailant choked out.

Axel turned toward the scared girl sitting in her bed. "Azrael, leave now! Go downstairs, find your parents and wait in the street till the police arrive."

She nodded in fear and ran out of the room. Axel turned toward his foe. "Lars Grossman… I should have known. Thaddeus betrayed me long ago."

Lars laughed hysterically.

"Why are you laughing?"

Axel lifted him up again with his chest wound.

"You still don't realize," Lars told his opponent.

"Realize what?"

"Look at me. Look at my eyes."

Axel looked at the famous hitman closely in his eyes. "Russ?" He dropped him and stumbled away. "It can't be…"

Russ coughed up some blood and spat it to the side. "All I did was gain some muscle, shave my head, grow a beard and change my name. Then the brilliant Axel Fassbinder couldn't tell his best friend from his worst enemy."

Axel's reality was shattered. It couldn't be… "Why Russ? Why would you do this?"

"Why? Isn't it obvious? You self-centered asshole. You left me, man. You fucking left me. You were all I had. You and your family. You acted like Azrael was all you had. When she died, I called you every single day for a year. Eventually, I gave up. And yes, I grew to hate you. I didn't just lose you. I lost Peter, I lost Karl, I lost me. So, I became something else because you did."

He coughed up more blood. They both realized he only had a few moments left based on the size of the hole in his chest. Axel looked out the window to see dozens of police cars show up. He looked back to see Russ had passed. He jumped out the window to the neighbor's roof and sprinted off. He continued to his old sacred place, running as fast and hard as he could out to the country. Between a circle of trees, a giant boulder faced a tree he knew too well. The tree he had carved their names on their first date. It lay plain and uncarved.

CHAPTER 14

The Golden Days

Have you ever met your wit's end? Been devastated by the pain of grief, rendering your conscience lost? As I sit on my pedestal of guilt between a rock and a hard place. I debate the hardest decision of many lives. The world is an utterly dark place, barren of hope, but there is still a glimpse of potential in its lasting endurance. This place where we are now. I can see a beautiful world before us. A child-like first perspective of this reckoned reality. Subjective innocence. Surrounded by the bane of my accomplishments, my life haunts me.

As the rain falls, hitting my forehead, it trickles down my mind. Passing my tears, it continues downwards as my thoughts transcend. What is justice but an immunity to understanding? Circumstances are not neatly defined as one or the other. Black or white. We live in a contentious world of gray. We live in a nation where our wants compete with the value of our needs. Only those who have experienced true loss understand what they need. No ecstasy in excess is true. Life is about finding your balance. Where discontentment thrives, bad things will follow.

My immunity to human sympathy has bred a new more dangerous logic. My intentions come to light. I pull out the atom scrambler that I brought with me. There is only one individual that connects all of this. The independent variable. I have become a cancer to mankind. My deeper ruling was meant to create. But all that has come from my life was to destroy. I have one last attempt to undo our fate. Perhaps this invention I hold in my hand has a greater divine purpose. This invention can kill even the immortal. What a coincidence. This very concept of its existence leads me to believe subliminally this was meant for one man… myself. If I were to take out the leading variable in the destruction of this world then maybe, just maybe, there is still hope.

I drop the weapon in my pocket and pull out Karl's journal. I read about his travels through time. I decide I must finish it. I must leave my brother with something to try and understand why this is the only option. I write for some time. The story of two brothers. My tears become heavier as each stroke of the pen lines the paper. Going through hardships in life is like hammering a nail into wood. If hammered improperly, that nail will bend to be weaker and weaker until it breaks. But if it's done the right way, the nail will become stronger each hit until it reaches its full potential.

I find a stone and turn toward the tree from my dreams. I carve our names once again. This is it. I exit the woods for my next and final destination. I remember this year. I must have been a freshman in high school. Karl would have been a senior. Only a few years after I had discovered my abilities. I walk down the road of guilt and shame. I am in no hurry to get to this last stop. I reach my hand in my pocket and feel my prototype of the atom scrambler. Even if I sacrifice myself there is no way to know for sure. Preventing Azrael's parents murder may have changed what I will become. This new version of me could be different. I weigh the costs. Maybe this alternate version of myself could be better.

I approach the driveway to see the old house. I missed this. Industrialization and technological adaptation changed us. I remember gas-powered cars. Owning the land your house was built on. Using cash that wasn't part of a digital system to regulate spending and your life. Long before the people watching your daily routines were in any position of power. Back in this day, people were afraid of machines running the world. Later on, they pray for it.

If only I could stick around to see how it plays out. I remember Karl's last words. "This is where my king dies. Now it's your move." I stop in my tracks. My brother loved me even more than I could ever love myself. Maybe he was trying to teach me to love humanity more than I love myself. Or more than I love those who I hold dearest. The thought of all these dreadful 'what ifs' taint my mind. I've made it this far. There is no going back. All of the death on my hands… This new timeline would reinvent my exit. Everyone could have a different ending. We started as a brotherhood. We will end on a greater level than this. My existence was a means to an end. Perhaps removing myself from this timeline is no guarantee. To act as if it is certain is foolish. For in life there are very few certainties. What is guaranteed today, may be but the withered hope of a past dream tomorrow. I roll the dice.

I stop at the driveway of my old home. Karl, if only we could have a good brotherly talk like we used to. It would make this all so much easier. This is the end of my story. Yet it is merely a new beginning. Though all journeys come to an end. There is always something new. Through the loss and sorrow something else breeds, hope. A new story and only you hold the pen. Always remember, there is order and there is chaos. There is nothing between them.

I approach the garage we used to hang out and practice in. From the sunroom, Karl hears me outside, just as I expected he would. He prepares to engage as I dash through the door, obliterating it. I knock my brother down to the ground. I follow up with an inhumanely strong taser I brought from the lab. Karl lies on the ground, incapacitated. He looks at my face, confused as my eyes fill with tears.

I lay my journal next to him and tell him, "It will all make sense soon, brother." I turn toward my younger self standing in the garage fifteen feet away. He stands frozen, shocked. Not knowing what to do or how to react.

"You have nothing to be afraid of, Axel," I tell my younger self. I walk toward him and hug him. I whisper in his ear, "Everything is going to be alright."

These are my last words before I hit the detonator. And then I see it. This was never my story at all. It was yours, Karl. I press the button disintegrating both versions of myself into nothingness.

CHAPTER 15

Karl's Letter

Dear Axel,

I know you're in heaven and I'm not sure if angels can read letters. I'm older now than I ever was in your world. I wanted you to know how everything played out. I read the book. Grandpa never showed up. I don't know a thing about time travel, but I'm sure he is in a better place.

Russ went on to become a big deal. He had some brilliant app idea for these new things called smart phones and he ended up donating all his money to help kids struggling with divorced parents. Dad is still well. Healthwise. Losing you hit him a little harder than the other losses. But I decided to live with him, and we keep each other company.

Ten years to the day we lost you, I finally decided to visit her. When I approached her door, I could hear children's laughter. I thought I was lost. When I knocked on the door, a beautiful woman answered. She didn't seem anything like you had described her but that made sense, considering.

I asked if she knew where Azrael was. She said, "I'm Azrael." She married a firefighter at age twenty-two. They have a young boy and another on the way.

I told her, "This isn't going to make much sense. But someone from another life who cared about you very much wanted you to have this."

I handed her a copy of the book you gave me. A couple of months later I received a letter in the mail. It was from her. She said that the book told an interesting story. She wanted me to know that she is naming her son Axel after you. I thought that would mean something to you.

As for me, brother… I decided to continue where we left off. Something about Army of one just didn't feel right for a name. Though I found a new one that caught my eye. Now one story ends, and another begins. The story of Karl Bronze and the Army of Three.

www.ingramcontent.com/pod-product-compliance
Lightning Source LLC
Chambersburg PA
CBHW032256310726
48973CB00008B/2429